HOPE REKINDLED

STRIKING A MATCH, BOOK 3

HOPE REKINDLED

TRACIE PETERSON

BETHANYHOUSEPUBLISHERS

Minneapolis, Minnesota

Published by Bethany House Publishers
11400 Hampshire Avenue South
Bloomington, Minnesota 55438

Bethany House Publishers is a division of
Baker Publishing Group, Grand Rapids, Michigan.

Printed in the United States of America

Library of Congress Cataloging-in-Publication Data

Peterson, Tracie.
    Hope rekindled / Tracie Peterson.
        p.   cm. — (Striking a match ; bk. 3)
    ISBN 978-0-7642-0891-1 (hardcover : alk. paper) — ISBN 978-0-7642-0614-6 (pbk.) — ISBN 978-0-7642-0892-8 (large-print pbk.)
    I. Title.
    PS3566.E7717H66   2011
    813'.54—dc22
                                                                                    2011008203

To Dr. Peter Kelleher
with thanks for your
generous heart and fantastic
surgical skills.

Books by Tracie Peterson

www.traciepeterson.com

A Slender Thread • *House of Secrets* • *Where My Heart Belongs*

BRIDAL VEIL ISLAND*
To Have and To Hold

SONG OF ALASKA
Dawn's Prelude • *Morning's Refrain* • *Twilight's Serenade*

STRIKING A MATCH
Embers of Love • *Hearts Aglow* • *Hope Rekindled*

ALASKAN QUEST
Summer of the Midnight Sun
Under the Northern Lights • *Whispers of Winter*
Alaskan Quest (3 in 1)

BRIDES OF GALLATIN COUNTY
A Promise to Believe In • *A Love to Last Forever*
A Dream to Call My Own

THE BROADMOOR LEGACY*
A Daughter's Inheritance • *An Unexpected Love*
A Surrendered Heart

BELLS OF LOWELL*
Daughter of the Loom • *A Fragile Design* • *These Tangled Threads*

LIGHTS OF LOWELL*
A Tapestry of Hope • *A Love Woven True* • *The Pattern of Her Heart*

DESERT ROSES
Shadows of the Canyon • *Across the Years* • *Beneath a Harvest Sky*

HEIRS OF MONTANA
Land of My Heart • *The Coming Storm* • *To Dream Anew* • *The Hope Within*

LADIES OF LIBERTY
A Lady of High Regard • *A Lady of Hidden Intent*
A Lady of Secret Devotion

RIBBONS OF STEEL**
Distant Dreams • *A Hope Beyond* • *A Promise for Tomorrow*

RIBBONS WEST**
Westward the Dream

WESTWARD CHRONICLES
A Shelter of Hope • *Hidden in a Whisper* • *A Veiled Reflection*

YUKON QUEST
Treasures of the North • *Ashes and Ice* • *Rivers of Gold*

*with Judith Miller   **with Judith Pella

TRACIE PETERSON is the author of over eighty novels, both historical and contemporary. Her avid research resonates in her stories, as seen in her bestselling HEIRS OF MONTANA and ALASKAN QUEST series. Tracie and her family make their home in Montana.

Visit Tracie's Web site at *www.traciepeterson.com.*
Visit Tracie's blog at *www.writespassage.blogspot.com.*

CHAPTER 1

EAST TEXAS, MARCH 1887

Y ou . . . you can't marry him," Jake Wythe declared, taking Deborah Vandermark by the arm. He swayed for a moment, then pulled her with him to the far side of the porch. "You can't."

Deborah broke loose from his hold. "Jake, don't be ridiculous. We've been through this. I love Christopher. This is a celebration of my upcoming wedding, and I will thank you not to embarrass me by making a scene." Deborah hoped her words would somehow sober him a bit. "Let's return to the others."

"You only wanna . . . wanna marry him because he's a doctor. You want to be a doctor and figure this is . . . is the way to get that done."

"Nonsense," Deborah said, putting her hands on her hips.

"If I only wanted to train to be a doctor, there are other ways to accomplish the task without committing my life to someone. Now, if this is all you came to tell me, I'm going back inside to be with my guests."

"He's an Irishman!" Jake declared, stumbling forward.

Deborah stopped and looked at him. The fact that Christopher Clayton was truly Christopher Clayton Kelleher was well-known in her family and circle of friends, but why Jake thought it important to bring it up now was beyond her.

She shook her head. "I'm sorry, Jake. You've saved my life more than once, but I don't love you. We're just good friends."

He pushed her back against the house. "But I love you. Don't you understand? I want to marry you. It should be me." He took hold of her face rather roughly and covered her mouth with his own.

Deborah fought against his hold. His breath reeked of beer as he sought to deepen his kiss. She tried to claw at his face, but Jake quickly pinned her arms.

"I can make you . . . happy," he murmured against her lips.

"Stop or I'll scream!"

She didn't need to. In a flash, G.W. had yanked Jake away from her and onto his backside. Standing over the smaller man, Deborah's brother shook a fist at him. "Of all the dumb things. What in the world is wrong with you, Wythe?"

"I love her. She shouldn't . . . shouldn't marry the doc. She . . . she . . . she should marry me."

"You're drunk." G.W. reached down and pulled Jake to his feet. "You're drunk and you attacked my sister. Get out of here and don't come back. You're fired."

Jake looked at him, confused—as if the words didn't make

sense. He stumbled back against the porch rail, then lurched toward Deborah.

G.W. grabbed him and threw him off the porch. "I said to get on out of here. We don't tolerate drinkin', and we sure don't allow for drunks to attack our women."

Jake landed in a flurry of dust. "I didn't mean to hurt you, Deborah. I love you."

Christopher came to her side. He put his arm around her shoulder and gave her a quizzical stare. "What's this all about?"

"Jake wants me to marry him instead of you. He's been drinking and he . . ." She paused a moment, unsure of what to say. "Well, he forced a kiss on me." She tried to sound casual, but in truth it had really shaken her.

Christopher frowned and looked to where Jake was just picking himself up off the ground. "Are you all right?" he asked, his hand stroking her arm in concern.

"I'm fine. Let's just go back inside." Coming alongside her brother, Deborah put her hand on his shoulder. "Thank you, G.W." She refused to cast even the briefest glance at Jake, which only caused him to call after her.

"Do you hear me? Deborah? I love you, Deborah. I love you."

Mercifully, as she drew nearer to the house, the music drowned out Jake's pathetic cries. A little band of local talent played while others danced and laughed in celebration of her upcoming nuptials. Apparently Jake had decided to forgo making merry, preferring to numb his pain and bolster his courage with liquor. She glanced around the room, wondering if others were also imbibing.

"Why were you outside?" Christopher asked.

She shrugged. "Jake asked me to step onto the porch with

him so he could tell me something. I had no idea that he'd been drinking."

Christopher led her to where the refreshments were laid out and poured her a glass of punch. "I'm sorry I wasn't with you."

"There was no reason to believe you needed to be." Deborah took the glass from him. "It's best we put it behind us now."

He narrowed his gaze and tilted her face to the light. "You may have a bruise."

She touched her free hand to her jaw. "Oh, bother. Well, it's a week until the wedding, so it should fade."

"Just a week," he said with a grin. "Seems like an eternity."

Deborah laughed. She sipped the punch and gazed out at the people who'd come to her family's home to share their revelry. Mother and Arjan were dancing, as were others. G.W. and Lizzie stood to one side. As Lizzie drew her husband's hand to her lips, G.W.'s deep scowl softened. No doubt his thoughts were still on Jake Wythe. At Lizzie's kiss, however, his outlook appeared to change. Deborah could see that her friend had a soothing effect on G.W. Lizzie motioned to his leg and he rubbed it, but nodded. G.W. had nearly lost the limb and his very life when he'd fallen from a tree over a year ago. He'd worked hard to recover, although he still was not up to dancing.

"Would you like to waltz with me?"

Deborah looked at the man who would soon be her husband. "I would like that very much." She allowed Christopher to take the glass from her and place it on the table. He extended his arm and she smiled. They might live in the seclusion of the Big Piney Woods, but they were still quite civilized when it suited them.

Christopher placed his hand upon her waist, and Deborah found girlish joy bubble up from within as they swayed to the music. She remembered the first time she'd been at a barn dance—the first time she was actually allowed to stay up for the dance itself. She had been fourteen and quite enthralled to discover what went on at such events. Her steps had been more awkward back then, and she'd mashed and bruised her fair share of toes. The gangly girl she'd been had grown up, however, and she easily kept stride with her husband-to-be. She had never been happier.

"I wish we could bring your family here for the wedding."

Christopher shook his head. "It's far too costly. I promised my mother we would come for a visit in the summer if all went well."

The music ended and the fiddle player declared he needed a break to smoke his pipe. The band disbursed and the dancers headed for the refreshment table.

"I can hardly wait to meet your mother. She sounds like a wonderful woman," Deborah whispered as Christopher led her to the side of the room.

"You two are very much alike," he replied. "You are both very intelligent, although my mother never had the chance for school—at least nothing more than grade school. But she's a determined soul, nevertheless, and taught her children to read and encouraged them to attend school. She would appreciate your stance on education being of the utmost importance." Christopher leaned closer. "It looks as though there are ladies who would like to speak to you. I'll go talk to G.W. and thank him again for rescuing you."

Before she could reply he was gone, and Deborah found herself half circled by several women. Mrs. Perkins and Mrs. Huebner were on her right, while Mother and Dinah Wolcott were on her left. Lizzie and the pastor's daughter, Mara, made their way to join her, as well.

"So is your gown finished?" Mrs. Huebner asked. "I understand you're reworking your mother's wedding dress."

"Yes," Deborah replied, giving her mother a quick smile. "Mother's gown was designed in the late 1850s, and as you know, the fashions have changed considerably. I have to admit, however, my contributions have been minimal. Mother and Sissy have been the ones to transform it."

"Have you changed it to a great degree, Euphanel?" Mrs. Huebner asked.

"Yes. You must remember, I married in Georgia. The skirts then were quite voluminous. We have been able to drape the tiered flouncing up and back over a bustle. Sissy is a genius when it comes to such handwork."

"She is," Deborah agreed.

"We need to hem it, but otherwise, we're very nearly done," Mother added.

Mrs. Perkins glanced around the room. Her husband founded the little sawmill town of Perkinsville, which left Mrs. Perkins as its unofficial matron. "Oh, a wedding is just the thing to cheer up our little town. Look what this party has done for our spirits." She continued, "I'm certain you have more than enough flowers for the wedding, but should you need any additional blooms, please feel free to visit my garden. You are free to take anything you need."

"That's so kind, Rachel," Mother replied before Deborah could answer. "We will keep that in mind. I have to admit, however, that I've been far more concerned about getting everything to the church in one piece. I'm beginning to think we should have just planned to have the wedding here."

"It will all work out, you'll see." Mrs. Perkins patted Mother's arm. "So will you and the doctor take a wedding trip?" she asked Deborah.

"We're planning a brief trip to Galveston," she replied. "Neither of us wants to be gone for too long, however. Just in case someone needs a doctor."

"Galveston is lovely. The water is so refreshing." Mrs. Perkins looked around the room. "It's such a pity that there aren't more folks in town these days." She shook her head and gave a *tsk*ing sound. "Since the mill fire, so many have left to find work elsewhere, and who can blame them? Mr. Albright and Mr. Longstreet will not give my husband any definitive terms for rebuilding. I wish he'd never taken on partners. In the old days, we could just assure folks that they'd still have a job and that the mill would be up and running before they knew it.

"Remember the early days of our little town, Euphanel? We weren't much of a community, and certainly the mill was very small, but each of our men ran their own business affairs. Now we are dependent upon others to let us know what the plan will be."

"Have they given no indication?" Mother asked.

"None. When Mr. Perkins confronts them, they merely tell him that he is a lesser partner and that they will be the ones to make the decisions about rebuilding. Mr. Albright did say he was seeking advice on whether the current location was most advantageous or if he should build elsewhere."

"Seems going somewhere else would be foolish," Lizzie threw in. "The rails are here—the town's already in place."

"That's exactly what Zed told them, but they weren't very inclined to concern themselves with such things. Mr. Albright said that the town could be disassembled and rebuilt."

"Seems like a lot of work when a little could suffice," Mrs. Huebner declared.

Deborah agreed. The entire matter seemed to be nothing more than a delaying tactic to torment her family.

"Miz O'Neal will no longer run the boardinghouse," Mrs. Perkins added. "She said without guests, there's really no need for her to stay on, and Zed can't afford to pay her out of his own pocket."

"When does Mary plan to leave?" Mother asked. "Where will she go?"

"Plans to join her sister in Ohio. I heard her say that she'll stay on until after the wedding. She wanted to see Deborah married."

Mrs. Huebner nodded. "I told Curtis the same thing."

"Surely you'll stick around until the school term is concluded," Deborah said. She was surprised the Huebners were considering a move, but if Stuart and Mr. Longstreet were not inclined to get the mill up and running again, what choice did they have? Perkinsville would simply continue to diminish until no one was left—not even its founding family. Those in need of a school would simply have to send their children to the county school some distance away.

"I heard that your sons moved their families elsewhere, Mrs. Perkins," Lizzie said as if reading Deborah's thoughts.

"Yes, it seems things will never be the same again. I never thought to leave this place, but now . . ."

"Surely Zed isn't going to pull out." Mother looked at her friend, as if to ascertain the truth in her eyes.

"He said it will completely depend on the decisions of Mr. Albright and Mr. Longstreet."

Deborah saw Lizzie clench her jaw and look away. Deborah recognized the emotion on her face, for she, too, had her own moments of guilt. After all, she had encouraged her friend to leave Mr. Albright at the altar, and in turn, Lizzie had left her home in Philadelphia to come to Texas with Deborah. Then Lizzie fell in love with and married Deborah's brother. It was hard not to feel at least a bit responsible for the fact that Stuart Albright wished to make them pay for the embarrassment he'd endured.

But it had never been about embarrassing Stuart. It wasn't even about denying him the inheritance that they later learned he would have received upon wedding Lizzie. Deborah had never wished Stuart harm; she had only wanted to see her dear friend happy.

And Lizzie could never have been happy married to Stuart— of this Deborah was certain. But now the price being imposed was not only intended for the Vandermarks, but for all of Perkinsville. Stuart was hurting them all because his pride was wounded.

"He didn't even love her," Deborah muttered.

"What was that, my dear?" Mrs. Perkins asked.

Deborah realized she'd spoken aloud and shook her head. "It was nothing. I'm sorry. I'm just pondering the past again." She gave a smile. "I hope very much to forget that which is behind me."

Mara Shattuck nodded. "There is great wisdom in that Bible encouragement." The pastor's daughter was often compared in looks to Deborah, but tonight they were nothing alike. Mara had pulled her hair into a tightly coiled knot at the nape of her neck and had dressed in quite a sedate fashion. It was a concession that she'd even come to the party. Deborah understood that when Mara had lived with her grandmother in New Orleans, they had observed the Lenten period with reverence and piety. They weren't of the Catholic faith, but even so, they took the opportunity of those weeks preceding Maundy Thursday, Good Friday, and Easter to remember the poor and needy and reflect on

God's ministry. Mara had come to the party only after spending the day helping the people of color who remained in Perkinsville.

Deborah admired the young woman who she was quite sure would one day marry into the family. Rob Vandermark, Deborah's other sibling, had set his sights on Miss Mara Shattuck, and once he concluded his studies at the seminary in Houston, she felt certain they would wed.

The musicians began to return to their instruments. "It looks like we'll soon be dancing again," she said with a smile. "My feet already ache, but I have to say, you've all made this one of the happiest nights of my life."

Mother gave her a hug. "I'm sure it's just the first of many."

೧೦೧

Christopher made his way to Deborah as she bid the last of the guests good-bye. It was getting quite late, and he would have to leave, as well. He leaned against the wall and watched his fiancée, amazed at her ease. She was so accomplished, and not only in this. He'd seen her stitch up a wound or help set a bone without a moment's hesitation. He'd always hoped to marry a woman who was as capable as his mother. Deborah Vandermark was certainly that and more.

Her grace and calm soothed him in ways he didn't fully understand. And tonight, she was radiant in her joy. He couldn't help but admire her fine figure and stylish attire. Just seeing her stirred his blood. He longed to pull her into his arms and spend the rest of his life in her presence.

"You look spent," Euphanel Vandermark told him. "Are you sure you wouldn't just as soon spend the night here? You are welcome to sleep in Arjan's old cabin."

Christopher was more than a little tempted. He suppressed

a yawn. "No. I need to head back to town. I'm trying to inventory everything for Stuart Albright. He wants a complete list by Monday, and I figured all week to devote Saturday to it. If I stay here tonight, I won't want to leave in the morning."

Euphanel smiled. "Just another week—and then you two will have the rest of your lives together."

He nodded. "I hadn't known a week could last so long."

Arjan moved to Euphanel's side and put his arm around her shoulder. "We'd best let these two say their good-nights, Wife."

She smiled up at him and nodded. "I suppose so. Be careful on your ride home, Christopher. I wouldn't want anything happening to you."

He chuckled. "If I get hurt, I understand there is a fine woman doctor in these parts. Well, I suppose she's not a full-fledged doctor . . . yet," he said loud enough to catch Deborah's attention, "but I understand she's quite capable."

"That she is," Euphanel said with a quick glance over her shoulder. "That she is."

Christopher waited until Euphanel and Arjan had gone before approaching Deborah. He pulled her into his arms without warning and captured her lips in a lingering kiss. Deborah melted against him and sighed. Just another week and she'd be his. A few more days. Part of him longed to change his mind and stay the night—if only to be that much closer to her.

He felt Deborah's fingers on the nape of his neck toying with his hair. He would have to get a trim before the wedding, he thought. He touched the soft skin just under her ear and thought of what it would be like to place kisses there.

Pulling away, he grinned like a mischievous child. Deborah arched a brow in question, but he only laughed and dropped his hold. "One week, Miss Vandermark. A week from tomorrow—you will be mine."

"Why did we decide to wait so long?" she asked with a pout.

He roared with laughter. "The date was your idea. As I recall you wanted spring flowers and warmer weather." He walked to the door and lifted his hat from a nearby peg. "I would have married you last fall without flowers or warm weather. I would have married you during the awful cold months of the winter when all of the plains states were buried in snows and hideous cold. I'd marry you tomorrow if you'd just say the word."

For just a moment, he thought she looked tempted. Then she squared her shoulders and stepped forward. "Good evening to you, Dr. Kelleher. I will see you in one week, at which time I will say the only words necessary to seal our arrangement. Until then, enjoy your inventory."

He shook his head. "You're a cruel woman."

She gave him a wink. "I promise to make it up to you."

eborah stood on a dining room chair while her mother and
Sissy pinned a hem in the white silk of her wedding gown.

"I can hardly believe it's the same dress," Mother declared. "I
remember when the huge hooped skirts were all the fashion, and
now this." She motioned to the straighter sleek lines of the gown.

"It was made good," Sissy commented. "Easy 'nuf to work
with quality."

"I'm still amazed. It looks so much like the one in the maga-
zine," Deborah commented, gazing down at the delicate silk.

The original gown had been skirted with three tiers of lace
flouncing over white China silk. Mother and Sissy had crafted
those flounces into a waterfall draping the bustled back. They
modified the belled skirt to fit with the fashion of the day, which

gave women a sleeker, more slender appearance—at least in the front. The back was another story. Voluminous amounts of material were fashioned over what seemed to be larger and larger bustles. Deborah was glad they'd chosen only a modest bustle. Anything bigger would have made her feel even more self-conscious. Still, she would have worn a bustle three times larger if required. She was marrying Christopher, and the gown was perfect. She felt like royalty—at least what she imagined royalty would feel like.

Deborah had always planned to wear her mother's wedding gown, and with the need to conserve money these days, it fit their plans all the better. Thanks to her mother's and Sissy's skill and the latest copy of *Godey's*, the masterpiece looked as if it had come from an expensive shop in Paris.

"Now turn and let's see if we have the hem pinned straight," Mother commanded.

Deborah took hold of her mother's hand and carefully turned on the chair. She let go and gripped the back of the chair as she made a full circle.

"It looks perfect." Mother sounded quite satisfied. "The train is so lovely."

"Won't be no problem to finish it up in time," Sissy said.

Deborah allowed them to help her from the chair. She ran her hands down over the overlaid bodice and basque waist. "I feel like a queen." She went to the cheval mirror they'd brought into the dining room.

Gently plucking a piece of lace that had twisted on the sleeve, she set it right and smiled. "I have never seen anything more beautiful, and just knowing that you wore this gown first . . ." Tears came to her eyes as she turned to face her mother. "I'm so very blessed."

Mother embraced her gently. "As am I. I can hardly believe this day has come."

Deborah pulled away and gave a light-hearted laugh. "Neither can I. It seemed forever in arriving." She gently touched the modest sweep of the scooped neckline. In just a couple of days, she would be Mrs. Christopher Kelleher. Dr. and Mrs. Kelleher. She giggled. One day it would be Dr. and Dr. Kelleher. Or maybe just "the doctors Kelleher." She giggled.

"You are getting giddy," her mother teased. "Let's get you out of the gown before you do something foolish."

"I wouldn't be so silly."

"Oh, look at you!" Lizzie and Jael declared as they entered the room, each carrying one of Lizzie and G.W.'s twins. Rutger wanted out of his mother's arms the moment they stepped into sight of his grandmother, however. At nine months of age, Rutger and Emily Ann, or "Annie" as she had quickly been dubbed, were getting into everything and charming everyone.

"I swear, they grow by inches each and every day."

"I agree with that," Lizzie said, wrestling her son. "Especially now that they eat from the table, as well as nurse. I can hardly believe they'll soon have their first birthday. Here it is the end of March; June isn't that far off."

Jael cuddled the calmer Annie. "I certainly wish I had a baby so sweet." Annie laughed and reached up to take hold of Jael's chin.

"Maybe you and Deborah both will have a baby this time next year," Lizzie said, her face revealing her delight at such a thought. "Then all of our children could be close in age and play together."

"I doubt we'll even be in the area," Jael said sadly. "Stuart doesn't like the influence you have over me. He's jealous of how close we are." She sighed. "He wouldn't be if it weren't for all his revenge nonsense." She shook her head and shifted Annie in her arms. "Sorry. I shouldn't have said that."

"But it's the truth," Lizzie said. "I'm afraid our lives will never be the same because of my bad decision to leave him."

"Leaving Stuart at the altar wasn't a bad decision," Deborah countered. "You should never marry someone you don't love, and I know you don't regret doing otherwise." That comment brought to mind the fact that Jael had married Stuart for less than love. She hurried to redirect the conversation. "Are you both as impressed as I am at what Mother and Sissy have done with this gown?"

"It's remarkable," Lizzie said, walking a few steps to see the back. "I can scarcely believe it's the same piece."

"We have the hem and waxed orange blossoms yet to sew," Mother said, "but I'm quite pleased with how it's turned out."

"Did the waxed blossoms survive the train trip?" Jael asked.

"They looked perfect," Mother replied. "The florist in Houston packed them quite carefully. They will make a grand finish to the dress."

A loud knock on the front door caught everyone's attention. Rutger immediately wanted to investigate and Lizzie battled to keep him in her arms.

"I'll get it, since Rutger seems to insist," she told them.

"Come, let's get you out of this gown," Mother said to Deborah.

Deborah nodded and followed her mother from the dining room. They were in the hall near the front foyer when she recognized the sound of Christopher's voice. Sissy turned, eyes wide.

"Groom ain't supposed to see you in your weddin' dress afore the ceremony."

Deborah froze in place, uncertain what to do as Christopher came into the room. Sissy tried to shield Deborah from sight. "Bad luck for you to be here, suh," she told Christopher.

"I'm afraid bad luck has preceded me."

Deborah moved from behind the older woman. "What is it? What's wrong?"

He noticed her gown and his frown deepened. "I'm so sorry."

She touched his arm. "What is it, Christopher? What has happened?"

Holding out a telegram, Christopher's gaze never left her face. "I've had bad news. Apparently something has happened to my family."

Deborah took the telegram and read it. The message was short and yet sent a wave of icy cold through her body. " 'Family tragedy.' " She looked up. "What kind of tragedy? It says nothing about the cause—about what's happened."

"I don't know. It was sent by the neighbor who lives across the street from my family. She and my mother are good friends."

Glancing again at the telegram, Deborah suddenly grew fearful. The second part of the message was simple.

Come quick.

Mother came to her side. "Do you have any way of contacting the woman to learn what has happened?"

"No. Not really. I could send her a reply, but I'm certain this must have cost money she didn't have. Even if she got the money from my folks, telegrams aren't cheap. They could never afford to send a lengthy explanation."

Something in his expression caused her to tremble. He was going to postpone the wedding. He was going to leave her and go to his family. She braced herself and waited.

"I . . . I have little choice . . . but to go." The look on his face seemed to plead with her to understand. "I . . . I'm so sorry."

Light-headedness washed over her. She wondered if Christopher would change his mind if she fainted dead away.

The twins began to fuss, and Deborah heard Lizzie suggest that she and Jael take them to the kitchen. Mother and Sissy offered to help, and before she knew it, Deborah was alone in the foyer with Christopher. A part of her wanted to break into tears and cry aloud at the unfairness of it all. Here she was, just days away from her wedding, and the groom was leaving her at the altar. Well, not exactly.

She thought of Stuart Albright and how he would most likely find this news quite satisfying since she'd played such a big role in ruining his wedding. Perhaps it was justice. Perhaps God was getting her attention—reminding her of the pain she'd caused when she encouraged Lizzie to leave Stuart.

That's not how God works, she told herself, trying to gather her wits. *God is just and righteous, and even now, I must see that He is in control of the situation.*

"Deborah?"

She lifted her chin ever so slightly. "When will you leave?"

Christopher reached out and cupped her quivering jaw. "I'm hoping to catch the train tomorrow. If not, I'll take my horse to Lufkin and catch another there."

Deborah nodded. "I understand."

He studied her intently. "Do you?"

She blinked several times, hoping to keep her tears at bay. "Your family relies upon you. What choice is there?"

"You could come with me to town. We could have Brother Shattuck marry us now," he said. "I'm not running out on you. I will return as soon as humanly possible."

His words offered little comfort; dread gripped her like talons. She wanted to believe that everything would be all right, but nothing seemed further from the truth.

She toyed with the idea of a rushed ceremony, then dismissed it. Mother and Sissy had worked so hard on the dress and other preparations. Surely the wedding would only be delayed a short time—a week, maybe two. It would be pure selfishness to demand Christopher marry her in a rush.

"You won't be gone for long," she said, trying to convince herself more than him. "I can wait."

He shook his head. "But you shouldn't have to, Deborah. I feel that I've put my family before you, and that's not at all what I want to convey. If I thought I could easily exchange telegrams with Mrs. Maynard, I would. It's just that I know the financial situation—my mother barely runs the household on what she gets. There's no money for such things."

"I understand."

"And I don't know anyone else who could afford to act as messenger and shoulder the cost until I could reimburse them."

"I understand," she repeated softly.

"I've thought about this all the way out here, and I don't know what else to do but go and see for myself. Perhaps my father has died—or maybe one of the children. If that's the case, then I'll have to help with the funeral expenses, and that will take the money I've put aside for our trip to Galveston."

Deborah lifted her finger to his lips. "Christopher. You must go. It's all right."

He pulled her into his arms. "But I don't want to. I've looked forward to our wedding day, just as you have. I've longed to make you my wife, to share my life with you."

"And you will . . . we will," she murmured. Deborah held

back her tears. She had to show Christopher that she could be the strong woman he needed.

She let him hold her for a few moments, then pulled away. Stepping back, she held up her hands, as if to ward him off. "You'd better go."

Christopher looked at her for a moment. "You look beautiful. I can hardly wait to see you in that gown again."

She smiled, but felt no joy. "That day will come before you know it. Just hurry back to me."

He nodded. "May I kiss you good-bye?"

She winced, but ducked her head quickly so he wouldn't see. "I think it might be better if you just went. I have no desire to ever bid you good-bye."

"Deborah . . ." He let her name fade without saying anything else.

She looked up and could see the battle raging inside him. "I'll tell everyone that you had to go to Kansas City. Please let us know as soon as you can what has happened. And be confident that we will be praying for you and for your family."

"They are soon to be your family, too," he said.

"Yes. In many ways, they already are. I know that if the situation were reversed, you would understand. Family has always been important to us—and always will be. That's one of the things I love about you, Christopher."

He stepped forward and pulled her back into his arms. He gave her a brief but sound kiss. "That wasn't good-bye," he said, turning to go. "That was a promise of my return."

∽∾∽

Deborah kept a brave face all through supper and into the night, even while her family plied her with questions she could not answer. Now, however, in the quiet of her room—away from everyone else—fear overcame Deborah in a way that she had not anticipated.

What if the tragedy were such that he couldn't return?

What if it wasn't his father who had died, but rather his mother? After all, the neighbor had sent the telegram. Perhaps she had to do so because Mrs. Kelleher was dead. If that had happened, Christopher would be forced to make some sort of arrangement. After all, his father's injuries from an accident in a rail yard kept him from working and Christopher's younger siblings certainly couldn't fend for themselves.

Deborah rolled restlessly to her side and tucked her knees up to her chest. What if he had to stay there and help his family for an indefinite period of time?

What if he never came back?

Overwhelmed by the weight and fear that had settled squarely on her chest, she muffled her sobs against her pillow and tried to pray. Words failed her, however. And the comfort she often found in talking to God remained elusive.

"Deborah?" her mother's soft voice called out.

She hadn't heard the door to her room open—hadn't seen the glow of her mother's lamp. Mother put the light on the dresser, then sat beside Deborah on the bed.

"I'm so sorry that this has happened, honey. But take courage. Christopher loves you dearly. He will be back—of that I'm certain."

Mother stroked back damp hair from Deborah's face. "I don't know why it had to be like this, but the world is full of heartache and tribulation, just as Jesus said it would be. Yet He reminds us that He has already overcome the world."

Deborah shook her head. "But that's because He's the Lord. What does that mean for us? For me?"

"I believe that because He lives within our hearts—because we belong to Him—we have victory. Satan would steal everything from us. He would take our joy, our hope, our contentment. He desires to destroy us, and what better way than by interfering in our lives and loves?"

"But God has more power than the devil. You've often reminded me of that," Deborah replied. "Why doesn't God keep these bad things from happening to us?"

Mother gave a sad smile. "Oh, how many times I've asked that very thing. Why did God give Satan power in this world? Why does God allow evil to corrupt and destroy the things He's created?"

"And what conclusion did you come to?" Deborah asked, sitting up. "What peace can you offer me now?"

Taking Deborah's hand in her own, Mother sighed. "The same peace that brought me through those long nights after your father's death—the peace that comes in knowing that all of this is temporal. Nothing here will last forever. God gives us earthly life for a brief time, and while it is ours, we should cherish it as a gift. We should live life to His glory and love one another in the richness of the love He holds for us.

"Christopher isn't lost to you—he's merely delayed. His love for you goes on, as does yours for him. This time apart is temporary. Use it for God's glory and not your own sorrow."

Her mother's embrace reminded Deborah of being a young child again—a child that held no responsibility or worry.

O God, she prayed, holding fast to her mother, *would that I could trust you like a little child. Would that I could let go of my worry and fear and trust that you will hold me.*

CHAPTER 3

APRIL 1887

C hristopher glanced at the clock. It was still early, but not unreasonable for a house call. He wanted to let Zed Perkins know what was happening and why he was suddenly leaving again.

He made his way through the quiet streets. Perkinsville was hardly more than a ghost town now. Most of the families had moved on, for there was no sense in waiting around, hoping that the mill would be rebuilt. There were mouths to feed and children to clothe, and those things couldn't be done with hopes.

The unnatural silence only seemed magnified by the clear skies and clean air. When Christopher had first arrived, the mill smoke and dust put so much debris into the air that he was hesitant to even open the windows in his home and clinic. Now that was gone, but at what cost?

He made his way up the walk to Zed's house, stifling a yawn. He'd not slept much at all the night before, fears overwhelming his thoughts. Whatever had happened must be grave, or his mother would surely have sent word herself. Still, uncertainty baffled him and burdened him with a sense of dread. This, coupled with the postponement of his wedding, had left him unable to sleep.

Knocking on the door of Perkinsville's finest two-story house, Christopher was surprised when Zed himself opened the door. Apparently they had let their hired housekeeper go.

"You're just the man I wanted to see," Christopher declared, extending his hand.

Zed waved off the formality. "None of that. Come on in and have some coffee with me. Better yet, have you eaten breakfast yet?"

"No, I didn't want to heat up the stove."

"Then we'll just head back to the kitchen. I was finishing up, but there's plenty left."

They made their way into the tastefully appointed house. Christopher caught the sound of female voices arguing from one of the rooms as they passed. Zed led him to the kitchen and motioned him inside before offering an explanation.

"I'm afraid my daughters have it in their mind that we should move to Houston. They have been pleading their case to Mrs. Perkins."

Christopher could well imagine the spoiled Maybelle and Annabeth nagging their mother. Around town, those two were known to get their own way in most every matter, but perhaps this time would prove the exception.

"What brings you here today?" Zed asked. "Have a seat," he said as he pointed. "I'll grab you a plate and silver." He went quickly to the task and plopped the utensils in front of Christopher. "This is one of Mrs. Perkins's everyday dishes. She'll chide me for not breaking out the good china and serving you in the dining room, but I figure you won't mind." He put the plain white plate in front of the doctor and added, "Now help yourself to the food."

Taking up a platter of bacon, Christopher chose several pieces. Zed left him to fill his plate while he fetched a mug for coffee.

"We've got cream if you need it." Zed put the cup in front of Christopher and waited for him to comment.

"No, black is fine. This is really far more than I expected. I certainly didn't mean to impose."

Zed laughed and took his seat. "No imposition. It's always good to have the company of another rooster—especially when the hens are raising a squawk." He shook his head as one of his daughters protested loudly. "Those girls are spoiled by my own hand, and now I'm paying the price."

Christopher waited until Zed had a long drink of his coffee before replying. "I'm going to get right to it. I've had bad news from my family in Kansas City. I don't know much other than what the telegram told me, and that was only that tragedy had occurred and I was needed." He sipped the strong black brew and let the warmth steady him. "I'm leaving when the train comes through, and I felt you should know."

Zed put his own cup aside. "I'm sorry to hear about your family, Doc. I wish I could offer some sort of assistance. I feel bad that you've gone without wages the last two months."

"It couldn't be helped. You were good to keep me paid long after the mill fire. That and the money I've earned by riding around to the various folks in need of a doctor's skills have kept me well enough." It wasn't exactly the truth, but Christopher didn't want the older man bearing the guilt of what he couldn't help.

Christopher sampled a mouthful of cheese grits and reached for the salt. He seasoned the grits as well as the eggs before continuing. "I don't know when I'll be back."

Zed slathered butter on a piece of corn bread. "You were right to alert me. Knowing Albright, if he sees that you've gone, he'll either take over the clinic or sell off the furnishings."

"Albright had me inventory everything that belonged to the company. I gave him that information the day before yesterday. It came later than he wanted, but I got called out on an emergency before I could finish it." He took a long drink, then gazed into the cup. "I figure it's just a matter of time before Albright demands I vacate the house anyway."

"Not as long as I have any say!" Zed sounded quite angry, but he quickly sobered. "Although, to be honest, I have little leverage anymore. I never figured to find myself in such a predicament. Never thought the day would come when I wouldn't be my own boss."

They ate in silence for a few moments. Christopher felt sorry for the older man. To have a younger man—an Easterner, at that—sweep in and deplete you of your livelihood and all you held dear would be humiliating and heartbreaking. The town of Perkinsville was only a shadow of its former glory. At one point, the town was growing fast enough to rival nearby Lufkin. Funny how things had changed overnight. Life was ever-changing, and property and possessions were easily destroyed. Since the devastating fire, the few who remained were mostly black families that had no choice but to stay and try their best to survive. If you could call it that.

A handful of white families remained, but it seemed they had plans to leave soon enough. The Huebners would go since there was no money to pay a schoolmaster. Mrs. O'Neal had already made known her plans to leave. The Wolcotts, Greeleys, and Shattucks remained in town, along with Mr. Perkins and his family, but most of the other residents had moved on. Mr. Perkins's sons had even relocated to other cities. It was really no wonder his daughters wanted to do likewise.

"Has Albright or Longstreet given any indication as to what they plan to do?" Christopher finally asked, pushing away the empty plate.

Zed shrugged. "They claim they will let me know when they have decided. They aren't even askin' for my opinion. I curse the day I ever took on a partner, much less two. If I hadn't gotten it in my head to expand, I wouldn't be in this position."

"I can't imagine that it's financially advantageous for them to do nothing," Christopher countered. "I suppose Albright could have felt the need to delay due to the bad winter. The plains states were devastated with the snows and cold weather. I read that hundreds of thousands of cattle and other livestock were lost. My guess is that buying extra building supplies isn't a luxury most can afford."

"That was just his excuse," Zed said, scowling. "Most of our buyers were back East." His expression changed almost instantly. "Say, what's this going to do to your wedding plans?"

"We're having to postpone. I spoke briefly to the pastor, and of course went out to see Deborah yesterday. She understands my need to go, although we both wish I could do otherwise. If only I knew the degree of the tragedy and whether or not a day or two would make a difference, I might simply stay until after the ceremony."

Zed nodded thoughtfully and rubbed his chin. "Well, these things have a way of workin' themselves out. I certainly didn't mean to burden you with my own troubles."

"Nonsense. Your troubles affect the entire community." Christopher placed a hand on Zed's shoulder. "I can well understand your concerns. You're a good man, and you care about your neighbors."

"Those folks trusted me for employment, and now that's been taken away. And for what? Albright somehow got the insurance company to agree it was an 'act of God.' The mill supposedly caught fire from a lightning strike, but I know different. That fire started from the inside. Someone set it—of that, I'm certain."

"I suppose without witnesses to say otherwise, money talked for Albright. He could have even offered to cut the investigator in on the deal." Christopher put his cup aside. "Well, I should head back to my place. Jude Greeley arranged for someone to send him a telegram when the train pulls out of Burke so that I can be ready. I told him I'd be at home. Thanks again for breakfast, and I'd appreciate it if you would keep Albright from throwing my things into the street."

"You have my word on it," Zed replied.

The two men got to their feet just as someone went wailing down the hall. Apparently one of the girls was quite distraught. Christopher turned to Zed with a hint of a smile. "If you need to stay at my place, feel free."

The older man laughed and slapped the doctor's back. "I just might take you up on that."

They were nearly to the door when Mrs. Perkins stepped into the hall. "Doctor Clayton—I mean, Kelleher. Goodness, but it will be hard to get used to that. Why you ever thought we would hold being Irish against you is beyond me."

Christopher gave her a slight bow. "I apologize for that, ma'am. It wasn't so much you and the folks of Perkinsville that concerned me. It was my decision long ago when I went east to medical school. However, you feel free to call me whatever you like."

"Oh, pshaw." She glanced back over her shoulder. "I'm the one who must apologize. If I'd known we had a guest, I would have put an end to the girls' fussing much sooner."

"Think nothing of it," Christopher replied. "But as I told your husband, I must be going."

"Oh, surely not. You should stay for breakfast."

"I've already fed him, Mrs. Perkins." Zed put his arm around her waist. "You have no need to fret."

"Indeed he did, and I must say, it was all quite delicious."

She smiled. "Well, you are welcome to stay and visit anyway."

Christopher shook his head and opened the front door. "I'm afraid I can't. Zed can tell you about my situation, but I thank you for the invitation." The last thing he wanted to do was spend additional time trying to explain.

"Do come back soon," Mrs. Perkins declared as she and Zed followed him out onto the porch. "You know you don't have to wait for an invitation."

"Thank you." Christopher made his way from the porch and had just started down the street when he caught sight of Pastor Shattuck.

"Good morning, Christopher. Do you still intend to leave today?"

Christopher nodded. "Just waiting for the train."

"Looks like you'll have a decent day for travel," the older man said as he looked upward. Overhead, the blue skies were void of clouds. "Hopefully the rain will hold off until you make it back."

"I hope so. What with the winter melt, I was told some of the tracks in the north are washed out and won't be repaired for some time to come. Hopefully it won't interfere with the line to Kansas City."

They climbed the steps to his porch and Christopher motioned. "Would you like to sit?"

"I would," Pastor Shattuck said, easing into one of the chairs. "I couldn't help but feel the need to come and just encourage you. I know this has been a difficult choice to make."

Christopher frowned. He never really felt there was a choice in the matter. He supposed there was, however. He could have refused to postpone the wedding in order to head north. Did it make him less worthy of Deborah that he didn't?

"Do you think I'm making a mistake?"

The pastor considered the question for a moment. "It doesn't really matter what I think. How did your bride-to-be take the news?"

Deborah's disappointed expression came to mind. "She understood, but I could tell she wasn't happy. What bride would be? They've all gone to so much work to arrange this wedding."

"And you think that's all she'd be worried about?" He threw Christopher a grin. "If you say yes, then I'm not gonna marry the two of you when you get back."

Christopher shook his head. "Of course that's not the only issue. I know Deborah loves me. I love her, too." He took the chair beside Brother Shattuck. "Did I do the wrong thing?"

"What do you mean?"

"All of my life I've had to be responsible for my loved ones. I was the firstborn and had to grow up quickly. It was impressed upon me that family came first—that my loyalty to them was a mark of my manhood. When I got the telegram, I never considered doing anything but going to them. Now I'm wondering if that was wrong. If I've somehow betrayed my love for Deborah."

"You're a good man, Doc. I can't fault you for caring about your folks. The delay is unfortunate. I suppose you two could have wed and she could have gone with you to help. There are always other alternatives."

"Maybe I'm not the man Deborah needs me to be." The thought troubled Christopher more than he cared to admit. He hadn't given her feelings nearly the consideration that he should have. Being a husband would be quite different than being a single man who watched over his mother's and father's needs.

"Well, the Word does say that you are to cleave unto your wife. Now, I realize you aren't married just yet, but that is something to consider. If you can't separate yourself from your mother and father, you won't be honoring the vows you make before God. Your wife must come first—not your mother and father. That doesn't mean you don't go on honoring them or caring about them."

"And if I can't put her first, then I shouldn't take a wife." Christopher stated matter-of-factly.

Brother Shattuck nodded. "That's about the size of it. Husbands are admonished to love their wives as Christ loved the church. He died for the church—for us. His heart wasn't divided."

Is my heart divided?

Christopher gave a heavy sigh. "I feel like I'm making a mistake, but I don't know what else to do. It's not like I can pick up one of those new telephones and call to see what the problem is."

The pastor smiled. "Those things surely are somethin' else, aren't they? I heard tell there are over a hundred thousand folks with telephones. I suppose someday everyone will have one, though I can't imagine they will ever take the place of speaking face-to-face."

"Neither can I," Christopher agreed. "Still, such a thing would certainly make occasions like this much easier."

"If it's any consolation," the pastor told him, "I've been praying for you through the night. I knew your heart was troubled, but you can trust God to direct your steps."

"I fear what awaits me," Christopher said, turning to the older man. "I feel like a coward."

"A coward wouldn't head into the heat of the battle. It's only natural that the unknown should offer some concerns, but you needn't let that build into fear. The Lord has promised to be with you wherever you go. He won't abandon you to face this on your own. I want you to know that I'll be praying for you while you're gone."

"The Vandermarks said they would do likewise," he admitted. "I can't say that I won't be thoroughly prayed over."

"Doc!" Jude Greeley called as he bounded down the street from the commissary. "Train's just left Rhodes." He stopped and shook his head. "No, I mean Burke. I can't get used to them changing the town's name. I mean, why was that necessary? Oh, and there's a rumor that they're getting a Farmer's Alliance store." He smiled and waved a piece of paper in the air. "But I digress. I got the telegram just now. You'd best get on out to the main track. They'll do little more than slow down for you."

Christopher got to his feet, as did Pastor Shattuck. "Well, I suppose I should make haste. I wouldn't want to make the train wait on my account."

Jude laughed. "Train makes everyone else wait on its account."

He turned and headed back down the dirt street. "Gotta get back. The missus hates it when I leave her in charge."

"I'll take my leave, too," Pastor Shattuck said. His expression softened with compassion. "There's no way of knowing at this point what you'll face in Kansas City, but you need to remember you won't face it alone."

Christopher drew strength from the words and stood a little taller. "I know you're right. I'll remind myself of that at every turn."

But deep within there was a nagging sensation that, in spite of the prayers and the knowledge that God would be at his side, Christopher was about to fall into a dark abyss—an abyss that promised to consume him, body and soul.

CHAPTER 4

. W. Vandermark tied his horse to the hitching post outside the house Stuart Albright had taken for himself. The nervous bay sidestepped—almost sending G.W. to the ground—and he winced in pain. His leg injury was good to remind him of how quickly life could change. Who could tell? Maybe there would be another change after his discussion with Albright. The important thing was to keep a tight rein on his temper.

After regaining his footing, he stroked the horse's mane. "Easy, boy. There's no sense in either of us gettin' our head up."

Drawing a deep breath, G.W. gave the horse another couple of pats, then made his way to the door. He knocked and, while he waited, rubbed the tops of his boots on the back of his trouser legs just in case any dirt clung to them. No sense appearing shoddy.

A young Negro woman dressed in a simple black gown and white apron opened the door and smiled. "Mornin', Mr. Vandermark."

"Mornin', Essie. I'm here to see Mr. Albright. Is he in?"

"Yessuh." She stepped back and reached for his hat. "Please step inside and I'll fetch him."

G.W. entered the house, none too surprised at the extravagant decor. Statues and paintings adorned every possible space. While completely out of place in Perkinsville, no doubt Albright felt right at home.

Essie disappeared for several minutes and G.W. continued to study the interior of the entry. A marble-topped receiving table near the center of the room was graced with a stylish silver vase and a huge arrangement of flowers.

"Mr. Albright say you can come to his office," Essie said from the hallway arch.

G.W. squared his shoulders and let the young woman lead him. There would be nothing pleasant about this meeting—of that he was certain.

Lord, he prayed silently, *please go before me. Give me the right words to say.*

As they made their way, G.W. noted that the rest of the house was just as elaborate as the foyer. When Essie ushered him in to Stuart Albright's office, he noted the room boasted pieces of art, including a huge oil of Jael dressed in a daringly low-cut gown. Embarrassed at the risqué piece, G.W. quickly glanced at the book-laden cases that lined one entire wall.

"Do you not care for my painting?" Albright chuckled. "I believe beauty should be appreciated. You can hardly appreciate what you cannot see."

G.W. felt at a loss for words. He shook his head, but still couldn't find his tongue.

Albright was not a patient man. "Why are you here?"

G.W. turned to address the man. Stuart sat behind a massive mahogany desk that very nearly reached from wall to wall. Of course, the room wasn't all that big, but it was made even smaller by the ridiculous furnishings.

"We need to talk," G.W. finally said.

Albright's icy blue eyes seemed to lend a chill to the room. He motioned to the red leather chair. "Sit down, Vandermark, and tell me why you've come to disturb my day."

G.W. tried not to let his temper flare at his host's rudeness. He took his seat and folded his hands. For a moment, he wished he had his hat back so that he could twist the rim, as he often did when feeling edgy. Instead he rubbed his leg.

"I've come on behalf of Vandermark Logging. We want to know what your plans are for the future."

Albright looked at him for a moment, then shrugged. "I'm afraid there is little to tell. We have been trying to decide what is most advantageous to our associates. Obviously much of the work force has already left the area. Getting them back might be difficult. Building another mill here . . . well . . . I haven't yet been convinced that it would be to our advantage."

"Then I'm here to demand you release Vandermark Logging from our contract. If the sawmill isn't operating, we've gotta sell our logs to someone who *is* operating."

The man laughed. "Whatever makes you think I would release you?"

G.W. leaned forward and narrowed his eyes. "You seem to be concerned with what's best for you and yours. I'm thinkin' this would be one of those things."

"Is this your way of threatening me?" Albright fixed him with a hard stare. "Because if you think to intimidate me, you might as well give up. I've crossed better men and won."

G.W. eased back in the chair. "Without a mill up and runnin', neither of us are makin' money."

Stuart laughed. "You may not be making any money, but I'm doing quite well for myself. A wise man diversifies, Mr. Vandermark. It's hardly my fault you've failed to do so. You're the one who agreed to provide your logs exclusively to my sawmill."

It was hard to remain seated, but G.W. managed somehow. "You need to know that we've talked to a lawyer. He tells us we are well within our rights to sue for breach of contract. You've taken longer than needed to make a decision regardin' the mill. A court would most likely release us from the contract and allow us to team up elsewhere. We're willin' to take this as far as we need to if you won't see reason."

"My, my. You certainly get right to the point." Albright leaned back in his chair as if completely unconcerned. "I suppose you think this comes as a surprise to me. That I have failed to plan for this possibility."

"I don't reckon I care one way or the other. If you're surprised, then that's the way it is. We still plan to do what's necessary to take care of our business."

"I see. Well, let me assure you, Mr. Vandermark, I'm not a man to be threatened or forced. When I feel backed into a corner, I simply come out fighting."

G.W. shrugged and rubbed his leg. "That's your right. I've cornered many a wild hog that felt the same way. The results weren't in their favor."

Albright clenched his jaw and narrowed his eyes to mere slits. G.W. knew the man was trying to intimidate him, but the only thing G.W. feared from Albright was the way he was bent on hurting the Vandermarks. And even then, it wasn't so much fear as irritation.

"Mr. Vandermark, do you suppose that a country bumpkin such as yourself could best me at anything?"

G.W. couldn't resist. He grinned smugly. "I got the gal, didn't I?"

Albright's face flushed scarlet, and his eyes seemed to bug out of his head.

With nostrils flaring, Albright got to his feet. "You think you can throw that in my face and win? It only serves to strengthen my resolve to see you destroyed. You have no power to stand against me. I will crush you like so many ants beneath my feet."

G.W. crossed his arms against his chest and hoped he looked as though he hadn't a care in the world. "Seems to me, Albright, that you're the one without a leg to stand on. You're used to bul-lyin' folks to get what you want—includin' women. Folks out this way don't much appreciate that kind of thing. You might have all the power in the world back East, but here in Texas, things are done different and folks look out for one another. My sug-gestion is that you get over losin' Lizzie and love the woman you married. You'd think with all that money you're always braggin' about, you could afford to buy her whole dresses."

Albright rounded the desk and stared down at G.W. with intense hatred. "I will see an end to you and your family."

G.W. got to his feet and stood nose to nose with the man. "This is between you and me. It's got nothin' to do with my family, and I'd thank you to leave them out of this."

"Your family took in Elizabeth when she ran away from me. They deserve to pay for their part—especially that sister of yours. If she hadn't interfered, Elizabeth would never have changed her mind. Your sister is as much my enemy as you are."

"I'm warnin' you, Albright. Leave Deborah out of this. You have a problem with me, then deal with me. Otherwise, back off."

Stuart's face seemed to relax and to G.W.'s surprise, he smiled. "You really have no idea what I'm capable of doing. I find it rather amusing."

"I hope you're just as amused when I beat that smirk off your face." G.W. felt a hint of satisfaction as Albright took a step back. "You've threatened my family and imposed your will on the good people of this community, but I'm gonna see that it comes to an end. Hopefully, I can do it with legal means, but if not . . ." He let the words hang in the air before turning for the door.

"Your threats mean nothing! Nothing!" Albright yelled after him. "I have more friends and power than you can even imagine. I'll see you destroyed if you dare try to break this contract."

G.W. paused at the door and shook his head. "Don't seem I have much to lose then, seein's how your actions threaten to destroy us if we sit idle. I'd rather go down with a fight. We've got a saying around here when things seem darkest. 'Remember the Alamo!' "

Stuart took three steps forward. "As I recall, Mr. Vandermark, your precious Texans lost that fight."

With a smile, G.W. nodded. "But I reckon we redeemed ourselves at San Jacinto. You mighta won the first battle, but you only managed to get our dander up to win the war."

∞

"I can't help but feel like all of this is my fault," Lizzie said, tears forming in her eyes.

Deborah embraced her. "Now, we've had this talk before. Stuart Albright is a vindictive man, and he is the only one to blame."

G.W. placed Rutger on the floor and came to stand beside

his wife. Deborah backed away to let her brother take charge. She knew his love for Lizzie ran deep and he would protect her and their family no matter the cost. Would Christopher offer her the same support? He gave it readily enough for his family.

"We're not gonna let him win, Lizzie." G.W. stroked her cheek. "We've got the Lord on our side. His evil ways won't stand against God's truth."

"Oh, G.W., you don't know how Stuart can be. He has all the money he needs to ruin us."

Annie started fussing, as if sensing her mother's fear. Deborah went to the little girl and picked her up. "There, now, you mustn't fret. Your mama and papa are right here." She bounced the child on her hip and looked to Lizzie. "G.W. is right. God is stronger than any Albright. We need to put this to prayer and trust that God will help us. It's not like we're seeking to hurt Stuart; we simply want what's right."

Lizzie took her daughter from Deborah and hugged her close. "I wish that I had your faith, but I don't." With that, she all but ran from the room.

Deborah looked to her brother and sighed. "She has no blame in this, but only time and the Lord will convince her."

Rutger crawled to his father and began to whimper, pulling himself up by G.W.'s pants leg. G.W. lifted the boy and rubbed his head. "I think it's nap time. I'll take him in and help Lizzie get them to sleep."

She smiled. "You're a good father, G.W. I always knew you would be."

He shook his head. "Sometimes I question whether I am or not. It seems Pa would never have allowed Albright to have this kind of control over us. I wish I had his wisdom."

"You can have the wisdom you need, G.W. The first chapter

of James says that if anyone lacks wisdom they have only to ask God and He will give it freely."

G.W. put Rutger to his shoulder. "Maybe I should spend a little bit of time in that book."

Deborah patted his shoulder. "It couldn't hurt."

She waited until he'd left the room to let down her guard. Her shoulders slumped. "I would do well to take my own advice."

Christopher's absence weighed heavy on her mind even though it had only been a few days. She tried not to let her heart lose hope. Surely everything would soon be back to normal.

"You certainly are deep in thought," her mother said from the door.

Lifting her face, Deborah gave a brief nod. "That I am."

"Christopher?"

She crossed her arms against her chest. "I can't help but worry. I try not to, but with something like this . . . well . . ." She shrugged. "I suppose times like these are meant to grow my faith."

Mother crossed to where Deborah stood. She pushed back an errant strand of her daughter's dark hair and smiled. "He's a good man who loves you. He'll be back before you know it."

"It seems like he's been gone months instead of days. I can't help but feel that Christopher's family troubles are going to be more than either of us can deal with."

"Nonsense. There is nothing the two of you can't face with God's help."

Deborah wrapped her arms around her mother's waist. Mother hugged her close. "I just hate not knowing what the future holds in store."

"Oh, my darling girl, it's not necessary for us to know the future. All that matters is that we know the One who holds it. God has already made provision—you'll see."

CHAPTER 5

Arriving in Kansas City three days later than he'd hoped due to heavy rains that had washed out part of the tracks, Christopher immediately hired a cab to drive him to his parents' home in the poorer section of town. The ramshackle dwellings where the more unfortunate residents lived were poorly constructed—some looking as if a good wind would surely cause their collapse. His overriding impression of his parents' house from his last visit was that it was in need of demolition more than anything. Perhaps if the present complications weren't too grave, he could help his mother spruce up the place a bit.

Christopher winced as the carriage found every rough spot on the road, and he banged from one side to the other. Hopes of comfort abandoned, he instead fought sleep as the driver continued through the city. It had been a long time since he'd been this tired. It was almost as if someone had placed a heavy weight atop him. He told himself it was just the humidity and threat of rain, but he knew different.

He closed his eyes and saw Deborah's dark eyes filled with sorrow. She had tried so hard to be assuring when he'd delivered the news of leaving her. Her willingness to support his decision only served to remind him of how much she loved him.

And I love her. I love her more than I ever thought possible to love another. She is everything to me.

Leaving her that day had been so hard. He pounded his fist against the carriage in a series of frustrated strokes—or at least he thought he had. Startled by the noise, he sat up and opened his eyes. Somehow, he'd dozed off. The carriage had stopped and the cabbie or someone was pounding loudly on the roof. He hadn't thought it possible to sleep, but apparently his body could simply take no more. Opening the carriage door, Christopher felt like his legs were leaden. His body rebelled at the interruption of rest and he hit the ground with a groan.

"Are you sure you want me to leave you here? Looks like rain," the driver told him. Christopher nodded, suppressing a yawn, and took the single suitcase the man handed down.

"I can wait for you, if you like?" the man added.

"That won't be necessary." Christopher settled the price of the ride and waited until the cab pulled off down the street before turning to face his family's home.

But it wasn't there.

He stared in shock at the charred frame. Brick chimneys rose out of the remains like strange sentinels guarding what had been left behind. Christopher dropped the suitcase. A fire had destroyed not only his family's home but the homes on either side. Family tragedy, indeed. This was a complete catastrophe.

He twisted around to see if the Maynard house was still standing. It was. He started for the door, then remembered his case and went back to retrieve it. Christopher couldn't keep his gaze from the blackened debris. How had the fire started? Was anyone hurt? Were they all dead? He felt sickened as the breeze blew the undeniable scent of destruction his way.

"Dr. Kelleher! I thought that was you," Mrs. Maynard called from her now-open front door.

Christopher forced himself to turn and face the thick-waisted woman. "What happened? Where is my family?"

∽

Stuart Albright was sulking. At least that's what Jael called it. He was clearly miffed about something. Probably the fact that G. W. Vandermark didn't roll over and play dead at his threats. She smiled and gave a slight shrug. Her father had tried to warn Stuart. He told him some men would not be motivated by intimidation, and clearly he had met his match.

"Have you decided when we are going back to Houston?" she asked with only a brief glance up from her needlework.

"No."

He didn't offer another word, and Jael allowed the silence to continue for a good ten minutes before pressing another question. "Have you decided to rebuild the mill?"

"No."

She frowned and fixed him with a look. "So you won't rebuild?"

He glowered. "It's none of your concern. Stick to your sewing."

Clearly agitated, he got to his feet and retrieved his newspaper. "I'll be in my office."

Stalking from the room, Stuart left Jael to wonder if this was the way her future would always be. She hadn't married for love, she reminded herself. Love wasn't real—not for her anyway. The man she'd given her heart to so long ago had also given her that realization, just before he deserted her and left her to carry, and later lose, his unborn child. Promises made in the heat of passion were seldom trustworthy, she supposed.

The needle pierced her finger, causing Jael to jump. She hurried to suck the droplet of blood to keep it from staining her work. Putting the hoop and threads aside, Jael got to her feet, still nursing her finger. She walked to the window and pulled back the heavy drapery to stare out into the night.

With so many people having left the town, there were very few lighted houses. She wondered why Stuart had allowed this abandonment of Perkinsville. He would stand to lose a great deal of money, and that was truly the only thing he cared about. This thought gave her resolve to seek him out once again. She wasn't afraid of his pouting and belligerence. In fact, she wasn't afraid of much anymore. Living without love had been her worst fear, and since that had been realized, nothing else seemed all that important.

She entered his office without knocking. Her gaze immediately went to the awful painting he'd demanded she pose for. He'd picked out the most scandalous dress, not caring at all that it made her feel immodest and uncomfortable. The memory only served to bolster her resolve. Jael fixed him with a silent stare.

"What do you want now?"

"I want answers, Stuart. I want to know why you insist on

tormenting the Vandermarks and the people of Perkinsville—at least those few who are still around to be tormented."

"As I've said before, my business is my business. Stay out of it and you'll be much happier."

"I didn't marry you expecting to be happy." The words dripped sarcasm. She crossed the room and put her hands on his highly polished desk. She knew the action would irritate him, but she didn't care.

"If you are so lovesick for Elizabeth Decker Vandermark, why do you even bother to keep up the pretense of devoted husband?"

He smiled. "Because you are so charming, of course."

Jael straightened. "Stuart, we both know what a farce our marriage is. I didn't ask you to pretend to love me or even care for me. It's just as you told me when we agreed to this arrangement—this marriage was for the sake of convenience and nothing more. Oh, I'll admit I fooled myself into believing that love might grow, but now I see it cannot, for the soil is poisoned."

"And what of it? I have not played you false."

She looked at him and shook her head. "I suppose you haven't. You said there would be no love and that is certainly true."

He pounded his fists on the desk. "And why should there be? You came into this marriage carrying another man's brat in your belly. You were just as desperate to save face as I was to reap my inheritance."

Stuart's words had the impact of a slap on the face. Jael steadied herself by taking hold of the back of the chair. "I want a divorce."

"No." He stared at her as if daring her to challenge him.

"I'm sorry, Stuart, but I was a fool to marry you. I should have faced my father's wrath and dealt with the consequences. I could have come to Deborah. I suppose I always knew that. You were simply a convenience."

He jumped to his feet. "As were you. And now you are an inconvenience."

"Then let me go. Give me a divorce."

"I will not, and you will not pursue this subject any further. In fact, should you dare to bring it up to your father or the Vandermarks, I will make you pay."

His words seemed suspended in the silence that followed. For just a brief moment, Jael had hoped he would agree to end their marriage and let her go on her way—perhaps even settle a small amount of money on her. But it was clear he would not.

"Why, Stuart? Why do you insist on remaining in a marriage where there is no love?"

"Marriage was never about love, and those fools who think otherwise are as simpleminded as you." He crossed to where she stood. "Marriage is nothing more than an arrangement to benefit those joined together."

"But I'm not benefiting."

He grabbed her roughly and forced Jael against him. She fought to free herself, but Stuart buried one hand in her hair and wrenched her head back to expose her face. Kissing her hard and without feeling, he pulled her head until Jael thought her neck would snap. Perhaps that was what he had in mind. Perhaps he would kill her and put her out of her misery—tell everyone she had fallen down the stairs. She went still in his arms and waited for the end. When it didn't come, she opened her eyes to find Stuart staring at her with an odd expression such as she'd never seen.

"Well? Why don't you finish it?" she taunted. "Kill me now so I might at least be free of you that way."

He let her go as if she'd suddenly become painful to touch. He staggered back, looking like he'd been gut punched. Jael righted herself. "I will have my divorce, Stuart. You won't stop me."

She turned and walked out the door. Her only thought was to pack her things and go to Deborah. The Vandermarks would take her in. She knew they would.

Jael had made it to the stairs when Stuart caught up with her. "If you dare to try leaving me—divorcing me—your beloved Deborah will pay with her life."

The words froze her in midstep. Could he possibly be serious? Jael turned and faced him. Evident satisfaction played across Stuart's expression.

"I thought that might get your attention."

"You could kill another person?"

Stuart's maniacal laugh left Jael doubting his sanity, but his reply removed all doubt. "It wouldn't be the first time." He narrowed his eyes. "And I seriously doubt it will be the last."

∞

"Sit and rest. You look quite weary," Mrs. Maynard said as she ushered Christopher into her sitting room.

The house was simple but clean. Christopher took a seat where the older woman pointed and waited to hear what was sure to come.

"The fire started in the middle of the night. The weather had been cold and fires were necessary to keep the house even slightly warm," she began. She sat nearby and studied him with a mother's gentle expression. "They believe the chimney flue got too hot and something caught afire."

Between his shock and exhaustion, Christopher could only

nod at the explanation. Thunder rumbled in the distance. The storm had finally arrived.

"Your mother, God rest her soul . . ."

"What?"

"Oh, my dear, I hardly know how to tell you, but they're gone. Your ma and da. They perished in the fire."

This wasn't happening. Christopher felt as if he might be sick. He forced back bile. "And the children?"

"The children? Oh, gracious me, they survived. Your ma saw to that. She got them out first and then went back for your da. Of course, the fire had grown by that time. Your brothers tried to go into the house to bring them both out, but the neighborhood men stopped them. They knew it was too late. The house began collapsing, and even the chief of the fire brigade said that nothing could be done but to try and contain it. As you can see . . . well, it claimed two other houses, but no other lives."

His mother was dead. His father, too. He had never once allowed himself to really consider the possibility. Oh, he had certainly expected his father to pass sooner than later. The man's health had been precarious, and the last time Christopher had seen him, it was clear to him as a physician that time would take its toll and Da's life.

"I wish I could have given you some forewarning," Mrs. Maynard continued. "The telegram took every free cent I had, and I couldn't afford to say anything more." She leaned forward. "As it was, they gave me the word *quick* for free. I told the telegraph operator what had happened, and he felt it imperative to get you here in a hurry."

Christopher could hardly believe what he was hearing. It seemed like a bad dream. Perhaps he had fallen asleep in the carriage and was even now simply caught in a nightmare. He looked up and refocused his eyes. No, this was happening. He was fully awake.

It just didn't make sense. He wanted to know so much more—wanted answers. How could this kind of thing have happened? Instead, he nodded, making a mental note to see that the woman was repaid for contacting him. "Where are . . . where are my brothers and sisters now?"

"They've been staying here with me, but at this moment, they're in school. I told them it was better for them to go than sit around here mopin'. Your ma and da were laid to rest day before yesterday. We considered waiting for you, but I had no way of knowing if you'd even received the telegram."

Burying his face in his hands, Christopher tried hard to think. Exhaustion clouded his thoughts and pain filled his heart.

"Why don't you take a rest? The children won't be home for another three hours. I have a room ready for you at the top of the stairs."

He looked up. "What? A room?"

She nodded and got to her feet. "I figured you'd need a place to stay."

"I can go to the hotel."

"Nonsense. I have the space and you needn't spend your coin that way. There will be plenty of other expenses. The accommodations ain't much, but the bed is comfortable. Now, come along. I'll show you the way."

Christopher looked at her for a moment and then got to his feet. "Are the children . . . were they hurt at all by the fire?"

"Only their hearts," she replied. "The wee ones, especially. They cry in the night, and though she won't say it, Miss Darcy frets about this house catchin' fire, too. I tried to comfort her, but she's a force to be reckoned with, that one."

"And the boys? Jimmy and Tommy?"

She nodded with a knowing look. "They're angry. They couldn't save their ma and da. They're madder than any two young men have a right to be. The days to come won't be easy for any of you."

Christopher was silent, for what could he say? Nothing made sense, no matter how hard he tried to force coherent thought.

"Come along, now. I'll fetch your suitcase later. You have a rest while you can." Her voice was soothing and gentle. "I loved your dear ma. Bertha was my best friend." She wiped at a tear as it trailed down her cheek. "The days are much darker now."

He nodded and followed her up the rickety wooden stairs. The polished finish had long since dimmed with continued wear; a clear path marked an outline on each step. At the top, Mrs. Maynard paused only long enough to regain her breath.

"I'm . . . getting too . . . old." She offered him a smile. "This is your room right here." She managed to cross to the door and open it. "Sleep and when you wake, I'll have something for you to eat."

"Thank you," Christopher said, barely able to form the words. He entered the room and turned in surprise at the sound of the door closing.

He stared at the wall for several moments trying to clear the cloudiness that dimmed his ability to reason. The truth wearied him. Christopher turned to take in the rest of the tiny room. A single bed had been pushed up against one wall. An open window displaced the musty odor of a room long closed and unused with scents of the pending rain. Christopher sat on the edge of the bed, pulled off his coat, and threw it over the footboard. He took off his shoes and eased back onto the bed. Mrs. Maynard had been correct—it was quite comfortable.

Christopher gazed upward at the unmistakable evidence of a leaking roof. The stains made strange patterns—hazy pictures, really. His vision blurred, and he blinked hard. He could make out what looked like a profile of Queen Victoria, and to her right, a rather sorry looking rabbit. But tears soon overwhelmed his eyes.

With a moan, he rolled to his side and drew the pillow to his mouth to muffle his cries. He was a grown man, but at the thought of his mother burning to death, he was once again a young boy. Why couldn't he have saved her?

CHAPTER 6

L izzie's father, Brian Decker, sat across the dinner table and marveled at his grandchildren. "They are a perfect delight." He reached over to wipe a bit of applesauce from Rutger's mouth. "I must say, they remind me very much of you when you were small, Lizzie."

"I'm so glad you are here to share in our joy of them," Lizzie answered. "Oh, Father, they have been the biggest blessing amid this adversity."

Mr. Decker had only arrived that afternoon, and Deborah knew her brother and Lizzie were overjoyed and relieved to have him present. G.W. had been soliciting advice from his father-in-law, a lawyer, and now the man had come to share some answers with the family.

Lizzie handed Annie a small piece of buttered corn bread. "We've all been quite beside ourselves."

"I gathered as much from your last letter. It seems that Mr. Albright is refusing to yield any kind of advantage to you."

"I went to talk to him," G.W. interjected. "Just like you suggested in your telegram. He wasn't in any mood to discuss options."

Mr. Decker straightened. "I'm sorry to hear that. Did he say why?"

"No. He only told me that should we dare to sue him for breach of contract, he'd tie us up in court for years to come. Seein's how he's gotten his way in any other legal issues regarding the mill, I'm inclined to think he's got powerful friends and can do just about whatever he likes."

"Well, I reviewed the contract several times, as well as shared it with colleagues to get their professional opinion. The fact of the matter is, Vandermark Logging does have an agreement to sell your lumber exclusively to Zed Perkins's sawmill. Still, while there should have been some noted date on how long they could force you to remain idle due to their 'act of God,' it's water under the bridge. At this point, we need to find a way to make a mutual agreement benefit both sides."

Deborah immediately felt guilty. While the contract had been Zed's requirement, she had been the one to make many of the changes. She'd never thought to add any kind of time frame on such a matter. After all, they were dealing with a man for whom their father held nothing but the highest regard. A handshake had always been good enough in the past, but when Zed needed a signed contract in order to secure his bank loan, Deborah had seen no reason not to comply. Neither could the rest of the family. It wasn't their fault that Zed had found it necessary to take a partner at a later date. And it certainly wasn't their choice to have Stuart Albright involved in any part of the business. Still, guilt gnawed at Deborah's conscience. If she had been more knowledgeable about contracts, perhaps she could have prevented this.

"I don't think you'll ever talk Stuart into doing anything beneficial for us," Lizzie replied. "He hates me, so he hates the Vandermarks. It's just that simple."

"Well, I will speak to him nevertheless," her father said as Rutger reached out to offer his grandfather a handful of mushed corn bread. Mr. Decker laughed and rubbed the boy's head. "No thank you, little one." He glanced to Annie and shook his head. "I can't get over how they look like you, Lizzie."

She smiled and glanced G.W.'s way. "So my husband continues to remind me. I suppose that isn't as surprising, however, as the unexpected arrival of two babies instead of one. This double blessing came as quite the shock."

"Oh, it shouldn't have," her father said. "You were, after all, a twin."

All gazes turned to Mr. Decker, and the room fell completely silent. Even the twins looked at him in noiseless wonder for several heartbeats, and then Annie let out a squeal of delight and Rutger followed.

"What?" Lizzie asked.

Her father blew out a long breath. "I thought your mother had told you."

"Told me what?" Lizzie looked most perplexed.

Lizzie's father put down his fork. "That you were the first-born of two baby girls. You had a twin sister who died at birth."

"Why did no one tell me before now?" Lizzie asked. "Even when I wrote to Mother about the babies, she never said a word."

"I suppose I should have expected as much," her father answered. "You mother swore everyone to secrecy when the child died. The baby was taken away and buried without fanfare. It was as if there had never been a twin. Your mother refused to speak about her and forbade anyone else to so much as mention the situation of your birth. She wouldn't even let us name the child. The tiny gravestone I purchased simply says *Baby Decker*."

Putting her napkin to the side of her plate, Lizzie got to her feet. "How can this be? How could Mother do this to me? She had only to be honest. I asked her once if she'd ever had other children, and she told me no."

"The death of that baby really upset her, but she would never talk to me about it. I asked the doctor, but he said it was best to let her deal with it as she found fit."

"And what of you, Father?"

He shrugged. "Men are not encouraged to worry overmuch about such things, but it cut me deeply. I have to admit, I was quite upset with your mother's manner of handling the situation. For her sake, however, I said nothing."

"And my poor little sister didn't even have a name," Lizzie said, shaking her head. "Was she so unimportant?"

"Not to me." He glanced away for a moment. "I called her Elsa. I thought it went well with Elizabeth."

"I think I need to be alone for the moment." Lizzie hurried from the room and Mr. Decker gave G.W. a look of alarm.

"I never meant to upset her. I honestly thought her mother would have mentioned it at some time or another."

G.W. shook his head. "There never was any mention of it. Her ma seldom writes—especially now that she's gone to England to help the women with their cause. When she heard about the twins, she sent a short note and two silver rattles. She said nothin' more—certainly nothin' about the past."

"Leave it to Harriet to send something useless and hide the truth," Mr. Decker said.

Deborah could hardly believe the news. It shouldn't have been so startling. Everything she'd read about twins said that being one increased the chances of reproducing them. Even just having twins in the family seemed to strengthen the appearance of other sets. She frowned. There were twins in Christopher's family, too—his sisters Mary and Martha. She knew how busy the twins kept Lizzie. Had it not been for the help of Deborah, her mother, and Sissy, Lizzie would never have been able to manage.

What if I have twins?

The thought of just one baby was startling, but two babies? How would Deborah ever find time to further her medical studies and help her husband?

Deborah forced her mind to focus on the people at the dinner table. It was foolish to let such wild thinking discourage her. She and Christopher hadn't even wed yet.

"If you can talk him into such a thing, then could we act right away?" Arjan was asking.

"I don't know that we should even bother to approach Albright on the matter," Mr. Decker replied. "We can ask his intentions, talk about the possibility of a lawsuit for breach of contract, but as for the other, I don't believe I would even mention it. In fact, you would do well to hide it from him all together."

G.W. frowned. "That won't be easy."

Deborah realized she'd missed most of the conversation. "What are you saying?" she blurted out.

Everyone looked at her rather oddly at her outburst. "He's talking about trading logs for other things," her mother replied.

"You sure we wouldn't be in any kind of legal trouble if we decided to go that route?" Uncle Arjan asked.

Brian Decker leaned back in the chair and smiled. "Mr. Albright seems to be a man who twists the law to suit his needs. I'm not suggesting that we do anything that breaches the agreement. Your contract states that you will sell logs exclusively to the Perkinsville Sawmill. It says nothing about you giving logs to other mill owners. Nor does it prohibit them from gifting you in some manner."

Arjan considered this a moment and nodded. "I suppose you make a good point."

Deborah felt as if her head were in a cloud. "How would this work?"

"As I stated earlier, you could give a shipment of logs to another mill and the owner could in turn give something to you. He could give you goods such as food, material for clothing, lamp oil, equipment; he could even make a payment on your mortgage. No money need ever change hands directly. It wouldn't even be a formal barter. You would simply gift the mill owner. He in turn would give you a gift." Mr. Decker shrugged slightly. "There's nothing in the contract that even hints that gift-giving would be unacceptable."

G.W. exchanged a grin with his father-in-law. "It would be just the kind of thing Albright would do to us if the shoe were on the other foot."

"But that's not the attitude I want us to have in this," his mother chided. "We are Christian folk, and as such, we do not want to lie or cheat."

"I do not recommend either of those options," Mr. Decker agreed. "As I said, the contract has nothing in it to suggest this would be a breach. You agreed to provide Perkins and his mill with logs. There is no mill at this time, and Perkins's associates have not decided whether they will rebuild. To be certain, they have made it clear that they will not pay for log deliveries. Therefore, I see no reason that you cannot do as you like with your own timber. So long as you aren't selling, you should be fine. I've run this by the best legal minds."

"But that was back East," Uncle Arjan countered. "Texas isn't exactly known for doin' things like the rest of the country. I've seen the book of rules get thrown out more'n once."

"And that might very well work to your benefit." Mr. Decker paused and picked up his fork once more. "The most Mr. Albright could do is demand you begin log distribution to him again. That, of course, will mean he'll have to pay for those logs, and you will have the money you need. I do not see a problem with the situation."

"We've got good friends to the north who own mills and would probably agree to the arrangement," Mother said. "They go way back with this family."

"Why don't I go with G.W. and Arjan, and we'll visit these folks," Mr. Decker suggested. "I could assure them of the legalities and put to rest any concerns."

"We can use the excuse of picking up our horses in Lufkin. Jefferson Marshall was expecting us to fetch them most any day now," Arjan said. "And if anyone asks, we won't have to lie about why we're there."

G.W. nodded. "We can also pick up a few supplies."

Deborah could hear a collective sigh of relief from around the table. She certainly hoped this was the answer they were looking for. If not, G.W. had made it clear serious financial problems would soon befall them. She had offered the money she'd set aside, but G.W. refused it. He told her the day might well come when they'd have no other choice, but for now, there were still alternatives. It appeared Mr. Decker had just widened the possibilities considerably. Now, if Christopher would just return or telegraph to let her know what was going on, all would be well.

"We can leave tomorra," G.W. declared. "We'll start up in Lufkin. The logs won't even have to pass through town at all; no one even needs to know what we're doing." He got up from the table and looked to their mother. "Could you watch the babies for a spell? I want to make sure Lizzie is all right."

Mother nodded. "Of course. She needs you."

Deborah watched her brother leave, wishing she could go with him. Lizzie was her dear friend, and she wanted to offer her comfort. But Mother was right. Lizzie needed G.W. more than anyone else.

She let out a heavy sigh and picked at her food. If she didn't hear soon from Christopher, she might well go mad.

∽

After sleeping a little more than two hours, Christopher arose and went quickly to work. He decided it would be best to be gone when the children came home. That way, Mrs. Maynard could let them know he was in town and that he would be back to speak with them. Christopher hoped it would allow them a little time to deal with the surprise of his presence, given that Mrs. Maynard had not mentioned to them that she'd sent a telegram. Not only that, but there was plenty to be accomplished.

First, he needed transportation, and Mrs. Maynard assured him a livery was just a few streets away. As he walked, Christopher made a mental list of what needed to be done. He should telegraph Deborah, then make his way to the funeral home to see what kind of debt was owed. Mrs. Maynard had also informed him that the children had little more than the clothes on their backs. Something would have to be done about that.

The livery was exactly where Mrs. Maynard had directed. A tall beanpole of a man welcomed him.

"Name's Rothberg. Need a saddle ride or a buggy?"

"A horse for now," Christopher replied. "I'm Christopher Clay . . . Kelleher. Mrs. Maynard sent me over."

The man nodded and sobered. "Sure was sorry about your folks." He motioned Christopher into the stable. "I have a gelding over here. One of my best."

"That will be fine." Christopher noted the sturdy-looking chestnut. He was a tall one, just like the man, and looked to have some Arabian blood.

"Your folks was good people." He quickly cinched the saddle. "Your brother Jimmy used to help me out during the summer. 'Course, when school began, he was only able to come for a few hours after classes. A smart one, your brother."

Christopher knew from his mother's letters that Jimmy was quite interested in his education. He hoped to promote that interest and keep his brother motivated to continue his education.

"Yes, sir. Good people. Your ma was one in a million."

"Thank you for saying so," Christopher said, the ache in his heart becoming more pronounced.

"She'd send over a loaf of just-baked bread from time to time. Probably the best I ever ate. And cookies as big as dinner plates." He smiled and shook his head. "Everyone in the neighborhood is going to miss her."

It touched Christopher to hear this tribute to his mother, but he felt as if his own emotions might boil over at any moment.

He paid the man for two days. "I don't know how long I'll need him, but I'll return and pay additional fees should it be longer."

"No problem. You're staying with Mrs. Maynard, and I can always check up on you there." He smiled and handed Christopher the reins. "Colleen owes me a hot meal. I think she's sweet on me anyway."

It was the first time Christopher had felt like smiling in days. He could well imagine the stocky Mrs. Maynard and the tall, skinny Mr. Rothberg. "Could you direct me to the closest telegraph office? I need to send a message to Texas."

Rothberg walked with him and the horse to the front of the stable. "Just turn right at the second street. You'll go down about six blocks and then you'll see a row of businesses. The telegraph office is on the corner."

"Thank you." Christopher stepped into the stirrup and mounted the horse. The gelding was well behaved and stood stock-still. "I'll be in touch."

The horse acted as if they were old friends. He quickly complied with Christopher's directions and seemed completely at ease with the city traffic. The area had changed a great deal since the last time Christopher had been back. Everything looked foreign to him—felt foreign, too. Of course, most of his adult life had been spent elsewhere avoiding his Irish heritage—avoiding the pain of seeing his father helpless.

"Helpless is exactly how I feel," he muttered.

His parents were dead. His mother gone—truly gone. He hadn't even been able to say good-bye. He thought about his last letter home. What had he told his mother? What kind of affection had he offered? His eyes blurred, but he refused to give in to the pain of his loss. He could grieve later. For now, there was work to be done.

He thought again of the children who barely knew him. It wouldn't be easy for them to see him as their authority or rescue.

"Nothing will be easy for them now."

∞

"And this is your youngest brother, Jonah. He just celebrated his seventh birthday two days before the fire," Mrs. Maynard declared. She finished the introductions and took a seat beside the boy.

Christopher let his gaze travel over the ragged quintet. Jimmy and Tommy glared at him with expressions that suggested they wanted nothing he had to offer. They were angry and hurting, and the appearance of a big brother offered no comfort. Darcy, at the age of thirteen, was quite a young woman. She admonished nine-year-old Emma to sit up straight and reached over to straighten her sister's pigtails. The three youngest were quite petite—perhaps even underfed. No doubt they had less to eat than their older brothers. Christopher shook his head, feeling guilty for not having done more.

Jonah continued to watch him with wide eyes and a look that seemed almost fearful. The boy's intensity caused Christopher to rethink how he would approach them. Somehow he had to win their trust—had to help them to see that he was there to help.

"I realize that none of you know me very well, but I can tell you honestly that I grieve our mother's loss as much as you do." He paused and added, "Our father, as well."

"Mrs. Maynard said they went up to heaven," Jonah offered, then buried his face in the stocky woman's waist.

Christopher was rather at a loss as to how to deal with the situation. His discomfort stymied rational thought; he could have more comfortably performed surgery while wearing a blindfold.

Drawing a deep breath, Christopher knew he would have to be strong. Strong and firm. He'd already decided that he would take the children back to Texas with him. There was certainly nothing for him in Kansas City, and while it would be stripping away the last remnants of all that was familiar, a new start would be good for all of them. Of course, Jimmy and Tommy would have plenty to say on the plan.

"I asked Mrs. Maynard to gather you all here," he began, "because I wanted to explain what will take place in the next few days. Since the house has burned down and the landlord had no insurance to rebuild, you have no home here in Kansas City."

"We got a home with Mrs. Maynard," Jimmy said in a terse clipped tone. "I can see to it that we manage. I'm almost seventeen." He was clearly used to being in charge of his siblings.

Christopher met his brother's gaze. "I'm sorry, but I cannot allow that. You see, I know our ma wanted to see you continue your education. She was very proud of you—proud of each one of you. She wrote to me all the time about what you were accomplishing. I know she would want you to be happy, but she'd want you to be safe and cared for above all. Mrs. Maynard cannot continue to care for you—that isn't her job."

Jimmy folded his arms against his chest but said nothing more. Tommy, too, remained silent, while Darcy had little difficulty posing the questions they no doubt all had on their minds.

"So where are you gonna take us?"

He smiled, hoping it would ease their fears. "I'm going to take you back to Texas with me. I'm soon to be married, and I know my wife would love having each of you." At least he hoped she would. He hadn't been able to explain everything in the brief telegram he'd sent her and had already decided he would wait until they returned to let her know the full impact of the fire.

"I ain't gonna go," Tommy declared, getting to his feet. "You can't make me. I'll be fifteen in a couple of months, and that's old enough to take care of myself."

"Me either," Jimmy said, joining his brother. "You can't just come in here and expect us to leave. We've lived here all our lives. We'll go on livin' here."

It was just as Christopher had expected. "I'm sorry, but that won't be possible. You are underage and cannot fend for yourselves. You cannot earn a living to support the little ones, and even if you were allowed to roam off on your own, the county would come in and take the rest of your brothers and sisters."

Jimmy let out a breath that was something between a growl and a sigh before storming off upstairs. Tommy opened his mouth as if to speak but then closed it and stomped off. At this, the two youngest began crying and Mrs. Maynard gathered them in her arms.

"I'll tend them in the other room," she told Christopher.

That just left Darcy. The blue-eyed, redheaded girl looked at him rather matter-of-factly. "Looks like you got a big problem."

CHAPTER 7

On Saturday, Deborah accompanied her mother to the commissary. The building was poorly stocked and able to satisfy only the most basic of needs. Her mother hoped to purchase at least several spools of thread, and two or three bags of flour, cornmeal, and coffee.

Deborah walked the aisles, looking for anything useful. There had been a time when the place had been brimming with supplies and trinkets. Now it was just the basic needs, and hardly much of those.

She heard footsteps fall behind her and backed up to let the other person pass. To her surprise, Deborah was immediately taken in hand by Jael. Her friend hurried them to the far end of the store, catching her skirt for a moment on a rough spot on the wood floor.

"Oh bother." She tugged the material loose, not at all mindful of its delicacy. She pulled Deborah behind a stack of barrels. "Stuart is livid. He apparently had a falling out with G.W."

"I know about it. G.W. asked Stuart to let Vandermark Logging out of the contract since they aren't moving ahead to rebuild."

"But now Stuart has decided he will rebuild. He figures if he's rebuilding and your family files for breach of contract, he can get a judge to rule in his favor because . . . well, something about there being a tangible effort to rectify the situation." Jael rolled her eyes. "It was all rather muffled as I was eavesdropping on Stuart and my father."

"So he plans to rebuild?" Deborah questioned. "That's wonderful news."

Jael shook her head. "I don't trust Stuart to be doing a good thing in this matter. The man still hates you and your family. He even threatened you."

Deborah looked at Jael and shook her head. "What in the world are you saying?"

"I told Stuart that I wanted a divorce. He refused, of course, though I can't imagine why at this point. He has all that he wants—his inheritance, the ability to hurt Lizzie and your family. He's extremely wealthy. Anyway, when I mentioned that I wanted a divorce, he told me no. Then he added that if I dared to try to leave him or divorce him, he'd make you pay—with your life." Jael reached out and took hold of Deborah's arm. "He means it, too."

"I'm not afraid of Stuart Albright," Deborah replied. How dare he deliver such a threat!

"Perhaps you should be. Stuart made some comment about having killed before. I don't know exactly what it was all about, and he certainly offered no details, but Deborah—I'm scared of what he might do."

Deborah felt her brows knit together. "He boasted of killing?"

Jael nodded and glanced around to be sure no one could overhear. "When I asked him if could really kill another person, he said it wouldn't be the first time or the last. It might well have been nothing but lies—just words spoken in anger to frighten me."

Deborah shivered as if a sudden icy breeze had blown into the store. "What an evil man."

"I fear if I do not stay with him and cooperate fully, he will carry through his plans to harm you. I couldn't bear it if that happened."

"But if you left him, where would you go? Were you planning to leave Perkinsville?"

Jael looked toward the floor, then back to Deborah. "I thought I might stay a while with you."

Deborah could see what her friend had in mind. "Of course you would be welcomed. You needn't stay with him because of his threats. I'll let G.W. and Uncle Arjan know. Christopher, too, when he returns. Perhaps they will speak to the constable."

"Stuart probably has the man paid off. I wouldn't trust anyone but family at this point. Have you heard from Christopher? Do you know when he'll be back?"

"There was a brief telegram. He said he'd arrived safely and that his parents' home had been destroyed by fire, but little else. Certainly nothing about when he planned to return." She shrugged. "I suppose he will have to see them moved to new lodgings before he can leave."

"Stuart talked of us moving back to Houston, at least for the summer. He has no desire to be here, where he believes there is a greater chance of disease breaking out. I'm not sure why he believes this, but I think it would be good to get him away from here and your family. Especially from you. He still blames you for taking Lizzie from him."

At this, Jael's expression changed to one of betrayal and hurt. Deborah wanted to comfort her but didn't know what to say. Jael continued, however, before Deborah could offer so much as a single word.

"I knew he didn't love me when we married. I didn't love him, either, but I thought I might come to. Now I know that won't happen. It grieves me to know that I made such a hasty mistake."

"You did what you felt you had to."

Jael nodded. "And I'm paying the price for it." She squeezed Deborah's hands. "He's forbidden me to see you at all. I don't know what I shall do or if I'll even have a chance to say good-bye."

Deborah thought for a moment. "You can leave messages with Mara Shattuck. If you go to Houston, you can even correspond with me, through her. I'll speak to her today and let her know what's happening."

"I should be able to manage that," Jael agreed. She glanced around once more, fidgeting like a treed coon. "I need to go."

"Please be careful. We know now that Stuart is dangerous. We must be on our guard."

Jael nodded.

"Go out the back way and I'll keep watch."

"That's a good idea," her friend agreed. "Where is the door?"

Taking Jael by the hand, she led her to the storage room, careful that they should not be seen. "The door is there—to the right."

Deborah waited until her friend had fled and then went to find her mother. Whispering, she relayed the information Jael had shared—all but the threat on Deborah's life. She would talk to G.W. first. He wouldn't overreact, but her mother might be inclined to do something out of pure emotion.

"I need to speak with Mara," she told her mother. "Would it be all right if I did it now?"

Mother nodded. "I can visit with Rachel until you're ready to head back. Just come to the Perkinses' house when you're ready."

Deborah nodded and hurried out of the commissary, nearly colliding with the constable. She straightened just in time. "Mr. Nichols, good morning."

"Miss Vandermark," he said, tipping his hat. "It looks to be a mighty fine day."

"It would be finer if you would tell me you'd caught the men who beat up and hanged George and David Jackson. Have you any leads? Has anyone stepped forward, seeking the reward my mother and uncle—I mean stepfather—have offered?"

He frowned and looked quite sorry he'd even addressed her. "Miss Deborah, it's been over a year. Nobody's gonna say nothing about what happened. They're too afraid. The White Hand of God has folks runnin' scared. There were some lynchings up north not but a week back and some twenty folks witnessed the scene, but no one is talking."

"That's ridiculous. How can an entire community allow a mob of masked men to cause such disruption?" She fixed him with a hard stare. "It seems to me you aren't doing your job."

He took umbrage and struck a defensive pose. "Now, see here. I'm doing my best. What with the mill burned out and all, my guess is that anyone who saw what happened or heard tell of it is long gone. We simply gotta accept that this is one of those things that can't be resolved."

Deborah stiffened. "I refuse to accept that nothing can be done about murder."

"She makes a good point, Ralph."

Looking around the constable, Deborah could see Pastor Shattuck sitting at a barrel where an unfinished game of checkers awaited. She smiled sweetly. "Mornin', Pastor. I wonder, is Mara at home?"

"She sure is. I know she'd love to visit with you. Ralph and I are trying to solve the problems of the world over a game of checkers. I'm afraid you caught us right in the middle."

"Pardon me," Deborah said, glancing back at Ralph. "I can see more important things await you."

She hurried down the steps, narrowly missing one of the constable's hound dogs. Anger and irritation followed her all the way to the pastor's house, and while she wanted nothing more than to explode over the matter, Deborah held her tongue.

When Mara opened the door, she offered a smile and a warm greeting. Deborah gave Mara a brief hug. "I wonder if I might speak with you. I have a bit of a problem."

∞

"Did she say when he plans to start rebuilding?" G.W. asked Deborah.

She shook her head. "No. Jael told me before she headed back to her house that she thought he was already arranging supplies and laborers."

"Well, that is good news," Mother said, crossing the room to where Uncle Arjan stood. They had been married less than a year, and their happiness and contentment in each other's company was evident.

"I'm going to go back to work in the kitchen. Give a holler if you need me, but Sissy has lunch nearly ready for us, so don't be long." She gave her husband a quick peck on the cheek and exited the room.

Deborah breathed a sigh of relief. "There's something more. I didn't want to say anything in front of Mother, but I feel I should tell you both."

G.W. frowned and rose from behind the desk. "What now? Albright go and threaten to tear out the train tracks?"

She shook her head. "No. Not that I know of, but Jael asked him for a divorce and he told her no. He was quite angry and added that if she tried to leave him or get a divorce, well . . . he would . . ." She hesitated and looked at her uncle, now stepfather. She had planned all along to let them know of Stuart's threat, but now it didn't seem like such a good idea. What would he say if he knew the truth? Would he and G.W. forbid her to leave the house? Would G.W. go challenge Stuart to a fight? She didn't want to lie, but neither did she want to be the reason that even more harm was done to her family.

"He would what?" her brother prompted.

Deborah didn't know what to say. She wanted someone to know the truth besides Jael, but what good would it do? It was only a threat, and nothing could really be done.

"What was it he said he'd do?" Arjan asked.

Deborah swallowed hard, her decision made. "He said he would make us pay." It wasn't exactly a lie.

G.W. shook his head. "Like he's not already doing that. I tell you, if Jael wants to leave the . . . the . . ." He blew out a heavy breath and held his tongue.

"I think what your brother is trying to say is that Jael would be welcome here if she needed help in getting away from Albright. We aren't afraid of him. What else could he possibly do to cause us harm?"

Deborah nodded and offered them a weak smile. "Indeed. What could he do?"

But Deborah knew Stuart Albright was a powerful man. He could do a great deal to cause them trouble. If he was willing to threaten her life—he would no doubt find it a simple matter to harm the others. And what if he decided to hurt the twins? She could never bear that.

What should I do? If only Christopher were there, she could confide in him. A thought nagged her. Knowledge was power, she'd always been told. Her family deserved to know the dangers that could be possible. They deserved to know the truth. Guilt coursed through her. Guilt for her part in developing the contract and not having the foresight to avoid such issues. Guilt for the harm that might come to her family. Guilt for not telling the truth.

The truth will set you free, a voice seemed to speak in the depths of her heart, but Deborah turned a deaf ear. The truth, in this case, seemed much too dangerous.

∞

Christopher had delayed as long as he could before seeking out Jimmy and Tommy. He figured that waiting until Sunday after church should have given them ample time to consider the situation and let the news of the move sink in.

"We need to talk," he told them as soon as the noon meal was completed.

"I hope you can spare Darcy, Emma, and Jonah," Mrs. Maynard stated. "I need them to help clear the table and wash up the dishes."

She had promised this excuse to allow Christopher to speak with Jimmy and Tommy alone. Christopher nodded and smiled.

"Thank you for a wonderful meal. I'll sit with the boys in the front room."

He motioned them toward the archway that led into the hall. Tommy and Jimmy looked at each other for a moment, then got slowly to their feet. They seemed to realize that the discussion was inevitable.

Christopher waited until they were both seated before continuing. He lowered his voice. "We have to talk about Texas."

"I don't wanna go," Jimmy declared. "I have the highest marks in school and my teacher says I can graduate by next year—maybe sooner."

"And I have a job. I can't leave." Tommy looked at Christopher. "It's important I stay here."

He didn't want to remind them of their age and helplessness and chose another tactic. "What about the little ones? What about Darcy? Have you considered their needs? Would you have me split up the family and take them south while you—the only brothers they truly know—stay here?"

The boys looked at each other, apparently not having considered this possibility. Christopher shook his head. "I know you don't want to leave, but I need your help. I'm willing to make you both a deal."

"What kind of deal?" Jimmy asked.

"I want you to continue your education. I will see to it that you further your studies. I only ask that you give Texas—and me—a chance. Come with me and stay for a year. If you graduate and are ready for college, I will find a way to send you. And Tommy, I'm certain that my fiancée's family could help you find a job—maybe something to do with their logging company."

"Truly?" Tommy asked. "That would be great." He immediately regretted the outburst and gave Jimmy an apologetic look.

"Nothing has to be forever. I'm just asking that you come and help the little ones to adjust. You two can't take care of them. They need far more than you can provide. The girls need a woman's guidance, and Jonah needs mothering, even if you two don't. Please . . . help me out in this." He paused as he searched for what to say next.

"Even though I was gone most of the time you were growing up, you were never far from my thoughts. All of you were with me no matter where I went; I held you in my heart and mind. I prayed for you and did . . . well, whatever else I could." He fell silent, not wanting to boast of how he'd cared for them over the years. "You've always been important to me."

Jimmy looked to the ground as if ashamed. "I know. Mama told me how much you did for us."

"I believe God made us a family in order to help each other in times like this." Christopher placed a hand on each boy's shoulder. "You will grow up soon enough. You'll move off and marry and have your own little ones. But right now you owe it to them, as well as yourself, to take a little time to grow up."

Tommy frowned. "We're not babies."

"I never said you were," Christopher replied. "But I promised our mother that I would always be there for you, should anything ever happen to her. I promised her that you would finish school if I had anything to say about it."

The brothers exchanged a glance and then looked back to Christopher. Jimmy was the one to speak. "And if we don't want to stay after a year, you'll help us get somewhere else?"

Christopher breathed a sigh. "I will. You might even be able to go live with one of our sisters and their families, but I know money has always been difficult for them to come by, as well.

I'm not even all that sure where to find them these days. Perhaps you know?"

"They haven't moved," Jimmy said. He looked to Tommy and gave a brief nod. "But I don't think we'd be any better off with them. I guess we can go with you. If that's the only way."

"For now it is," Christopher said. "That doesn't mean God won't provide another at a different time."

"God?" Jimmy asked and shook his head. "I got no interest in Him. He's obviously not interested in us."

Christopher shook his head. "You know that's not true. God has always been there for this family."

Jimmy got to his feet. "Well, He sure has a funny way of showin' it."

CHAPTER 8

I can't say I've ever heard of such an arrangement," Bertram Wallace said, "but your family and ours go way back. I'll do whatever I can to help."

Wallace's family had once worked for the Vandermarks before heading out to start their own logging and sawmill company. G.W. knew they had long since cut out their acreage of forest, however, and now only managed the mill.

"We want to keep this fair, but not let anyone else know what's going on," G.W. explained. "Mr. Decker, my father-in-law, assures me that if we give you the logs you need and no money changes hands, we'll be legal."

Decker leaned forward. "It's true. The exchange of gifts should not create a problem of legal means; however, it would be better not to throw it in the face of Stuart Albright and his business associates. Their delay in deciding to rebuild the mill or move elsewhere has caused difficulty, but it is their right."

Wallace nodded. "I don't have a problem with the plan." The older man looked at Arjan. "We had plenty of secrets in the good ol' days, didn't we?" He gave them a broad smile. "Sounds like this Albright fella wants to see you folks on your face in the dirt. I can't abide that."

G.W. had known Mr. Wallace would feel that way. It was the reason he'd put the man at the top of their list to visit. "We thought," G.W. continued, "that we'd talk to Mr. Kealty and maybe Mr. Danview, too."

Wallace considered this for a moment. "There's talk that Kealty is selling, but he might be interested in hearin' what you have to say. He's a good man."

"I'd like to involve as few people as possible," Arjan added. "We just need enough to keep the mortgage paid and food on the table. We can live and have lived frugal. We know what's necessary."

"We all have had a taste of that. Don't want to go back to it, neither," Wallace replied. He held out his hand. "Let's shake on the deal. You write out the information for how you want things done, and I'll figure up what I can do for you from my end."

Later that day, as the trio sat down for dinner in one of Lufkin's nicer cafés, G.W. shook his head and smiled. "I'm thinkin' this is gonna work out all right."

"You've got a fine family reputation and folks seem to share a good history with you," his father-in-law replied. "I like the way people pull together out here."

"You can always join us out here," G.W. said with a grin.

"I know one little gal who would find that prospect awfully rewarding."

Decker laughed. "I'm sure she would. I was a little worried about her after unloading the news of her being a twin, but she seemed to bear it well."

G.W. picked up a spoon, intent on the bowl of chicken and dumplings the waitress had just brought. "We spoke for quite a while, and Lizzie said that learning about her twin explained so much. She always felt that there was something or someone missing in her life. She had thought it was just because of the way her ma treated her, but now Lizzie says she can finally understand why she's always felt that way."

Brian Decker shook his head slowly. "To think that I could have helped her long ago. I honestly figured Harriet would tell her; I mean, there was certainly no reason to keep it from Lizzie. I suppose the pain of remembering what had happened was something Harriet couldn't face."

"Lizzie plans to write to her ma and ask for an explanation. I don't reckon she'll reply if it's too much of a burden to bear," G.W. said and sampled more of his food. "This is mighty good."

Spying a familiar face across the room, G.W. waited until the man was nearly even with their table before addressing him. "Bart Perkins. I heard your father mention you were up this way."

Bart looked at the trio in surprise. "Well, I do say, this is a surprise. What brings you to Lufkin?"

"That sorry excuse for a train we have," G.W. said, laughing. "What about you? Your father said you were gettin' involved in politics, of all things."

Bart hooked his thumbs in his waistcoat pockets and rocked back on his heels. "That I am. I plan to be mayor of this town one day. The times have changed, and with it, we have many problems that need attending."

G.W. glanced around. "Seems like Lufkin is a well-managed town."

Bart leaned forward. "So long as we can keep the Negroes in their place. They are causing us all kinds of grief. I don't know why that pig Lincoln ever figured freeing them was a good thing. They're shiftless and lazy, uneducated and thieves—every last one of them."

G.W. frowned. He wasn't used to hearing friends speak so harshly about the blacks. "I'm sorry to hear you're having problems."

"Oh, there were problems in Perkinsville, too, but Father never wanted to deal with it in an appropriate manner. I reminded him on more than one occasion that he was letting the colored folks get away with too much. They weren't working anywhere near to capacity, but my father never wanted to interfere. That's as much why we're out of business today as anything."

"Well, the fire certainly put an end to production," Arjan said.

"It was set by the blacks."

"Do you have any proof?" G.W. asked.

"Well, I'm sure you know my father is certain the fire was set. No one but the blacks had any reason to set it afire."

G.W. leaned back to fix Bart with a hard look. "How do you figure that? Most of them worked at the mill."

Bart nodded enthusiastically. "Exactly. And everyone knows those people don't want to give an honest day's work."

"That crazy," G.W. said. "We have both blacks and whites working for us. They are all hard workers who give a good effort. George and David Jackson were two of the best workers we'd ever had before the White Hand of God killed them."

Bart shrugged. "They must have done something to offend. That's the trouble with colored folks—they just don't know enough to stay in their place and keep their mouths shut. We see it here, too, and they probably thought that if the mill was out of commission, they could laze about."

G.W. tensed and Arjan put his hand on G.W.'s knee.

Arjan looked to Bart. "We just got our food. Why don't you sit down and eat with us."

Bart shook his head but didn't lose the pose. "I've already eaten; besides, I have a business meeting to attend to. How long will you gentlemen be in town?"

Arjan answered for them. "I don't think it'll be much longer. We got what we came for."

"Which was what?" Bart asked.

G.W. slammed his empty mug down a little harder than he'd intended. "Horses. We came to pick up the team that we lent out last winter."

Arjan smiled and nodded. "Jefferson Marshall used them for freighting. He was waiting on a new team to be delivered from El Paso. Now they've arrived."

"I saw them," Bart said, looking glad to change the subject. "Nice looking pair." He glanced at his pocket watch. "Well, I must be going. Perhaps we'll cross paths again later."

G.W. watched as Perkins hurried from the café. "I wasn't exactly expecting his attitude."

Arjan looked to Brian Decker. "He's the son of Zed Perkins. We should have made introductions. I apologize."

"No need. The man sounds like he's the one who should apologize."

G.W. reconsidered the conversation. "You don't suppose he had anything to do with the lynchings in Perkinsville, do you?"

"I seriously doubt it, Son. Bart has always been good to go off at the mouth, but his follow-through leaves a lot to be desired. My guess is he's repeating somebody else's thoughts."

"Well, whoever they are, they're wrong," G.W. said with a glance at his father-in-law.

∞

Christopher couldn't sleep, despite the bed's comfort. He got up and sat staring into the darkness. Now that he'd convinced Tommy and Jimmy of the need to keep the family together, the time had come to press forward.

He thought of Deborah and wondered what her reaction would be to the arrival of a ready-made family. She would no doubt be shocked—maybe even angry—that he'd not consulted her first. But if there had been any other way, he would have taken it.

"I'm not cut out for this," he whispered. How was he supposed to take over the care of these children?

A sound echoed from somewhere in the house. Crying—of that he was certain. Christopher got to his feet and pulled on his clothes. Without bothering to tuck in the shirt, he made his way to the door and opened it. He listened for a moment. Mrs. Maynard's room was downstairs, so it had to be one of his siblings.

He crept into the hall and the sound grew louder. It was coming from the left of his room, where Emma, Jonah, and Darcy slept. He eased open the door. The sobs were coming from the bed where he'd tucked in the two youngest earlier that evening.

Christopher couldn't see very well, but didn't want to light a lamp. He retraced the position of the room's furnishings in his mind and carefully made his way to the bed.

"Emma and Jonah, are you all right? Are you ill?"

The crying softened. "I'm a-scared," Jonah said, sitting up.

Emma sat up, as well, and fought to speak. "I want . . . want . . . Mama. I miss . . . miss her."

This sent Jonah into a new round of tears. There was nothing to do but offer what comfort he could. Taking the boy in his arms, Christopher sat on the edge of the bed. Emma quickly scooted across and crawled onto his lap beside Jonah.

"I miss her, too," Christopher said as the children calmed in his arms. He sighed and held them close. "I miss her more than I can say."

Emma lifted her head. "Can't she come back?"

If she could, it certainly would simplify things. But instead of voicing his thought, he shook his head. "Mama is in heaven now. Da too." At least he hoped his father had trusted his soul to Jesus. After years of anger and bitterness, it was hard to say if his father had put faith in anything other than the bottle.

Christopher didn't want to dwell on that possibility. "Would you like me to tell you a story?" he asked.

"What kind of story?" Emma asked, sniffing back tears.

"About when I was a little boy."

"You were little?" Jonah asked.

Giving a chuckle, Christopher rubbed the boy's back. "I was indeed. I looked very much like you."

"Tell us a story about Mama," Emma said.

"Well, you and Jonah get back under the covers, and I will do just that."

They seemed reluctant to leave his lap. "Will you stay here?" Jonah asked.

"Just until you fall asleep." Christopher glanced to where Darcy slept soundly on a narrow cot across the room. He couldn't really see the child, but he heard her deep breathing. "Now, we must be very quiet so we don't wake up your sister."

"She won't wake up," Emma said. "Mama always said Darcy could sleep even with a freight train coming through the middle of her room."

Christopher smiled. He could imagine their mother saying such a thing.

He helped the children snuggle back under the blankets and then surprised them, as well as himself, by reclining on the bed beside them. It was a good thing the narrow frame was up against the wall. Otherwise they might have all tumbled off the opposite side.

Emma and Jonah snuggled up close to Christopher. Up until this moment, they had kept him at a distance, preferring Mrs. Maynard. It touched him that they felt safe enough to rest in his arms.

"When I was Jonah's age," he began, "Mama would tell me stories at bedtime."

"She told us stories, too," Emma interjected.

"Did she tell you about the time when she rode a train for the very first time?"

Emma shook her head against his arm. "Never."

"I ain't never rode a train," Jonah said.

Christopher smiled to himself. "Well, in a couple of days, we're all going to ride a train, so I think it would be good to tell you about Ma's first train trip. You see, she was almost a grown-up lady before she got to ride the train. She thought they were smelly and noisy and they frightened her."

"Da used to work on the trains," Jonah offered.

"That's right, and that's where Ma met him. Da was working to build a railroad track out of Chicago—that's a big city up north where Ma and Da used to live." Christopher smiled to himself as he remembered the way his mother's face would light up when she told the story.

"Our mama used to help wash clothes for the railroad men. Da used to tease Ma for being afraid of the trains. He told her they were just like big carriages with iron horses instead of real ones. He told Ma if she ever rode on the train, she'd never want to ride in a wagon again."

"And did Da take her for a ride?" Emma asked with a yawn.

"He did, indeed. He told her if she would come and ride the train with him, he'd give her something special—a big surprise."

"A surprise? What was it?" Jonah murmured. He sounded even closer to sleep than his sister.

"He wouldn't say what the surprise was, but he told Ma she'd be sure to like it. So Ma finally agreed to ride on the train. At first she was afraid, but Da helped her by holding her hand and telling her all about how he'd helped to build the track that they were riding on. Before she knew it, the short ride was over and she liked the train."

Emma yawned and snuggled deeper in the covers. "But what was Da's surprise?"

"Da gave her a big kiss—her first kiss, and our mama said she lost her heart to him." Christopher felt tears come to his eyes. For so long now, he'd only thought of his father as callous and sour. The accident had made him that way—the prejudices of people toward his ancestry had taken their toll, as well. He'd almost let himself forget the good man their da had been—the deep love he'd shared with their mother, the love she'd held for him. Had Ma forgotten, too? Is that why she'd never told the little ones how she fell in love?

Neither child said a word. Christopher listened to their steady breathing. One more sorrow had been laid to rest, at least for the moment. Would that peace of heart and mind could be his as easily.

And Deborah. How could he bring this responsibility to her? She planned to be his bride, to share his life as a physician and helpmate. It wasn't fair to saddle her with five grieving children. Of course, Tommy and Jimmy were hardly little ones anymore, and Darcy was quite the independent thinker. She even reminded him of Deborah. Even so, they were all still in need of guidance and direction. They weren't old enough, any of them, to be left to their own affairs. At least as far as Christopher was concerned.

Oh, God, what am I to do? I won't let them be sent to an orphanage. I won't abandon my own flesh and blood. But what if Deborah wants no part of them? What if she tells me it's her or them?

As soon as the whispered words were out of his mouth, Christopher shook his head. Deborah wasn't like that. She would never want him to leave the children to strangers or to seek their own way. She was a compassionate and giving woman—that was one of the reasons he loved her so much.

He let go a heavy sigh and eased from the bed. He wouldn't solve anything here tonight. Soon enough, he'd come face-to-face with Deborah and explain the situation for what it was. He was now responsible for five children, and if that was too much for her to bear with him, then he would have to let her go.

The very idea left him feeling empty inside. Perhaps even more empty and alone than he'd felt upon the news of his parents' deaths. To lose Deborah was unthinkable. He pushed the thought aside. He would not lose her. He was determined. There would be a way to make all of this work. Of that, he was confident. God would surely show him the answer.

CHAPTER 9

E aster weekend had been a stormy one, but the Vandermarks didn't let that stop their celebration of the resurrection. As they gathered for dinner after Sunday services, Deborah could only smile at the animated conversations around the table. Mother had invited Mr. and Mrs. Perkins, along with daughters Annabeth and Maybelle, as well as Pastor Shattuck and Mara to join them. The house was overflowing with glad hearts and good will.

Deborah found the atmosphere helpful for letting go of her worry about Christopher. She'd heard nothing from him since that first telegram. She would just have to be patient. As her mother always said, "God will show you the answer in His good time."

"This is a feast fit for a king," Arjan told Deborah's mother and kissed her check.

Deborah could see the joy her mother took in his praise. She was so glad that her mother had married again. Their marriage had made the family whole again, and Deborah knew that her father smiled down approval from heaven.

"These are the best creamed peas and potatoes I've ever had," Zed announced.

Mrs. Perkins smiled at Deborah's mother. "I never had much luck with them. I always manage to get the sauce too thick or too thin."

"Sissy made these. She can show you her tricks," Mother offered, nodding toward the woman who sat beside Deborah.

"I shore can, Miz Perkins. Ain't no problem. No problem at all."

Rachel Perkins nodded. "And you can also teach me how you made those wonderful hot cross buns. I've never had anything that tasted so good—especially slathered in butter. I haven't had decent butter or yeast bread in weeks."

"Well, Lizzie churned quite a bit of butter last week," Mother said. "I'll send some home with you when you go."

"That would be wonderful." Mrs. Perkins cast a glance at her two daughters. "Perhaps Lizzie can share her secrets with you."

Annabeth frowned. "I hate churning. I'd rather buy butter ready-made."

Maybelle nodded. "In Houston, they have stores that carry all sorts of foods, ready for the eating."

"Seems a waste of money to me," their father said. "If a person can make their own, why pay someone else to do it for them?"

"Because sometimes the product is much better than anything you can make yourself," Maybelle declared.

"That has not been my experience," Pastor Shattuck threw in. "I cannot tell you how much more I appreciate a homemade meal, prepared by loving hands—just like this. Why, I've never had food this good from any restaurant or packaged item."

Maybelle sulked but said nothing. Deborah felt sorry for her. No doubt the sisters were still encouraging their parents to move. Mother said that Mrs. Perkins was beside herself from their nagging.

Annie let out a howl of protest as Rutger reached over to take a portion of her bread. She slapped at him, but her brother was too quick. He snagged the food and yanked his arm back just before her hand slapped the table. This caused her to cry all the louder.

Lizzie took the bread from Rutger and handed it back to Annie. "Now, Son, you need to learn to leave other people's food alone." The boy looked up at her with a pout. Lizzie ignored it and buttered another piece of bread for him. She handed it to Rutger and gave him a pat on the head. "Now you have your own."

Mara laughed. "I used to fight with my brother for food. He was older and ate everything that wasn't nailed down. Aaron considered my plate free range."

Pastor Shattuck smiled. "I remember your grandmother writing to tell me of his voracious appetite."

The conversation moved to comments and stories of other childhood pranks and games. Deborah was glad no one seemed to notice how quiet she was. She truly was doing her best to just enjoy the day and the company of good friends. She didn't want to be sad or troubled, for Easter was a time of renewal and hope. Pastor Shattuck had spoken to them about the Lord's resurrection in terms of a new birth. Coming from the tomb was much like a babe being born, he had said. Jesus overcame death to be reborn into glory. She liked that thought—liked, too, that Pastor Shattuck said each of them were also reborn into eternal life when they accepted Jesus as their Savior.

"Eternity starts when you ask Jesus to forgive your sins and come into your heart. What a lovely thought." She hadn't meant to speak aloud and looked up, rather startled. "Sorry, I was just thinking back on the sermon."

Pastor Shattuck smiled. "So many folks think that eternity is something they are waiting for, and while heaven is yet to come, eternal life is found in Jesus and our accepting of Him."

"I agree," Arjan declared. "I look forward to heaven one day, but until that time I need to remember that God has given me a life right here—that I need to live it for Him."

"Exactly," Deborah agreed. "Live for and with Him eternally. It's a very pleasant thought."

"It helps us not to miss out on the blessings He has for us," the pastor added.

Deborah smiled and nodded. "Yes. I very much appreciated your pointing that out. It made me more mindful of not only my behavior, but of the very gift God has given in salvation."

"Makes me feel so safe," Mother said. "So cared for."

"Amen," Sissy said. "I's also so grateful you allowed us black folk to come and share Easter service."

"Miz Jackson, there is coming a day when folks of all colors will sit side by side in church and elsewhere," Pastor Shattuck replied. "I very much look forward to that day."

"So, Mr. Perkins, tell us about the new mill," G.W. interjected.

Zed leaned back in the chair. "I don't know all that much myself. My partners don't seem to think it necessary to keep me apprised. I don't know if they plan to rebuild on the old site or somewhere new."

"How soon do you think you'll need logs brought in?" Arjan asked.

"I can't rightly say. I was surprised to hear that Mr. Albright and Mr. Longstreet plan to bring in finished lumber from other towns. I kind of figured we'd set up an outside mill like the old days and process enough of our own lumber to build, but they wanted no part of that. I'm not exactly sure when they'll expect a delivery of logs."

Arjan seemed perplexed. "But it would be less expense to process your own logs."

G.W. frowned. "Sounds like more of Albright's games."

"That it does," Mr. Perkins replied. "I figure it's his way of holdin' all the cards."

"If they just get the mill up and running again," Mother said, "it will be such a benefit to everyone. I cannot imagine Mr. Albright can go on losing money like he has and not suffer."

"Stuart has more than enough money. His desire to have his revenge is worth whatever price he has to pay," Lizzie stated.

"Hopefully the man will tire of his games," Pastor Shattuck said. "We will pray it is so and that our little community can be restored."

"Have you heard lately from Dr. Kelleher?" Mara asked Deborah.

"No, I'm afraid I only had the one telegram that let me know he'd arrived safely."

"Oh, I feel like ten kinds of fool," Zed said, pulling a piece of paper from his pocket. "This came for you late on Good Friday. I was rather surprised to see it. Just so happened I was dealin' with some old railroad papers and happened to be in the office."

He handed the telegram to Deborah and smiled. "It's from the doc."

She glanced at the brief note. "He's headed back." Her smile broadened. "He sent this just as he was leaving Kansas City."

"What does it say?" her mother asked.

"Hardly more than what I said." Deborah passed the telegram to Sissy, who handed it to Euphanel.

"He left Friday and hopes to be back sometime this week," Mother announced. "That is good news."

"We've been blessed that there haven't been any accidents or problems in his absence," Annabeth declared. Maybelle nodded and both girls fixed Deborah with a rather smug expression.

"If there had been," their father countered, "I'm guessin' Miss Deborah woulda handled things just fine."

"She's a woman, Pa. It's vulgar for her to do such things," Maybelle said.

"Vulgar to heal a person? Vulgar to keep someone from dyin'?" G.W. asked. "Like she did for me? I can't see it as such."

Deborah was grateful for her brother's support. She gave him an appreciative glance and turned her attention back to the food on her plate.

"I think we're doing more talking than eating," Mother said, getting to her feet. "Perhaps if I bring in dessert, you'll feel more motivated. I have some mouth-watering strawberry shortcake, just waiting for our attention."

"Is that with that buttery pound cake you make, Miz Vandermark?" the pastor asked.

"It is indeed. Would you care to indulge?"

He laughed. "I'll be happy to have my portion and anyone else's."

Laughter filled the room. G.W. shook his head. "Nobody's gettin' my share. Ma makes the best pound cake I've ever tasted."

"I agree," Arjan declared.

"Then I'll be right back, and we can all indulge together."

ငာ၁

G.W. pushed back from the table some time later and patted his full stomach. "I could celebrate the Lord like that every day."

"Perhaps we should," Lizzie said with a grin.

"And we'd all weigh as much as Miz Foster's prized hog," Mother replied. "Now if you'll excuse me, I'm going to gather some of these dishes."

"No, Mother, I'll take care of them," Deborah said, getting to her feet.

Mara began gathering plates. "I'll help you."

"Well, Sissy, it looks like we get to retire with the others to the front room."

"Iffen you don' mind, I's gonna take me a Easter nap." Sissy got up from the table, a hand upon her back. "The weather's got my rheumatism actin' up sumpt'n fierce."

"By all means, go and rest. You've earned it." Mother motioned to the hall. "Why don't we retire to the living room, and I'll bring coffee."

"It's gettin' kind of late and the stormy weather has kept the skies overcast," Pastor Shattuck stated. "I believe once Mara is finished helpin' out, she and I will make our way back to town. I ought to go ready the buggy."

"We really should be going, as well," Mrs. Perkins said with a quick glance at her husband.

He nodded and stood. "Pastor makes a good point. Might even get back before the next storm moves in."

They heard the rumblings of thunder in the distance, and Mother moved to the end of the table. "I will miss your company, of course, but I completely understand."

Deborah looked to Mara. "I can handle this by myself."

The young woman inclined her head to the kitchen. "I'll . . . ah . . . bring these in and then go."

Something in her expression made Deborah realize she had something she needed to say. Deborah nodded and led the way with a stack of plates. She quickly discarded the dishes on the counter and turned to Mara.

"Has Jael sent word?"

"Yes. She sent this letter." Mara put the tableware down and reached inside her blouse. "I hid it so I could give it to you when we were alone."

"Probably a good idea. Maybelle and Annabeth have a tendency to run their mouths at the most inopportune times." Deborah took the letter. "Thank you for doing this. I know it's probably not the most comfortable thing. I certainly didn't want to put you in a compromising position."

"I don't feel that it's a problem." Mara smiled. "I also heard from your brother Rob. He hopes to come home for a visit this summer. Probably toward the end of next month. Won't that be wonderful?"

"Has he hinted about the two of you setting a wedding date?"

Mara blushed. "Not exactly. We both know that when the time is right, we'll wed. We're trusting God will show us when."

"I wish He'd show me when, as well," Deborah said with a sigh. "I don't understand this waiting, but I suppose in time God will reveal everything I need to know."

Mara leaned forward and kissed Deborah's cheek. "He will."

∞

Long after everyone had gone, G.W. checked in on the sleeping twins, then headed back into the room he shared with Lizzie. She was already in bed, and he had to admit, she made a most fetching picture with her long blond hair brushed out around her shoulders.

"You're the prettiest gal around. You never fail to make my heart skip a beat." He grinned and sat to take off his boots.

Just then, he heard the mules fussing, which wasn't like them. Getting to his feet, he reached for his rifle. "Sounds like we've got a varmint causin' problems."

"Do be careful," Lizzie said, sitting up. "It could be one of those wild hogs."

He nodded and headed out. Reaching the back door, G.W. wasn't surprised to find Arjan on his heels.

"What's goin' on out there?" his stepfather asked, holding up a lighted lantern.

"I don't know, but the girls sound mighty upset." G.W. opened the back door to agitated braying. He could see movement in the distance. "They're out of the pen. Somehow they got the gate open." The two men moved out to round up the animals. It was strange, G.W. thought, that they should be having this kind of problem. The mules had been confined since Friday and there hadn't been any trouble with them.

Arjan picked up a bucket and tapped the lantern base against it. "Come on, you old coots, I'll give you some grain." Several of the nearest mules began to wander toward them.

Without warning, G.W. heard a man call out, "Just wanted to get your attention!"

Arjan stopped. "Who's there?"

Several mounted riders approached. There were five in total, and each wore some kind of sack over their heads. Holes had been cut out to let them see, but otherwise their faces were hidden. "We're part of the White Hand of God," the leader announced.

"This here is what we call a friendly warnin'. Mind your own business or there'll be trouble."

G.W. felt the reassurance of the rifle at his side. He didn't move to expose the weapon, but stood stock-still. "Who are you to threaten us?"

"You Vandermarks have been nothin' but trouble. You need to remember your own kind and leave the darkies to themselves. I'm here to issue a warnin'. Stop offerin' that reward your family posted and keep that nosy sister of yours from pesterin' folks for answers. Otherwise, you'll be forcin' our hand."

"Kinda like you're forcin' mine," G.W. said, raising the rifle to his shoulder.

The leader pulled back on the horse's reins and the beast took several steps back. "Friend, you don't want to be doin' this. You don't know me, but I know you. I know where you live, and I know your family."

"Don't you dare threaten my family," G.W. said, moving a step forward.

"Bad things are gonna happen," the man said, turning his horse. "If you don't do what we've asked, the blood will be on your hands."

He kicked his horse and gave a blood-curdling yell, echoed by the other men as they moved back to the road. G.W. started to follow, but Arjan took hold of his arm.

"Let 'em go. There's no sense in goin' after them. We need to get the mules back in the pen."

"They threatened our family. It ain't right to just let 'em go."

"Maybe not, but if you go after them, they'll hurt you or kill you. They have the lead, and setting up an ambush sounds like just the kind of thing those cowards would do. Stay here, G.W. There'll always be another day to fight."

G.W. looked at his uncle for a moment, then lowered the rifle. "I suppose you're right." But the idea of letting such men roam at will didn't set well. "This leaves a bad taste in my mouth," he told his uncle.

"It does in mine, too, but it can't be helped just yet. Not without risking too much . . . not without endangering those we love."

CHAPTER 10

Christopher had been completely exhausted by the time they reached Lufkin. Rather than wait for a train to take them south, Christopher arranged to rent a wagon and an ancient pair of horses to pull it. Even though it was late in the day, he felt it was important to get the family home. The weather was clear, the roads dry, and he longed for his own bed.

It was the middle of the night, however, before he was finally able to make his way to that bed. Even then, despite the ache in his back and weariness in his bones, Christopher found sleep hard to come by.

Because the hospital was the only place with enough beds, Christopher had settled them there for the night, but Jonah was afraid of the small infirmary, and only an hour after Christopher urged the boy to give it a chance, Jonah found his way into Christopher's room. Emma soon followed, declaring that there were scary noises coming from outside. She was certain that bad fairies were coming to hurt them. The comment had made Christopher smile. Despite their Christian upbringing, Ma had no doubt shared the mythical stories she'd known as a child. She had wanted to hide their Irish beginnings, but Christopher knew his ma had been steeped in such superstitious tales. It would have been hard to bury them away.

The children crawled into bed with Christopher and quickly fell asleep. Throughout the remaining hours of the night, Christopher tried his best to doze, but it was useless. Each time he started to nod off, he worried about crushing Emma or Jonah. Finally, he gave up altogether and got dressed. A quick glance at the clock showed that it was nearly five.

With a sigh, Christopher went to the stove and got a fire started. The idea of strong coffee gave him hope that he could make it through the day. He put the pot on the burner and went to check on what food he had in the house.

There wasn't much of anything he could feed himself, much less five growing bodies. The only solution that came to mind was to take them to the Vandermarks. Euphanel would be more than capable of helping him figure out a solution, and he was anxious to see Deborah. Maybe breaking the news to her with the support of her family would make the situation easier. Maybe.

Christopher knew the Vandermarks would be up with the sun, but he didn't want to wake his siblings. They might as well get some rest, even if he couldn't. To busy himself while the coffee brewed, Christopher went to his office and pulled out a ledger. He didn't have a lot of money left, and that was the most worrisome challenge of all. How was he supposed to support a family? He had nothing of value to sell. He needed his gelding to get around the area to see his patients, and the crude wagon and horses he'd rented in Lufkin would have to be returned within the week.

He buried his face in his hands. *God, I just don't know what to do. I didn't think this through, and I didn't make provisions. All I could think about was getting back here.*

Guilt washed over him in waves. He'd put his own desires first. The children would suffer because of his need to return to Deborah. But it wasn't just Deborah. Christopher couldn't stomach remaining at Mrs. Maynard's much longer. Every time he caught sight of the charred remains of the family home, he was tormented by images of his parents burning to death. He couldn't get out of there fast enough.

Besides, there is nothing for us in Kansas City, he thought.

Christopher got to his feet. He needed the counsel of someone wiser, and Euphanel and Arjan Vandermark would offer reasonable solutions and godly guidance. They could help him figure out what to do. Heading into the infirmary, Christopher found Jimmy was already awake.

"I figured you'd still be sleeping."

Jimmy shook his head. "I kept thinking about everything. I can't seem to make my mind relax."

Christopher nodded. "I've got the same problem. Let's get the others up. I want to take you all out to meet some friends of mine. They'll be able to give us breakfast, and maybe some advice as to what we need to do next."

"Who are these folks?"

"My fiancée's family. The Vandermarks own a big logging

company and live north of here. We passed their place on the way down."

Jimmy nodded. "Okay. I'll get 'em ready."

"Good. I'll go hitch the wagon. Emma and Jonah are sleeping in my room, just off the kitchen. Have everybody out front as soon as you can."

Christopher made his way back into the kitchen and moved the coffeepot from the stove. Next he went to the examination room and took up his medical bag, just in case anyone needed his skills along the way.

He slipped out the back door and headed to the livery, where he found Peter Garby singing and shoveling hay. The old black man straightened and smiled at the sight of Christopher.

"Doc, I figured it was you what left me this new business. Where'd you get these sorry old nags?"

Christopher smiled. "Now, Peter, those nags brought me and my family all the way from Lufkin."

"Well, that 'splains it, then. They was probably in their prime when they started the trip. That old cow path you traveled ain't fit to be called a road." Peter laughed at his own joke and pointed at the wagon. "Ain't never seen kindlin' fixed up like that."

Laughing, Christopher nodded. "I feared it might well fall apart beneath us, but it was all I could afford to rent out."

Peter nodded and put his hayfork aside. "You headin' off, Doc?"

"Yes. I need to hitch up the wagon. I want to take my family out to the Vandermarks."

"That's the second time you mentioned family. What you jawin' on about?"

"It's a long story. I'm afraid my parents were killed in a house fire."

The older man took the hat from his head and placed it over his heart. "God bless 'em. I'm sure sorry, Doc."

"I have three brothers and two sisters who were still living at home. I brought them back to Texas with me."

Peter put the hat back on his head and went to the stall Christopher had used the night before. "You's a mighty good man, Doc. I'll get your wagon ready."

"I'm going to have to get some work quickly in order to pay you, Peter." Christopher hadn't thought even as far as to how he'd manage to care for the team of horses before taking them back to Lufkin.

"Don't you fret none, Doc. I know you's good for it." Peter worked quickly to harness the team and get them secured to the wagon. He managed it in half the time it would have taken Christopher. "They's ready for you."

"Thanks, Peter. I appreciate your help."

The old man grinned, revealing several black holes where teeth were missing. "My pleasure."

Christopher led the team from the livery and across the street. He stopped in front of his porch and found his siblings waiting impatiently. Jonah jumped down rather than taking the stairs. He hurried to Christopher.

"Where are we goin'?"

"To see some friends of mine." Christopher helped him into the wagon and motioned for the others to come.

"I'm hungry," Jonah declared, leaning down over Christopher's shoulder.

"I am, too," Christopher replied. "My friends will have food for us."

At least he was pretty sure they would. Times were hard for everyone, and maybe this wasn't his best idea. Still, he knew the Vandermarks—especially Euphanel. She would be madder than a nest of wet hornets if he let his family go hungry.

Jimmy helped load the girls into the wagon before he climbed aboard himself. Tommy followed suit, yawning all the way.

"Don't know why you had to wake us up so early," Tommy complained. He plopped down in the bed of the wagon. "Sure ain't as comfortable as a bed."

Christopher decided to remain silent. Getting them on the road would be a smarter solution than spending time trying to convince them of the benefit. He climbed up and took a seat. To his surprise, Darcy climbed over the bench and eased down beside him. She looked up at him with a smile.

"Can I help?" she asked.

Releasing the brake, Christopher maneuvered the reins between them. "Sure. I'll show you how it's done."

"I never drove a wagon before," she said, awed by the leather straps he'd handed her. Christopher showed her how to raise the reins to lightly slap them against the rumps of the horses.

"Now tell them to 'get along.' "

Darcy did so and began to giggle as the horses pulled in unison against their load. "Look at 'em go!"

Christopher chuckled. The old mares were barely moving. He showed his sister how to turn the team when they came to the main road, and soon they were headed north out of town.

"That's not so hard," Darcy said, tiring of the game. She handed the straps to Christopher. "Can I learn how to ride a horse?"

"I would think so," Christopher told her. He glanced over his shoulder to see that Tommy and Emma had fallen back asleep despite the bumpy road. Jimmy had become a pillow for both of them with Emma sprawled across his lap. Tommy leaned at an awkward angle to rest his head on Jimmy's shoulder.

The trip to the Vandermarks passed without trouble, and Christopher was more than a little relieved to see Euphanel coming from the barn with a basket over one arm. He gave her a wave and pulled the wagon to a stop near the front porch.

She looked at him for a moment, and Christopher could see the confusion on her face. Walking toward them, Euphanel shifted the basket.

"Christopher, you're back."

"I just got back last night."

Darcy stood and eyed the woman. "Are you gonna marry my brother?"

Euphanel laughed. "No, darling. I'm already married." She looked back to Christopher. "This is your sister?"

"One of them." He pointed to the others. "Emma is back there with three of my brothers."

"I'm Jonah," the little boy announced. "I'm seven and I'm hungry."

She smiled. "Well, I believe we should feed you. Do you like ham and eggs?"

The little boy's eyes widened. "I ain't never had an egg."

Euphanel smiled and looked to Christopher. "Shame on you for not teaching this boy a love of eggs."

"Gotta have them to love them," Christopher replied.

Her smile faded. "That's true enough. Well, bring them all in. You know your way to the dining room."

Christopher stepped down from the wagon. "Mrs. Vandermark—"

"Now, I thought you were going to call me Euphanel." She raised a brow.

"Euphanel. I want to apologize. I had nothing in the house to feed them. Fact is, I don't know quite what to do—"

She held up a hand to silence him. "After we get everyone fed," she said.

Christopher had just helped Darcy from the wagon when he heard his named called. Deborah stood only a few feet away, a look of amazement upon her face.

"Christopher?"

His siblings were now standing beside him. "I want you to meet my brothers and sisters. Well, five of them anyway."

Deborah didn't know what to think. She looked at the children and assessed the situation. Christopher introduced each one.

"I'm pleased to meet you," she told them, then turned her questioning gaze back on Christopher. "How is it that they came to be with you?"

"Our ma and da burned up in the fire," Emma said matter-of-factly.

Putting her hand to her mouth, Deborah tried to hide her shock. She could see the pleading in Christopher's expression. "Well, come along and have something to eat. We can talk about what happened afterward."

Christopher led the way. Deborah watched as all but the one called Darcy followed him into the house. To her surprise, Darcy stood waiting for her at the door.

"Are you going to marry my brother?"

Deborah nodded. "I certainly plan to."

Darcy seemed to consider this for a moment. "Do we have to call you Mama?"

She couldn't hide her surprise at the child's question. "Are you going to call your brother Papa?"

The girl laughed. "Nope. He's Christopher."

"Then you should call me Deborah."

This answer seemed to appease Darcy. "I like that name. You can call me Darcy."

Deborah wasn't at all sure what had just happened. She followed Darcy into the house and motioned her toward the dining room. There they found her siblings already seated and waiting to be fed.

Hurrying past Christopher, Deborah went into the main kitchen to help her mother. There was very little left over from breakfast, but that was easy enough to rectify. Her mother was already slicing ham.

"Would you start frying the eggs? I'm going to get this ham on, then fetch Sissy to bring in some of the corn bread she's been baking this morning." Mother took up the largest of their cast-iron skillets and filled it with the meat. Setting it atop the stove, she checked the fire.

"I'll be back momentarily, but watch so that it doesn't burn." She was gone before Deborah could even comment.

Going to the basket, Deborah made quick order of things. She began breaking eggs and had them on the stove within minutes. Stirring in a little cream, Deborah tried not to let her emotions overwhelm her as she beat the eggs into a frothy mixture. She didn't know what to think or how to feel about this turn of events.

"I didn't know how to tell you," Christopher commented from the door.

She looked up. "I'm so sorry about your parents, Christopher." She knew he held a deep love for them—especially his mother. "I wish I could say something that would ease your pain."

He nodded. "Thank you. The children didn't have anyone else—no place to go. Mrs. Maynard had taken them in after the fire, but she couldn't afford to keep them."

Deborah stopped stirring. She put the spoon aside and slowly walked to where he stood. "They are your family. You had to see to their needs."

He pulled her into his arms. "I missed you so much." He buried his face in her hair.

Holding on to him tightly, Deborah couldn't help but wonder how their lives were about to change. Darcy's question came to mind and weighed down on her like a load of logs. Had she just inherited a family? Did Christopher expect her to mother his siblings?

She hated herself for feeling distress. How could she begrudge little children the comfort of their older brother after losing their parents? She drew a deep breath.

Lord, I'm going to need help with this. I don't know what you want me to do, but whatever it is, I know I'm going to need strength.

She raised her head and looked into Christopher's face. Seeing a glimmer of tears in his eyes, she knew it would be wrong to question the matter.

Leaning on tiptoe, she placed a gentle kiss on his lips instead. "Are you hungry?"

"Famished."

Deborah touched his cheek. "Then find a seat at the table, and we'll have the meal on in just a few minutes." She stepped away from him and hurried back to the stove as her mother came back to the kitchen with Sissy in tow.

"Welcome back, Doc," Sissy said.

"Thank you," he said, but his gaze never left Deborah.

She could see the unspoken questions in his eyes. There was no time to do anything other than offer him a weak smile before she turned her attention back to the food. He wanted to know that she was all right with the news. That she accepted his new responsibility. That nothing had changed between them. But in truth, everything had changed, whether she liked it or not.

CHAPTER 11

With Lizzie and Sissy busy helping Mother, Deborah decided to pull Christopher away from the table as soon as he'd emptied his plate. She needed to know how he was doing—what had happened, and what she should expect to come next.

"Could we talk for a moment? Alone?" she whispered in his ear.

Christopher nodded. "I want you all to mind your manners while I talk with Miss Deborah." He got to his feet and looked to Euphanel, who was cutting up pieces of ham for Jonah. "If that's alright with you, Mrs. Vandermark . . . Euphanel."

She smiled at him. "Go on. We're just fine here."

The other children were still busy stuffing food into their

mouths. Deborah thought they ate like they hadn't had a decent meal in months. From the look of how thin they were, they probably hadn't. She frowned at the thought of them being hungry.

"I hope that look isn't for me," Christopher said as they made their way outside.

"No, of course not. I was just thinking of how bad it must have been for your brothers and sisters . . . for you." She stopped on the porch and wrapped her arms around Christopher's neck. "I prayed so much for you, and now I see why. Perhaps it was God's prompting that kept me on my knees."

Christopher touched her cheek. "I never expected this to happen."

"Of course not. Who would ever imagine such a tragedy was possible? Can you tell me what happened?"

"The chimney flue got too hot and set the house ablaze. Mother got the children out, but she went back to help my father. They were trapped and burned to death."

Deborah shook her head and closed her eyes. She couldn't imagine a more horrible way to die. "And . . . were the children . . . hurt?" she forced herself to ask.

"No. They breathed in plenty of smoke but were otherwise fine. Mrs. Maynard lives just across the street, and she graciously took the children in."

"Thank God for Mrs. Maynard. I hate to think what might have happened if she'd not been there."

"I know. Jimmy and Tommy would probably manage all right, but the younger ones certainly would have been taken to an orphanage. I might never have found them."

Deborah hugged him close. "I'm so sorry."

"I'm the one who's sorry, Deborah. I never intended to impose a family on you like this." He pushed away from her and walked to the end of the porch.

"I spent every cent I had. Paying for the funeral expenses, reimbursing Mrs. Maynard, purchasing train tickets, and feeding them on the way down. Oh, and I rented that miserable excuse for a wagon and team," he said, pointing to where the horses still stood.

"I have some money," Deborah declared. "It's yours. I've saved it ever since coming back home and working for our business."

"I can't take your money."

"It's ours," she insisted.

"No. You earned it and put it aside for your own purposes."

Deborah put her hands on his shoulders. "And now that purpose is to help you."

He shook his head. "Look, there are some folks around here that owe me money. Let me see first if I can collect. If not, then we'll discuss your idea."

"What about our wedding?" she asked, almost afraid to hear his reply.

He sighed. "I don't know. I don't know what to do. I have to figure out how to arrange for my siblings first."

"I thought I might find you two out here," Mother said, coming from the house. She crossed the distance in a casual manner and smiled. "Solving the problems of the world?"

"Just my little corner of it," Christopher replied.

"I hope you won't think me interfering." She took a seat and motioned for them to do likewise. Deborah felt relieved at her mother's presence—her own thoughts were skewed with all sorts of ideas.

"Christopher," her mother began, "it's obvious that you need help with your family. We are more than willing to offer you that assistance. We have enough room for everyone—food, too. I'm sure Arjan wouldn't mind if you wanted your family to stay with us for a time."

"I'm ashamed to admit that I'd hoped as much. I've very little money—"

"Hush. We won't speak of such a thing. You're family, Christopher—or very nearly." She smiled. "Family takes care of one another—just as you have taken care of those children."

"I didn't know what else to do. I couldn't stay there; neither could I just leave them."

"Of course you couldn't."

"They have nothing," he added. "They got out of the fire with little more than their nightclothes. Mrs. Maynard said some of the neighbors offered up the articles you see them wearing now. But that's all they have."

"Well, don't you fret, Christopher. We have plenty of things around here we can use."

"I don't know how I could ever pay you. I just told Deborah that I need to go around and see what I can collect on debts owed me."

"You needn't worry," Mother reassured him. "Times are hard for everyone, but God has a way of working it all out. He multiplied the loaves and fishes in the Bible, and He will multiple the food and clothes here today."

"What's going on?" Jimmy asked as he stepped onto the porch. Tommy followed and let the screen door bang against the frame.

"We were just discussing how to keep you strapping lads fed and clothed," Euphanel said. "Why don't you come over here and tell us what you think of our plan."

Jimmy looked apprehensive. "What plan?"

"I have just suggested to Christopher that you could all stay here. There are lots of chores to be done and we could use the help. I have plenty of rooms in the house, and while we are a bit of a distance from town, there's no reason we can't arrange for you all to go back to school and finish up the term."

"I don't wanna live with strangers," Jimmy said, then looked to Deborah's mother. "No offense, ma'am."

"None taken," she assured him. "And we aren't really strangers anymore—are we? I figure it might feel awkward for you two, being the oldest, but the younger ones need to feel safe and protected. The best way I know to do that is by keeping their bellies full and their hands busy. That way they'll be too tired at night to worry overmuch about the past."

Jimmy seemed to think about this for several minutes. Tommy, too, seemed thoughtful on the matter, and Deborah couldn't help but feel sorry for them. How trapped they must feel just now.

"I need a job," Tommy finally declared. "I had one in Kansas City."

"We both need work so we can earn our keep and help support the others," Jimmy confirmed.

"Well, we can probably put you to work for Vandermark Logging. I can't promise, of course, but my husband and son will be back soon, and we can certainly ask them then. There's always something to do in the logging camps, and I believe it would make a good trade. However, there's also school to consider. I wouldn't want either of you forsaking your education. You can always help out after school and on Saturday."

"Sunday, too," Tommy offered.

Mother shook her head. "No, Sunday is the Lord's Day and

we rest. We refrain from working in order to honor Him for all that He's done for us."

Tommy and Jimmy exchanged a look. "Nobody works on Sunday?"

"Well, of course, some people do not honor the Lord that way," Mother replied. "And if there's an emergency, we do not hesitate to work. Even Jesus said it was good to help each other, even if it was on the Sabbath."

Deborah could see that Jimmy and Tommy were mulling over the idea. She leaned forward. "Mother, Christopher and I aren't exactly sure when we'll go ahead with the ceremony, but couldn't he stay here, too?"

Mother looked to the doctor and nodded. "I would encourage it, since the children are used to you. It might ease their fears."

"I . . . don't . . . I don't think I should," he said, glancing over his shoulder at Deborah. "I would still need to keep up my practice. Let me think on it."

Mother nodded and got to her feet. "I'll go see if Sissy and Lizzie need help."

"I'll come, too," Deborah told her mother. She had a feeling Christopher needed some time to talk to his brothers.

They made their way into the house, and Deborah reached out to touch her mother's arm. "Thank you for all you're doing to help him. He's so torn up by what happened, and caring for his siblings is a tremendous worry to him."

Mother nodded. "It's a huge responsibility, Deborah. You must also consider what it means. Perhaps you'll even desire to postpone the wedding."

Deborah squeezed her mother's hand to halt her steps. "Why do you say that?"

"Five children to oversee changes everything," her mother

said. "There's no shame in admitting that. Five children who are grieving the loss of their parents will be even more difficult. Grief makes folks act strange. They say and do things they don't mean because their pain is so great. You will have to have an extra measure of grace for each child."

"I am afraid," Deborah admitted. "I don't know if I can help them navigate their grief. I might be more trouble than help. They may see me as a threat—someone who is taking away their brother."

"They might. However, we must simply put this in God's hands, Deborah. We must trust Him to show us what we need to do and how we can best help Christopher and his siblings."

Deborah longed to say so much more. She wanted to tell her mother her true fears—feelings of how she wasn't at all certain she wanted children in her marriage. Of course, there was no possibility of avoiding that now once they were married. Perhaps they shouldn't marry if she was this confused.

"Mrs. Vandermark," Darcy called from the entryway to the dining room. "Emma's cryin' and she won't stop."

Mother looked at Deborah and smiled. "God will give you the answers you need, darling. Don't fret. He wasn't taken by surprise, and He has a plan."

Deborah watched her mother go and frowned. "I wish He'd tell me what it was."

"Wish who'd tell you what?" Darcy asked.

Deborah felt like a child caught sneaking something to eat. She thought for a moment to lie, but immediately put that idea aside. Darcy was a smart one. In many ways, the girl reminded Deborah of herself.

"I wish God would tell me what to do—how to help you and the others." She held Darcy's gaze. "I feel quite sad that you have lost your parents. It must hurt a great deal. My father died several years ago, and I still miss him."

Darcy nodded. "I don't miss my father, but I do wish my mama was here. My da was sick and in bed a lot, so I never spent much time with him."

"My father was very important to me," Deborah told the girl. "He taught me so many things."

"Like what?"

"How to ride a horse. How to cut wood. How to tend animals. Of course, my mother taught me some of those things, as well. But she also taught me how to sew and make clothes. Do you sew?"

"I do. My mother taught me."

Deborah smiled. "Then we already have something in common."

Darcy seemed to think of this for a moment, then looked at Deborah expectantly. "Do you think you could teach me to ride a horse?"

"I suppose I could. Of course, your brother will have to agree to it."

"I'll talk to him," Darcy said matter-of-factly. "I think he'll listen to me."

∽

"But I don't want to live here," Jimmy said. "It's not our home."

"Neither is my place in town," Christopher replied. "The owner may kick me out any day. I believe this is the best answer." He pushed back his hair and stood. "I know this is hard for you, but I need for you two to help me."

Jimmy looked at Tommy and nodded. "I know it's not easy for you, either. I just . . . well, I hate it."

"I do, too," Tommy added.

Christopher studied his brothers. They seemed so young to

130

him. Were they really nearly grown? "Come on," he encouraged. "I'll show you around."

The boys ambled along beside him while Christopher told them about the Vandermarks. "They really are the very best people you could ever know. I used to write and tell Ma about them, and she said they were just the kind of folks she'd cherish knowing better."

"And Mrs. Vanermark did say that we could maybe have jobs," Tommy added.

Christopher smiled. "As you can see, there're plenty of ways to earn your keep here. The garden alone takes many hours of tending." He waved his hand toward the area where Sissy was working even now. "Then there's canning and smoking food. Hunting and fishing."

"Do you suppose we could learn to shoot?" Tommy asked.

Christopher stopped walking and faced his brothers. "There isn't a single thing you can't learn if you put your mind to it. The Vandermarks can show you how to shoot, how to log, how to hunt, and do just about anything else you're of a mind to learn. If you give them a chance and agree to stay here, I promise I'll work quickly to come up with a more permanent solution. If we need to move to a bigger city like Houston or Galveston, I will need some time to make arrangements."

Jimmy kicked at a rock in the path. "They won't laugh at us 'cause we're from the city, will they?"

"I've never known them to be unkind to anyone, Jimmy. They are good God-fearing folks who practice what they hear each Sunday. I know you're feeling a bit angry with God right now, but I believe He has given us this opportunity for the safety and well-being of everyone concerned. I'm just asking you to give it a chance."

131

Jimmy and Tommy exchanged a glance. "Guess there isn't much of any other choice," Jimmy said. "Just remember, I want to go to college."

"I also want you to further your education," Christopher replied. "I won't forget."

ꙮ

Stuart Albright looked at the figures his father-in-law had just handed him. "I suppose if we're to rebuild, we'll be best to keep the present location."

"It will cost three times as much—just for start up—if we move the mill elsewhere," Dwight Longstreet told him. "More than that if we have to run a new siding for the train."

"I can see that for myself." He pushed the papers away. They fluttered in the air momentarily and fell onto the massive desk. "So have you arranged for workers?"

"I've put out the word. We need men with experience; otherwise, it will take forever to get the mill operational."

Smiling to himself, Stuart shook his head. "No, I want the blacks working on it. They are taking up space on my land—in company houses. Have them begin the construction work."

"And if they do not know how?"

Stuart shrugged. "Hire a foreman who does. One white man can handle it."

Longstreet looked at him oddly. "I suppose it could work."

"It will. I'm not in any hurry to see this mill running—I only want to prove that I'm actively pushing forward. That way, the Vandermarks won't have a leg to stand on should they decide to pursue a lawsuit."

"They will also expect you to begin purchasing logs again."

"I'll delay that until I have no other choice," Stuart replied.

"I want them to suffer, Dwight. I want them to know that I'm not a man to be toyed with."

His father-in-law said nothing, but the disapproval lined his expression. Just like his daughter—no guts for making bold moves.

"What of Houston?" Longstreet asked. "Are you still of a mind to move there?"

Stuart was glad for the excuse to change the subject. "I am. I think that it will keep your daughter away from the bad influence of the Vandermarks. She doesn't understand my desire for her to abandon her friendship with Miss Vandermark." Stuart leaned back and laced his fingers together. "She is too emotional to make a sound decision on this matter, so I must make it for her."

Longstreet shrugged. "I've never known Jael to practice poor judgment."

Stuart thought of revealing the truth of Jael's pregnancy to her father, then decided against it. It was much more powerful as a sword he held over her head. He smiled. "Well, I have. So this is how I will handle the matter. You are, of course, welcome to reside with us once we find a suitably sized home."

Jael's father nodded and picked up his hat. "I have my own place there, and I must return. There are banking affairs to see to."

Stuart gave him a curt nod and turned back to a stack of papers at his right. "I don't anticipate you'll need to visit Perkinsville anytime soon. Find a foreman and have him brought to me. I'll instruct him on what we want."

Longstreet looked like he might comment, but said nothing. Stuart hated the man. He was a coward, ignorant of the way modern business needed to be handled. He cared too much about people and the details of their lives. Such a waste.

Still, Longstreet had his uses. When those ceased to exist,

then perhaps Mr. Longstreet would, as well. For now, Stuart would tolerate the man, as well as his daughter. His father had put a stipulation on getting his inheritance and keeping it. He had to remain married to the woman for at least six years. It irritated him to no end, but he would prove to Father that even this wouldn't hold him back. He would remain married to Jael, and when six years had passed, then he would decide what was to be done. Until then, neither her nagging for a divorce nor her desire to help the Vandermarks would deter him from his duties.

CHAPTER 12

 thought you'd never get home," Mother said, pulling Arjan into a long embrace.

He gave her a quick kiss, then turned to G.W. "Tell her the good news."

G.W. stood with his arm around Lizzie and nodded. "We found enough folks to help us in our arrangement of tradin' logs. Longtime family friends, willin' to keep it to themselves. It won't be easy, but we'll manage. Mr. Decker made a good suggestion."

Deborah came alongside at this. "And what was that?"

"We'll abandon the current camp and set up to the far north," G.W. replied.

"It seemed to me," Brian Decker began, "that any travel done by Mr. Albright is usually to Houston. If that is indeed the case, he would most likely never pass this way for any reason. You can reduce the rail time by moving to the far northern reaches of your acreage, as well as keep it out of the sight of locals who might say something without realizing the harm."

"That will mean no more coming home in the evenings," Mother said with a frown.

"Maybe not every evenin', but we'll still make it home often enough," Arjan replied with a grin and a wink.

"And have you talked to the men about this?"

"We have," G.W. said. "Stopped at the camp for a brief time on the way down here. They understand what we're up to. I reckon those with families will move them north to live in tents at the loggin' site. Some will probably move on into Lufkin since it'll be close enough to get home at night."

"Well, if you're certain this is how it must be," Mother said. "It will be a great deal of work just getting the site set up. You'll probably need to build a corral and keep the mules there."

"True. We've been discussin' all of this," Arjan answered. "We have a plan."

"What will you need us to do?" Mother asked.

Arjan put his arm around her shoulders. "Keep us in grub and prayers."

Deborah looked to her mother. "You'd best tell him our news."

Mother nodded. "Christopher is back. He's brought us a bit of a surprise."

G.W. shook his head ever so slightly. "What kind of surprise?"

"Five of his siblings. A house fire killed their parents, and Christopher found himself in charge of the five youngest. They range in ages from seven to sixteen. The oldest two boys would like jobs this summer."

"Where are they now?" G.W. asked, looking around.

"Christopher took them to town to see about school," Deborah interjected. "He wasn't certain when Mr. Huebner was ending the term."

"I was hoping you wouldn't mind if they stayed here with us," Mother added. "Christopher certainly hasn't enough space or food. We can easily put them to work here. They can help in the garden and with other chores."

"They seem to be very well behaved," Deborah added.

"They are," Lizzie concurred. "Darcy is thirteen and very capable with the twins."

"I'd say you ladies have this worked out already," Arjan said, laughing. "I see no reason to interfere. How about you, G.W.?"

"It's fine by me."

"I did want to ask if you might be willing to let Christopher use the cabin." Deborah quickly added, "Christopher suspects that Stuart will force him to leave his house soon. I thought if you and Lizzie weren't planning to move into the cabin yet, it might make a good place for Christopher to stay and see patients."

"I have no objection to that," G.W. replied. He fixed Deborah with an ornery grin. "Just so long as you two aren't sneakin' around at night to meet under the moonlight."

Deborah felt her cheeks grow warm. Arjan and Mother laughed. If a hole in the floor would have opened to swallow her, Deborah wouldn't have minded. They had no way of knowing that such thoughts had crossed her mind. It would be wonderful to have Christopher just a short distance away. The cabin was where Uncle Arjan had lived for years, and it might even be suitable for Christopher and Deborah after their wedding.

"I guess we're all set, then. I'll look forward to meetin' the doc's brothers and sisters—and I'm sure we can find the boys some work. Pay might not be much at first, however. They'll have to understand that. And now," Arjan pulled Mother along with him, "how about tellin' me what kind of cookies you have in the tin."

Deborah smiled as the couple exited for the kitchen. Mr. Decker glanced at Lizzie. "Where are my grandbabies?"

"Napping," she told him.

"That sounds like a splendid idea." Mr. Decker looked to the trio. "If you wouldn't mind excusing me, I will join them—at least in napping. I believe I'll seek the comfort of the guest room rather than the nursery, however."

"You go right ahead," G.W. said. "I have some things to talk over with Lizzie."

Deborah made her way into the front room to allow them some privacy and took up her sewing. A million questions assaulted her peace of mind.

When would she and Christopher marry? What would they do for money? Would they have to relocate? She certainly didn't want to leave.

And then there were the children. What kind of needs would they present? How could Christopher possibly provide for them unless he secured another steady position as a doctor? Again, the idea of moving elsewhere crossed her mind.

"But Stuart is rebuilding the mill," she murmured.

But that didn't mean he would hire Christopher. Stuart hated the Vandermarks, and Christopher was clearly tied to the Vandermark he hated the most.

The most important question, however, was the one Deborah didn't want to ask. It frightened her. What if Christopher no longer wanted to marry her? Worse yet, what if she decided she couldn't marry him? No. She shook her head. She loved Christopher. A little bit of trouble wouldn't keep her from a life of happiness with the man of her dreams.

Of course, five siblings were hardly a little bit of trouble.

"Deborah?"

She jumped, startled by G.W. calling her name.

"I nearly forgot. I ran into Jake Wythe in Lufkin," G.W. said. "He wanted you to know how sorry he was. Gave me this letter for you." G.W. handed the envelope to Deborah.

She looked at the handwriting and then back to G.W. "Was he well?"

"He seemed to be. Better off than last time, for sure. He seemed sincerely sorry for the way he acted at your party and asked if there was any chance of getting his job back."

"What did you tell him?"

G.W. shrugged. "I figured it was up to you. You were the one most wronged. He said he's left off drinkin'. He realized his mistake there. Said he was mighty discouraged and never meant to cause you harm."

Deborah looked again at the envelope. "I'm sure he didn't. He's usually a very gentle man. I knew it was the whiskey that caused him to act as he did. I never intended to see him lose his job, but I also didn't want him taking liberties with me."

"Well, read your letter and let us know what you think," G.W. said, heading back to the foyer. "He's a good worker, but I don't want him back with us if he's gonna make you uncomfortable."

Once G.W. was gone, Deborah opened the letter and began

to read. Jake was full of apologies and regret. He assured her that he would never touch liquor again, and that he was quite disgusted with the way he'd acted.

She read his final words again. *I've been drawing closer to God, knowing that my behavior was in part due to having walked away from my faith. Please forgive me, even if you don't want to ever see me again. I know that you and Dr. Kelleher will be very happy.*

He seemed sincere, and she couldn't help but feel a sense of relief. As far as she was concerned, Jake deserved a second chance. She would ask Christopher what he thought, however, before giving G.W. an answer.

By the time Christopher and the children returned, Deborah had finished the final touches on a shirt for Jonah. She held it up and showed it to the little boy. "What do you think, Jonah?"

He looked at the shirt and then to his big brothers. Christopher smiled. "Tell her thank you, Jonah."

"Thank you," he said, still uncertain as to what he should do.

"Well, go and get it," Christopher added, laughing. "I don't think he's used to getting presents—especially new shirts. In our family, hand-me-downs were more common."

The little boy walked up to Deborah and gave a shy smile. "Is it really for me?"

"Only you," she replied. She could not imagine how these children must have lived in Kansas City. Christopher had told her how poor they were, but it was still hard to fully grasp.

"We also have a surprise for you girls." Deborah got to her feet. "Mother and I changed the furniture around from my room to yours. You will each have your own bed now."

"Our own bed?" Darcy asked in disbelief. "Emma and I used

to share before the fire, and at Mrs. Maynard's house, I just had an old cot."

"I hope that means you are pleased. We took the smaller beds from my room and put them in yours so that you and Emma wouldn't have to share the big bed. I will use your bed in my room."

"Can we go see?" Emma asked. "Right now?"

"I don't see why not," Deborah said, smiling. She looked to Christopher. "Is that all right with you?"

"Absolutely."

The girls shot out of the room without another word. Christopher shook his head and laughed. "You've made them very happy."

"It was an easy enough solution. Also, Arjan and G.W. are back with Lizzie's father. They are waiting to meet Jimmy and Tommy. I think they'll be happy for the extra help."

"We can help right away," Tommy added. "Mr. Huebner isn't gonna have but another week of school, so we're not gonna start until next fall."

"Hopefully, by next fall, the mill will be up and running. Did Mr. Huebner say whether they plan to stick around?" she asked, looking to Christopher for an answer.

"He mentioned the possibility. He plans to head down to Burke to see what kind of jobs are available there, as well. He needs to find work in case the mill isn't up and running by September."

"Surely it will be operational by then," Deborah said. "Most of the mills set up with an outdoor arrangement at first. If they build a covered area for the saws, then they should get workers back right away. If the same men bring their families back to Perkinsville, then Mr. Huebner will have more than enough students."

"I thought I heard voices." Uncle Arjan came into the room. "These must be the Kelleher boys."

"Yes, sir," Christopher replied. "This is my brother Jimmy. He's nearly seventeen and has a mind to go to college. This is Tommy, and he'll be fifteen this year." He put his arm around Tommy's shoulder. "The youngest is Jonah."

"I'm seven," Jonah offered.

"Well, that's half grown," Arjan said, ruffling the boy's brown curls. Jonah beamed. "Why don't you come with me into the office, and we'll talk with G.W. about puttin' you to work."

The boys followed Arjan from the room, leaving Christopher and Deborah alone. She saw the weariness in his expression. "What's wrong?"

He straightened and crossed to her. "First, this." He lowered his mouth to hers and kissed her with such passion that Deborah felt her knees give way. He caught her easily and pulled her against him. With a low chuckle, Christopher set her on her feet.

Breathless, Deborah opened her eyes. "Goodness . . ." She fell silent and pressed her hands to her chest. Her heart nearly pounded out of her body.

"Do you require a doctor's assistance?" he asked, grinning.

"I very well might." She shook her head. "I have to admit, I was sitting here contemplating whether or not we should move forward with the wedding right away."

He raised a brow and frowned. "You're having doubts because of the children?"

She shook her head. "I'm not having doubts after a kiss like that."

"But doubts, nevertheless," he said without smiling.

Deborah reached out and took hold of his arm. "Not doubts about my love for you. It's never been that. Neither do I doubt your love for me. I do admit, I am concerned about my ability to care for all of them."

"I have worried about putting this burden on you."

"Christopher, I want to share your burdens—your worries. The children need you, and I understand that. I feel . . . well . . . I don't know what to say." Deborah turned away, knowing it would be impossible to tell him about her fears. At least not yet—not before she could face them herself.

"What's wrong, Deborah?" He came up behind her. "Talk to me."

"I'm not sure I can. I feel . . . so . . . overwhelmed." She turned and he took hold of her. "I'm afraid. I know it sounds ridiculous, but I am."

"Afraid of what?"

"I don't feel I can say—not yet. Give me time to sort through my thoughts."

He touched her face. "Don't be afraid. We're together. We can figure this out, one step at a time."

Deborah wanted to tell him about her fears of motherhood. She wanted to explain that his siblings only served to remind her that a large family would need constant care. She could hardly be working at Christopher's side as a physician while mothering children. Mill town medicine was too demanding—too bloody. If emergencies came up, as they always did, she would have to be able to move on a moment's notice. There wouldn't be time to make arrangements for the children.

"You are fretting, and it's not necessary. If we love each

other and trust God to direct our steps, we needn't fear our future."

She knew the truth of what he said—at least in theory. In practice, it was something entirely different, and she wasn't at all sure how to make the two become one.

∽

Euphanel giggled like a young girl as Arjan led her to the crate on the back of the wagon. "I'm so glad you were able to get two of them." Peering inside the wagon she was rewarded with a yipping sound.

"Oh, they're so cute. What fun they will be for the children."

Arjan nodded and lifted two puppies from the crate and put them on the ground by the wagon. "Folks in Lufkin said they were ten weeks old." The lumbering little fur balls were part bloodhound and part collie. A strange mix, but it made for a sweet-natured animal with distinctive bloodhound ears and collie nose, coat, and tail.

Reaching down, Euphanel picked up one of the pups. "Oh, they're so soft." The puppy licked her face and nuzzled up to her ear as if looking for food. "I'll bet they're hungry."

"Could be. Long trip." Arjan nodded toward the house. "You want me to fetch somethin'?"

"Well, since we plan to have the children take responsibility, let's call them out here and let them be surprised. We can instruct them then and the puppies will bond with them more easily."

"Sounds good." Arjan headed for the house. "I'll call them."

Euphanel put the first puppy down and lifted up the second. "You will be the best kind of healing," she said, kissing the animal on the nose. This puppy was less excitable and seemed content to just settle into Euphanel's arms. She checked to see if it was a boy or girl. "Oh, so you're the little lady. And such a calm disposition." She glanced down to see that the male pup was already chewing on a piece of wood he'd found.

At the sound of the children approaching, Euphanel put the female on the ground to join her brother. Jonah was the first one to spot the animals. He stared in surprise, coming to a dead stop. Emma saw them next.

"Puppies!"

The three youngest siblings ran forward to take the pups in hand. There was a great deal of squealing, chatter, licking, and yipping as the introductions were made. Euphanel smiled when Jonah asked what their names were.

"I thought maybe you three would like to name them. This is the boy," she said, pointing to the pup with a splotch of black covering his right eye. "And this is the girl. See, she's a little smaller and doesn't have the patch."

Darcy picked the female up and looked at her seriously. "I knew some folks once that had a dog named Lady. She's just a puppy now, but do you suppose we could name her a grown-up dog name?"

"Of course. She'll grow into it. In fact, I was just remarking that she was quite the little lady."

"I like that name, too," Emma said, reaching out to take the puppy from her sister. Darcy tried to act like she didn't mind, but Euphanel thought she looked rather disappointed.

"I know there aren't three," she began to tell them, "but two of the barn cats are about to have kittens, so I think you'll all have plenty of animals to spend time with."

"I like cats better anyway," Darcy said.

"We ain't never had a cat or a dog," Jonah said, his eyes as big as saucers.

"Never?" Euphanel questioned.

"Mama said we didn't have enough food for people," Darcy explained. "We couldn't be feeding a dog or cat. Mrs. Maynard had a cat and sometimes she came to visit us when the mice were bad."

Euphanel felt regret for the children who'd grown up in such poverty. "Well, you can definitely help to take care of these animals. They will need a lot of love, and right now I think they're hungry. At least this little pup is." She reached out to scratch the male behind the ears. "So what shall we call this little boy?"

"Let's call him Man," Jonah said. " 'Cause we got a Lady and this can be the Man."

"That's a silly name," Darcy said. "Man isn't a dog's name."

Jonah looked crestfallen. "Well, you named Lady. Me and Emma get to name this one."

"How about Buster?" Emma suggested. "You know like Mama used to call you when you'd get into things you weren't supposed to?"

Jonah smiled. "Yeah. Buster. I like that—it'll remind me of Mama."

Arjan joined them about that time. "Ready for me to put the crate in the barn?"

Euphanel knew the children would want to live in the barn with the puppies, but it was time to explain the rules. "The puppies will live in the barn, and at night we'll keep them locked up. This way, the wild hogs won't get them. They can be really mean to animals and people who can't defend themselves."

"Can't the puppies be in our room?" Jonah asked.

Emma looked at Euphanel with great hope. "Please?"

She was ready for this. "No. Cats and dogs stay outside. The only time we let one of the cats inside is when there's a mouse we can't catch. You'll have plenty of time to spend with them, so don't fret. Right now we'll let Arjan take the crate for us and you can bring the puppies. After we get them settled, I'll show you what to feed them and you can come back to the barn with the food."

The children were quite excited at this prospect and forgot their concern about the puppies not being allowed in the house. Euphanel could only smile at their excitement. Her prayer was that the pups would help them in their grieving process . . . and so far her prayer looked to be answered.

CHAPTER 13

MAY 1887

The first week of May brought gentle hints of summer. After a wet and stormy April, the weather settled and the skies cleared. Even the heaviness of the normally damp air felt less imposing and brought a riot of flowery scents. Deborah loved this colorful time of year, when everything around her seemed alive and vibrant.

"Here's the last of those roses, Miss Deborah," Sissy announced, putting two pots on the ground beside her. "Your mama said to tell you she'll be bringin' some cookies out for the lil'uns soon."

Deborah straightened and reached for the first pot. She looked to where Emma had just finished digging the hole. "Are you ready for this one?"

"Yes. You can put it right here, and I'll pack the dirt around it."

Working the rosebush from the pot, Deborah maneuvered the plant into the hole. While Emma took care of securing the dirt, Jonah called Deborah's attention to the hole he'd dug.

"See how deep it is, Miss Deborah?"

She could see he was quite proud of his accomplishment. "It's very fine. I'm sure this plant will grow strong there."

"It's the best I ever dugged," Jonah said, rubbing his hands together to get some of the dirt off. "I never planted nothin' before."

Deborah thought of their life in the city and nodded. "I'm sure there wasn't much of an opportunity, living in town."

"Jonah, you've got to wash up before you can have something to eat," Darcy announced. "You too, Emma."

With the older two boys living at the lumber camp, Darcy took it upon herself to mother and direct Emma and Jonah, assuming the responsibility without it ever being suggested. She seemed to believe that her attention was not only needed, but expected.

She's so much like me, Deborah thought for about the hundredth time that day.

"Emma, if you're done, let's go wash." Directing her younger sister to the pump, Darcy helped Emma to get the water started. Jonah joined them, none too happy.

"I don't like to wash up."

Deborah smiled as she planted the second rosebush. She tapped down the dirt and dusted off her gloves. Standing, she watched Darcy help Jonah with the towel. They worked well together, and Deborah couldn't help but admire Darcy's patience.

"Can we play with the puppies now?" Emma asked, returning to where Deborah was getting to her feet.

"I'm sure that would be fine. Why don't you bring them up on the porch? That way we'll be ready when my mother brings out our treats."

"I'll help, too!" Jonah's enthusiasm sent him running for the barn. It was only a matter of seconds before the children came running back, arms full of roly-poly squirming delight.

Emma settled on the porch floor and let her puppy loose. She giggled when the animal climbed back up on her lap and licked her face.

"She sure likes the new puppies," Darcy said, coming to stand beside Deborah.

"I like them, too," Deborah admitted. "Don't you?"

Darcy shrugged. "I like horses better. Do you think we could have a lesson today?"

She looked so hopeful that Deborah couldn't resist. "Why not?"

Clapping her hands, Darcy all but danced away. "I'll change my clothes." She disappeared into the house without another word.

"Lady, stop!" Emma rolled to her side as the puppy held fast to one of her braids. "Lady!"

Jonah giggled hysterically at the sight. "She's gonna eat your hair." He turned to find his own pup about to wander down the porch steps. "Come back, Buster."

He rolled Buster on his back and scratched the pup's belly. Deborah sat down on the porch steps near Emma. "He definitely likes that," she told the boy.

Emma finally had Lady interested in something other than her hair. The pup sat calmly, chewing on the tip of the little girl's well-worn boot. The soles appeared paper thin and the leather was cracked and scuffed.

"We're going to have to get you another pair of shoes," Deborah said.

"Mrs. Maynard found them after the fire," Emma told her.

Deborah frowned. "Were they in the fire?" That would explain a great deal.

"No. They were somebody else's shoes. They gave them to Mrs. Maynard for me to wear."

"I see." Deborah glanced at Jonah's shoes and saw that they too were hardly worth wearing. "Well, tomorrow we will do what we can to get some new ones. The commissary might still have a few pairs. If not, then we'll order some."

"New shoes?" Emma looked at Deborah as if she were speaking another language. "I've never had new shoes."

"No? Well, it's about time, then." She smiled at the little girl. It made her feel good to know they could bless the children with a better life.

Mother came out on the porch with Darcy in tow. They carried refreshments and Deborah jumped up to help.

"We've got it all under control," Mother said. "I thought you might enjoy some cookies and milk," she said to Emma and Jonah.

The puppies were momentarily forgotten as the youngest Kellehers hurried to the table where Mother placed her tray. Darcy in turn added a plate of cookies and smiled.

"I helped bake these this morning," she announced proudly.

"Then I must have one," Deborah declared. "Oh, I see you've been practicing Mother's sugar cookie recipe."

Darcy nodded. "She said it was the easiest of them all. I got to mix the butter and sugar together. Then I added the cream and the eggs."

"I remember doing that myself," Deborah told her. "Did you roll out the dough, too?"

"Yes. My mama taught me to roll out crust a long time ago and it was just like that."

Deborah took up one of the cookies. She sampled it and feigned deep consideration. Darcy regarded her with wide, hopeful eyes. "Yes. It's as good as any I've ever tasted. You are a good teacher, Mother. And you, Miss Darcy, are an excellent student."

The young girl smiled with pleasure, then helped Jonah reach the cookies and waited for his approval, as well. When he reached to get a second treat, Darcy all but danced a jig. "He must like them."

"They are very good," Emma said in a most adultlike manner. She sat back down with her cookie and tears touched the corners of her eyes.

"Are you all right?" Deborah asked.

"I just miss Mama. She sometimes baked us cookies."

"Not very often," Darcy said. "We didn't have enough money for sweets."

Emma nodded and repeated her sister's words. "Not very often."

Darcy came to where Emma sat. "Stop crying. Do you want Miss Euphanel to think we aren't grateful?"

Emma wiped at her tears while Mother came to sit beside the little girl. "It's all right. Tears are perfectly fine. Your mama was a good woman and you loved her a great deal—just as I'm sure she loved you. You miss her, and that's only natural."

Mother hugged Emma to her side. The child relaxed against her, calming at the maternal touch. Deborah wondered if she would ever be able to offer similar comfort to a child. She did her best to be friendly and loving with the children, but could she really help to mend their hurts the way Mother had always helped to mend hers?

Jonah occupied himself once again with the puppy, while Darcy chose to indulge in another cookie. Deborah caught her mother's eye and motioned to Emma's feet.

"We need to get them some new shoes. These were given by neighbors after the fire."

Mother looked at the pair and nodded. "They look a little too small. Do they pinch your feet?"

Emma nodded. "But they was all we had."

"I'm sure we can find something else. Tomorrow, we can take the wagon and go into town to see what they have at the store."

Deborah smiled. "That's what I told them. I have some money set aside. We can use it and get what we need. Darcy, do you need a new pair, as well?"

The thirteen-year-old pulled up the hem of her dress and nodded. "These are too big."

The strange-looking brogans were indeed too big. Why hadn't Deborah or someone noticed it before now? She felt guilty for worrying about how to coexist with Christopher's siblings instead of truly recognizing their needs.

"We can take care of all of that tomorrow," Mother said with a smile.

Just then Lizzie came to the door. "I'm ready to pick herbs—Darcy, can you come and keep the twins out of trouble?"

Darcy looked at Deborah. It was clear that she was torn between playing with the babies and having a promised horseback riding lesson. Deborah waved her on. "If you want to help, we can always ride later. Just come find me when you're done."

Darcy darted for the door, forgetting all about the cookies. "Let's go," she said without so much as a backward glance.

Deborah had to laugh at the child's enthusiasm. "She certainly enjoys playing with the twins."

"Indeed. And I know Lizzie appreciates the help. Darcy can keep the children occupied and has more energy than we do," Mother replied.

"Can we go, too?" Jonah asked.

Mother shrugged and got to her feet. "I don't know why not. You and Emma, go put the puppies back in their pen, and wait for me by the well. We'll meet up with Lizzie and the others in just a minute." Jonah gathered Buster, while Emma wrapped her arms around Lady.

"Hurry, Jonah," Emma said, bounding down the stairs with her load.

"It takes so little to make them happy. I think of all they've gone through, and it amazes me they can find joy at all." Deborah sighed and looked off toward the mulberry trees.

"You seem troubled." Mother reached out to touch Deborah's chin.

Deborah lifted her gaze and met her mother's worried expression. "I'm really fine. I just feel a little confused. I don't know how to be a mother."

"Who has asked you to be one?"

She shrugged. "Well, the little ones need guidance and teaching. They need comfort when they get upset and cry. I feel completely inadequate to do that."

"But why? You have always had a compassionate heart," her mother chided. "I've never known you to be otherwise. You saw the need for new shoes; I certainly missed that. It's often the little things that offer comfort or distress. You are seeing to their needs in a practical, tangible way. If I had not been here, you would have offered Emma comfort and a kind word. Don't be so hard on yourself."

Deborah frowned and turned away. "I'm not like you, Mother. I don't know that I ever will be."

"What do you mean?"

Emotions threatened to strangle her. Deborah turned. "I don't know that I could ever be a good mother."

A gentle breeze blew across the yard, sending a sweet scent on the air, but even this had no calming effect on her spirit. "I try to imagine it," she continued. "I really do. But how in the world can I help Christopher and be a physician in my own right, plus have children to tend at the same time?"

"Are you saying you don't want a family?" Mother asked, her tone quite serious. "You do realize you don't get to decide about that fact. God is the one who creates life. If you marry Christopher, it will be God, not you, who blesses the union with children."

"Or not. Perhaps I cannot have children," Deborah replied. "Maybe the feelings I have are for a good reason. Maybe God has never intended for me to give birth to my own babies."

Her mother looked perplexed. Deborah immediately felt bad for even making such a statement. What was wrong with her anyway? What woman didn't naturally long to have a family of her own?

I hate the way I am, she said to herself. *I disgust even myself.*

She turned away and shook her head. "I'm sorry. I shouldn't have said anything."

"There's nothing wrong in speaking your heart, Deborah. Have I ever taught you otherwise?" Her mother took hold of her once more. "You don't need to hide your heart from me. I'm not appalled by such a declaration. I'm not troubled that you feel this way. Goodness, child, God has His own way for you. I wouldn't begin to tell you what that is."

"I find it hard to consider marriage knowing that Christopher probably wants a family," Deborah said. "I haven't had the nerve to even ask him about it. I mean, the fire happened and the children came, and well . . . it just seemed poor timing."

"No. Poor timing was that you hadn't discussed this long ago. Does Christopher know how you're feeling—even a little?"

"I don't know. He knows I love medicine, just as he does. He knows I love helping him treat patients. I worry he's brought his brothers and sisters here, expecting me to stop helping him and work with them."

"But why? Why do you think this?" Mother asked.

Frowning, Deborah raised her face. "He's not here asking me to assist. To me, his actions speak louder than any words. He's been heading out to tend patients for days now, and not once has he suggested I go with him." She drew a deep breath to steady her emotions. With very little urging she might burst into tears, and that was the last thing she wanted.

"Deborah, you must speak with him. This is not the way I raised you. If you are feeling out of sorts, then you must let Christopher know. He can't be expected to instinctively know your heart."

"I thought he already understood my heart." Her words were heavy with emotion. "I thought that was why we loved each other."

Mother embraced her for just a moment. "Oh, sweetheart, you need to tell him how you feel."

"But what if he doesn't want to marry me after that? What if we can no longer work together?" Deborah imagined all of her dreams suddenly dissolving before her eyes. "I don't know what I'd do."

"But you can't marry a man you don't trust."

"I trust him. I never said I didn't."

Mother pulled back and smiled. "If you trust him, then why

aren't you talking to him about this matter? Why are you bearing this alone—fearful of what the answer might be?"

Her mother's words hit hard. She *should* be able to sit down with Christopher and share her heart. She ought to be able to go to this man—the man she wanted to spend her life with—and explain her fears.

She nodded. "I'll talk to him tonight. If there's time and the children don't need him too much."

"You let me handle the children," Mother said. "I will have them help me with some task. You and Christopher need time to settle this. I don't want you to lose him out of fear—nor to marry him because of it. Fear is not a solid foundation upon which you can build a marriage."

"I know you're right."

Mother patted her cheek. "I must go now, but remember what I said."

"I will. I promise."

Deborah watched her mother leave and let out a heavy sigh. She made it sound so simple, and perhaps that was the truth of it. Maybe Deborah was just making it difficult. Either way, she couldn't be happy by settling for less than what she felt called to do. Christopher wouldn't want to marry her if Deborah was less than the woman God had created her to be.

"But what if I'm the one who's wrong?" she whispered to no one. "What if God is calling me to be a wife and mother—to raise a family and put aside all my book learning? What if I'm simply in rebellion against Him, and don't even realize it?"

CHAPTER 14

G.W., Stuart Albright just rode up. He's getting out of his buggy this very minute," Deborah announced. "You don't suppose he's heard about the trades, do you?"

Getting to his feet, G.W. shook his head. "I couldn't say, but I wish Lizzie's father had stuck around. I feel better when we have a scholarly man in our corner."

"Do you want me to stick around?"

G.W. considered this for a moment. His guess was that Stuart hated Deborah more than anyone—unless he counted himself. "No. I'll call for you if I think it's needed. Better let us men bang heads on this one."

Deborah nodded, but G.W. could see she was upset. He let her go without another word and looked down at his desk. He wanted to make sure there was nothing visible that might give away their secret dealings.

Sissy ushered Mr. Albright to the office and announced him. "Mr. Albright says he needs to speak with you."

"That's fine, Sissy." G.W. remained standing as Albright pushed the black woman aside and stalked into the room as if he owned it.

"Vandermark, I have a proposal for you."

"First, apologize to Sissy. You didn't need to be so rude. She's an older woman—please show some respect." G.W. knew he was setting the stage for Stuart's hostility to grow, but he didn't want Albright to think he could just barge in and treat people like that.

Albright cast a brief glance at Sissy. "I apologize." He turned back to G.W. "Will that suffice?"

G.W. looked at Stuart for a moment before taking his chair again. "Have a seat."

The man unbuttoned his suit coat and did as instructed. G.W. figured it was the last time Albright would do anything he was told. He decided that for now, he would hear the man out—then throw him out, if necessary. G.W. frowned and chided himself for his attitude. Maybe Albright had come to propose the start-up of log delivery.

"As I'm sure you've heard by now, we are arranging to rebuild the mill," Stuart began. He fixed his gaze on G.W. and settled back in his chair.

"I heard somethin' about that."

"It appears that the construction will take some time to complete."

"I suppose you'll set up saws out in the open and build around them."

Stuart shook his head. "You suppose wrong. There are far

more modern processes now for mills. We intend to have the latest equipment available. Steam power will cut costs, and I intend to see the latest innovations installed. However, such equipment is costly and requires a decent structure in which to house it."

G.W. ignored a wave of disappointment. If Albright was being truthful, it would no doubt be a while before he wanted logs from Vandermark Logging. "So why are you here today? I reckon you didn't come for logs."

"No, again you suppose wrong. I actually have come for logs."

"I see." G.W. tried not to sound hopeful. He took up a ledger and opened it. "How many do you want and when do you need delivery?"

Stuart gave a bit of a laugh. It wasn't one of joy, however, and G.W. closed the book and eased back into his chair slowly. "I suppose that was just your idea of a joke?"

"Not at all, but you misunderstand. I don't want a mere shipment of logs. I want to buy you out."

G.W. could hardly believe his ears. He narrowed his gaze. "I reckon you better explain yourself."

"Of course. Your company is completely tied to mine. I hold the key to your success or demise." He gave G.W. a smug smile. "You might say I control your destiny."

"You might, but it would be wrong. God alone controls my life." G.W. crossed his arms against his chest. "Vandermark Logging isn't for sale."

"Now, now. Let's not make rash decisions without hearing the details of what I am about to offer. I would like to present a legitimate business proposal. I will buy Vandermark Logging and all your land, houses, and equipment. You and your . . . family," he said, "can simply pack up your personal items and leave."

He made it sound like it were already a done deal. G.W.

shook his head. "You're barkin' up the wrong tree, Albright. Our company and land ain't for sale. Even if they were, we wouldn't sell to the likes of you."

"I hardly see how you have much of a choice," Stuart replied. "You have to be quite behind in your bank payments. I understand you received permission to sell off a small portion of land, but the bank will not allow further sale."

"And how is it that you know anything about our bank dealings, Albright?"

Stuart looked most satisfied, and G.W. regretted having asked the question. "I have my ways of knowing whatever I need to, Mr. Vandermark. I am a man of resources. I'm also a man of power."

"I suppose that's your way of sayin' that havin' money allows you to nose into other folks' business. Well, it won't do you any good this time."

"You can't hope to continue for long in this manner."

"I don't have to," G.W. said, taking a deep breath. "Our lawyer, my father-in-law, has it under control for us. I reckon he's just as smart as you when it comes to business dealin's."

"I seriously doubt that." Albright touched a hand to his impeccable suit. "Were he as capable as you say, Vandermark Logging would hardly be in this position."

"Albright, I didn't ask you here today, and I'd appreciate it if you'd state your business and go."

Stuart's icy blue eyes bored holes into G.W. "You are in a bad way, Mr. Vandermark. You are at my mercy. If I choose to, I can drag out the rebuilding of the mill until your family is dead in the dust."

"You do what you feel you have to," G.W. said. "I doubt Zed will be all that happy with it, however. He'll have something to say about all of this."

"Hardly. I'm buying him out, as well. He has no more say over anything."

G.W. couldn't hide his surprise. "Buyin' him out? It's his company."

"No, Mr. Vandermark. It is my company. Mine and Mr. Longstreet's. I hold the controlling interest. Mr. Perkins owes me a great deal of money. He had no insurance on his business, and no means to support himself apart from it except for the company stores—which are also now mine."

"So you're just gonna ruin the man? I guess I should have figured on that. It seems that stirrin' up trouble and makin' folks miserable is what you do best."

Albright shrugged. "It's a gift." He laughed and got to his feet. "I came in good faith to offer you a decent price on the business. It seems to me, a mill owner should handle his own logging. If you aren't of a mind to cooperate, I'll simply wait until the bank takes over your property, and then I'll buy it for a pittance of its former worth."

G.W. fought the urge to jump to his feet. He didn't want Albright to see that he was upset. He pretended to busy himself with the papers at hand. "I'm sure you know the way out."

Without another word, Stuart exited the office, leaving G.W. to contemplate the situation. He wished his father-in-law could have been there to help, but he figured he'd handled the situation well enough. G.W. really wanted to talk to Zed and find out what was going on. He couldn't imagine Zed had wanted to sell out. The longtime family friend would no doubt be devastated. With a sigh, G.W. pushed the papers aside and bowed his head. Prayer seemed the only hope any of them had.

∽∾

Lizzie sat on the porch, glad that the twins were off with Euphanel and the others. It would give her a few free moments to confront the man she'd nearly married.

When Stuart bounded out the front door, a scowl on his face, Lizzie knew her time had come. She stood and faced him. "Why are you here?"

Stuart stopped in midstep, unable to hide his surprise. He quickly recovered and masked any emotion in his expression. "You know full well."

"You once said you loved me, and now you treat me this way."

He shrugged. "I lied. I never loved you or anyone else. I wasn't raised to love—I was raised to prosper. You nearly cost me everything. Had Jael not needed my help as much as I needed hers, I might have seen the end to my fortune. All thanks to you."

"I couldn't marry a man I didn't love," she countered. "It wasn't my intent to hurt you—neither in leaving you on our wedding day nor going through with the marriage." She softened her tone and took a hesitant step forward. "Stuart, I didn't want us to live in misery."

He laughed, causing her to step back again. "I would not have been in misery. You wouldn't have had to be, either. I told you as long as you presented yourself in a positive manner socially, I would give you the freedom to live as you wished. You could have had everything your heart desired."

"Everything but love." She shook her head. "I feel sorry for you, Stuart. At first I worried about causing you pain, but now I just hold pity for you. You have no idea what real love is all about. I'm blessed to know it for myself, and there is nothing so wonderful."

Her words hit their mark. Stuart paled slightly and shook

his head. "I will crush you. You and your precious family. Mark my words, I will have my revenge."

"The world is full of folks who are seeking the same," Lizzie said sadly. "I thought you to be smarter and definitely more secure in your position than that. Seems to me you've been running scared most of your life."

His face contorted in anger as he took a menacing step forward. "Watch yourself, Lizzie. It would be a pity if something happened to you—or one of your children."

She closed the distance between them and narrowed her eyes. "You'd do well to watch yourself, Stuart Albright. If you ever open your mouth to threaten my children again, I'll . . . I'll. . . ."

He laughed. "You'll what? You can't hurt me."

Lizzie regained her composure. "I'll have my father help Jael get a divorce." She smiled at the look of surprise on Stuart's face. "That's right. I know Jael wants to leave you. I knew it from the first moment when I learned the truth about why she married you. Mark my words, if one of my children so much as scrapes their knee, I'll be eyeing you first to ascertain whether or not you pushed them."

Stuart opened his mouth to speak, then turned instead. He stormed from the porch and into his buggy, barely releasing the brake before applying a whip to the back of his horse.

Feeling rather strengthened by Stuart's reaction, Lizzie squared her shoulders. It felt good to stand up to the man who'd so often manipulated her in the past. She felt a sort of quiet resolution in their exchange. He would know now that she was not a weakling. She was a woman who loved her family. A mother who would guard her children with her life.

Lizzie shook her head and wished that things could have been different with her own mother. She couldn't imagine how different their relationship might have been had her mother been more interested in Lizzie than in working for women's rights. She was so disinterested in motherhood that she didn't even tell Lizzie about her twin sister.

Taking a seat on the porch, Lizzie felt tears form. How she longed for her mother to come and see the twins and explain about the sister she'd never known. She wanted her mother to tell her how sorry she was for the wasted years—that she wanted a new life with Lizzie and the others.

"But that won't ever happen," she whispered with a sigh. Regrets wrapped themselves around Lizzie like iron bands. For all the joy she knew now—for all the love—she couldn't find a way to put the demons of the past at bay.

"Are you all right?"

It was Deborah, returning from teaching Darcy about the horses. Lizzie forced a smile. "I'm fine. Stuart came for a visit with G.W." She wiped away a tear. "How was your ride?"

Deborah shook her head and came to sit beside Lizzie. "Only Darcy rode. I observed and counseled, but that isn't important. What happened with Stuart?"

"I stood up to him. I waited for him out here and when Stuart concluded his business I cornered him about why he was here—why he was determined to make us suffer."

"He wants to make you suffer for the sake of suffering."

"And he's accomplishing it," Lizzie replied.

"Don't allow him the upper hand, Lizzie. You know that he's cruel and has proven himself to be underhanded in his business dealings. There is no shame in putting such a person from your life. No fault, either. The Bible says we are to resist the devil and he will flee from us."

"Instead, I resisted and the devil hunted me down."

Deborah put her arm around Lizzie's shoulder. "Well, he may know where you are, but he cannot have you. You belong to God, and He will not tolerate this torment forever. God will not be mocked, and that is exactly what Stuart Albright is doing. He's mocking God and seeking to harm those whom God loves. You'll see. God's hand will reach down and destroy Stuart and all he's built for himself."

Lizzie shrugged. "But you know as well as I do that evil men prosper all the time. Wickedness abounds and the weak suffer."

"Yes, but we are not weak. We have Jesus and the armor of God. Remember those verses in Ephesians six that Pastor Shattuck spoke on several weeks ago? The armor of God will protect us. And above all, the Scriptures say, we need to take up the shield of faith in order to deflect the darts of the wicked. God has made provision for our protection. We simply need to trust Him."

"When Stuart threatened the children, I found more strength than I knew I even had."

"He threatened the twins?"

Lizzie nodded. "He threatened me, as well, but I told him if he ever so much as caused one of my children to scrape their knee, I'd have my father help Jael get her divorce."

"You should let G.W. know that he threatened to do you all harm," Deborah said. She looked away. "Stuart told Jael he'd hurt me if she tried to leave him. I should have said something sooner about it to G.W. and Arjan, but I was afraid of what kind of trouble it might stir up. Now, I know."

It was Lizzie's turn to offer comfort. "It wouldn't matter, Deborah. Stuart is a cruel man. He will do his worst, but as you said—we have God's protection. We must rest in that and trust Him to keep us from harm."

"We must also be as wise as serpents, the Bible says." Deborah gazed down the road. "That's especially true when it's a snake in the grass that's threatening to bite."

‹∞›

"He honestly thought he could just waltz in here and buy us out?" Arjan asked.

G.W. nodded. "That's what he said. Said he knew we had to be gettin' desperate. He has no right to know anything about our business, but apparently he has his sources."

Deborah left the room and discussion in order to find Christopher. She had promised her mother she would speak with him about her fears. Something deep within her mind warned her to remain silent, however. She loved this man, and surely she would love his children.

"I can be a good wife and mother," she murmured. "I know I can. I've always been able to do whatever I set my mind to."

Christopher was outside talking to Jimmy and Tommy. The boys had come back with Uncle Arjan, full of stories and excitement. She held back, not wanting to disrupt their obvious enjoyment of the evening.

Mother had taken Jonah and Emma with her to work in the garden, and Darcy was mucking out stalls in the barn. Deborah decided a walk might do her better for the moment. She needed to understand her own heart. After all, how could she talk to Christopher about her fears when she wasn't even willing to face them herself?

She slipped down the stairs and headed off toward the woods. There was still enough light, and perhaps Deborah could spend that time in prayer. She thought of the words she'd just shared with Lizzie.

"Here I am again. Why can't I follow my own advice? Why can I speak of hope and safety in God to others, but not grasp it for myself?"

Gazing heavenward, Deborah looked up through the boughs of a longleaf pine and sighed. There was such beauty here. Such peace. Why could she not find it within?

Father, I don't know what to do. I love Christopher and want to marry him, but I'm afraid. She startled at the thought. Was it merely fear that kept her from feeling at ease—from taking delight in the idea of marriage and motherhood?

CHAPTER 15

ith Christopher away on a medical call, Deborah took the opportunity to ride into town with Arjan and G.W. the next day. They had decided to see Zed Perkins and discuss the situation with Stuart Albright. Deborah wanted to check in with Mara to see if Jael had sent a letter. She hurried to the preacher's house and found Mara eager for a visit.

"I had a letter from Rob. He plans to come home at the end of this month and stay for several weeks. I'd like to surprise him with a party for his twenty-fifth birthday.

"I think it would be great fun."

Deborah took off her straw bonnet. "I think that would be wonderful. Mother would be thrilled to have you come by the house to discuss it." Deborah glanced around the house and lowered her voice. "We can certainly talk more about the birthday plans, but I was wondering if you'd heard from Jael."

"I have." Mara hurried to a small desk across the room. She slid open a drawer and removed a piece of folded paper. "She gave me this just this morning. I was planning to give it to you at church tomorrow."

Deborah took the paper and opened it. She scanned the lines and shook her head. "Stuart plans to move Jael on Monday. He's making her stay with her father in Houston so that she won't have any opportunity to be around me." She looked up at Mara. "She says we must speak before she leaves."

"How will you arrange it?" Mara questioned, then answered before Deborah could speak. "I could invite her here."

"No. Stuart might insist on coming, too." Deborah considered the problem for a moment, then tapped the side of her temple. "G.W. and Arjan are visiting Mr. Perkins at this very moment. They are discussing business. It would be quite appropriate for them to include Mr. Albright. Let me go speak with them and see if they would do this for me."

Mara followed her to the door. Deborah stuffed the paper in her reticule and then re-affixed her bonnet. "Pray that this works," she told Mara before leaving.

∞

"I'll fetch him right away," Zed told Deborah. "I'll say it's urgent and cannot wait."

"Thank you so much, Mr. Perkins. I can't tell you what this means to me." Deborah turned to her stepfather and brother. "Thank you, as well. I know his company is not desired."

"That's all right, Deborah. A discussion between us all is needed," Arjan assured her. "This is the perfect excuse."

"I'll take the long way around to their house. I can slip in right after you and Stuart head back here," she said, nodding at Mr. Perkins, who was already reaching for his hat.

Once outside, Deborah lost little time. She hiked her skirt just enough to give her legs the freedom she needed, then half walked, half ran to the northern edge of the town. She hurried toward the railroad tracks, doing her best to keep careful watch down the open roads for Mr. Perkins and Stuart. At one point, she heard them before seeing them and barely managed to dart behind one of the houses as they passed along the road just to the south.

With Stuart on his way to meet with the men, Deborah picked up her pace. She didn't hesitate before knocking on the door. To her surprise, it opened right away and Jael stood in welcome. "Come in quickly. Mr. Perkins managed to tell me what was happening."

The two women embraced briefly before Jael closed the door. "Essie is gone for the morning. We're alone. Stuart was quite angry to be disturbed. I doubt he'll stay long."

"Then we must hurry," Deborah declared. "Your letter said it was urgent we speak."

Jael nodded. She looked gaunt and pale. "Stuart is forcing me to go to Houston. He wants me to stay with my father until he can arrange a house for me. Oh, Deborah! Stuart is acting so strangely. I came across some letters he received, and I believe he has someone at the bank who is giving him information on your family. When advised that money appeared in Vandermark Logging's account, he ranted around here like I've never before seen. I'm not sure what he plans."

"Oh, Jael, I am so sorry. Are you sure you wouldn't want to come back to the house with me?"

The young woman shook her head. "That would only make him angrier. I am, after all, his wife." She frowned and looked away. "And there's another thing. I think I might be with child."

Too stunned to speak, Deborah waited until Jael turned back to face her. "I don't want to be. Please don't think badly of me, but I asked Stuart for a divorce and he refused. If I'm carrying his child, there will be no possibility that he'll change his mind. What will I do?"

The hopelessness in her voice caused Deborah to reach out and take her in her arms. Holding Jael close, Deborah let her friend cry. Nothing she could say or do would make this better.

Jael suddenly pulled away. "There isn't time for this. Stuart told me he wasn't about to stay for long. He'll be back before we know it. Deborah, I feel so desperate."

"Go to your father. He loves you and will keep you safe. Tell him what is happening between you and Stuart."

"I can't. If I do, Stuart has threatened to tell Father about my indiscretion with Ernest Remington and pregnancy prior to our marriage."

"What if he does? It's in the past, Jael. Your father will not hate you. The family name wasn't dragged through another scandal. He will see your sacrifice and hopefully feel bad for it."

Jael considered this for a moment. "He might at that." She wiped her tears. "But if he doesn't . . ."

"Why would he not? I think he's endured enough of Stuart to know what kind of man he's dealing with. If you are the one to tell your father, then Stuart loses his power over you. He's convinced you won't be truthful—that you're too afraid of the consequences. I, on the other hand, know you to be quite strong and capable. The truth will set you free, just as the Bible states."

"I fear Stuart, Deborah. I fear what he might be capable of doing to . . . you. He's already tormenting your family."

"Don't you fret over us. God is our stronghold. Stuart has caused problems to be sure, but our hope is in the Lord."

"I wish I knew more about such things. My family was never all that religious."

"You don't have to be religious. Just know that God loves you—that He gave His Son, Jesus, to die for you. He wants to be there for you—to comfort you and encourage you. Trust Him, Jael. He will be faithful to you."

Her friend shook her head. "I don't know how God can help in this when Stuart is so very evil."

Deborah touched Jael's shoulder. "God is more powerful than the devil. He may have allowed him a certain amount of control over this world, but God will defeat Satan when all is said and done. We need only to stand fast. Don't be afraid to put your confidence in Him, Jael."

They both startled at the sound of footsteps on the porch. Jael grabbed Deborah. "The back door—hurry!"

They fled through the house and into the kitchen. "God be with you, Jael," Deborah said, giving her friend a quick embrace. "Write to me through Mara."

"I will. I promise."

Deborah heard Stuart bellowing his wife's name as she hurried out the back door. She ran from the house, turning to dodge behind one of the other houses and a small stand of trees. Deborah felt the pounding of her heart and paused a moment to settle herself. There was no sense in returning to her family in a panic.

She was focused on heading to Zed Perkins's house when she saw that Christopher's door was open. He was back. She knew he planned to come out to the house that evening, but she wanted to have some time alone with him first. Speaking with Jael about talking to her father made Deborah realize that facing her fears was the best advice she could give herself. It was time to be honest with Christopher—to explain her concerns, even if she wasn't entirely sure what they meant. Making her way across the road, Deborah knocked on the examination room door and opened it.

"Christopher?"

He looked up from restocking supplies in his bag. "What a pleasant surprise."

"I came into town with G.W. and Arjan. They're with Mr. Perkins. I wondered if we might talk."

Christopher came to her. "What's wrong?"

Deborah closed the door and leaned against it. "Why do you never ask me to join you on your medical calls?"

"What are you talking about? I didn't ask because . . . well, I presumed there was more than enough work to be done, what with my brothers and sisters at your place."

"And does that mean you expect me to remain there to take care of them?"

Christopher looked uncomfortable. "I . . . uh . . . well, I don't know what I expected. You know how worried I've been, trying to determine how I can provide for them. It's my responsibility."

Deborah felt sorry for him. "Christopher, my mother loves having the children there. This is something she has taken on and enjoys."

"And you want no part of it?"

"I didn't say that," she quickly countered.

Christopher reached for her hand. "I'm sorry if you felt slighted. I don't seem to be able to do anything right these days."

"Nonsense. It's not about me feeling slighted." Deborah drew a deep breath. "Christopher, I want to be a physician. I love medicine—you know that. I love you, as well. I just need to know that I can manage both at the same time."

"Why would that be difficult?"

"Children." She felt her chest tighten. "Ever since you returned home with the children, you've not asked me even once to accompany you. In fact, you've hardly said much of anything to me."

She could see the regret in his expression and held up her hand. "I didn't say these things so that you would apologize. I am saying this because it will affect our life together. If you expect me to stay at home and care for your brothers and sisters, then I can hardly be out there assisting you."

Christopher pulled up a stool and sat. "And what about after we're married?"

"I understand that your siblings will be a part of our future. They must have a home and care—especially the younger ones. In the fall, however, school will start and they will be busy with that."

"I see. And what about any children we might have?"

Deborah straightened her shoulders and tried to firm up her determination, but to her surprise, she broke into sobs. Knowing she'd completely ruined any chance to explain this without emotion, she buried her face in her hands.

Without a word, Christopher pulled her close. Deborah hated the way she was acting. How could she hope for him to take her seriously about helping him when she couldn't even discuss this openly without tears?

After a few moments, Christopher lifted her face to his. "Deborah, are you trying to tell me that you don't want my children—our children?"

"I . . . I . . . don't know." She gasped for breath. "I love you.

I know I . . . would . . . love our children. I . . . oh, I don't know what I'm . . . trying to say." She tried to pull away, but he held her fast.

"Deborah, calm down and listen to me. You can't turn away from me. We have to talk about this."

"I know." She drew a deep breath and tried her best to settle her nerves. "I'm so sorry. This has been troubling me for so long now."

Christopher looked at her oddly. "You've held this in all along while planning the wedding?"

She felt horrible. Nodding, she reached out to him. "I'm sorry. I was wrong. I was swept away in my desires and dreams. You're the reason I love medicine. I love you, Christopher. I don't want to lose you."

"Who said you would?" He shook his head. "Deborah, we can't keep such things from each other."

Deborah sniffed and he handed her a handkerchief. "I'm sorry. I know I was wrong. My mother told me that I couldn't even think of marrying you if I didn't trust you with the truth."

"And what is the truth?"

"I want to use my knowledge and training. I want to continue to learn from you, and I want to marry you. I'm afraid, however, that once we marry and I have a baby, it will all end. I can hardly follow you around to the mills and logging camps with a baby on my back."

He smiled. "If anyone could, it would be you." He reached up and pushed back damp strands of hair.

For several moments, neither said a word. They stood quietly gazing into each other's eyes. Deborah fought back her doubts. "When I left to attend the university, I did so out of a love for learning and a love for my family. I wanted to help with the business, and my father often said that it would be wonderful to have the help. I thought that meant that it was expected of me. Here I am again putting thoughts and feelings into your heart and mind that may or may not be true. Please forgive me."

He smiled. "Only if you forgive me first. I knew it was going to be a shock to bring home the children. I wanted to consult you—to figure it out together, but there was no time to contact you. I was uncertain as to how you might react. I knew five children would be rather daunting. Of course, Jimmy and Tommy don't need our attention like the others do. Even Darcy is pretty self-sufficient."

Deborah thought of the thirteen-year-old. "She's very much like I was at that age."

"You said," Christopher began thoughtfully, "rather . . . your brother said that I could stay in the cabin on your property."

"That's true."

"Would it be possible for us to stay there after we marry?" he asked.

"I believe so. At one time Lizzie and G.W. had planned to move into it, but Lizzie prefers the big house, and Mother loves having them there, as well. Since they added on, there's really no need to move into the cabin."

"Then perhaps we could live there. I don't know how big it is or if we could add space for the children, but if we could, perhaps we could open an office there. We could put out word that people could come and be treated there for their ills and injuries. If we have a baby, you could run the office when I need to go out to the mills. Would that be acceptable?"

"And I could continue to train and attend patients with you until we started to have children?" she asked, feeling her cheeks grow hot. Talking about marital intimacy was hardly something a proper lady did.

"Exactly. And perhaps by that time, the mill here will be reopened and the area will need a full-time doctor again."

Deborah nodded. "I would think so. Goodness, but I never considered that." She looked at him. "And you wouldn't mind? Are you sure?"

He pulled her back into his arms. "I'm quite certain. Marriage is about compromise and working together. It's also about being honest. Please don't keep things from me, Deborah. We can work through anything . . . together."

She relaxed against him and sighed. "I'm so sorry, Christopher. I'm going to do better, I promise. I've been so afraid that perhaps I didn't even want to be a mother—that I would be awful at the job."

He laughed. "You would make a remarkable mother, and if God blesses us with a child, I've no doubt you will love him or her just as you love me. Right now you're afraid, but I intend to help you get over your fears." He drew her fingers to his lips and kissed them gently. "I can be most persuasive." He kissed the back of her hand and glanced up.

Deborah felt her breath catch. Goodness, but he was so very handsome, and he loved her. She felt her heart skip a beat as Christopher touched his lips to hers. Deborah wrapped her hands around the back of his neck and sighed. Her mother was right. Honesty and openness was much better than holding secrets and fears in silence.

CHAPTER 16

C hristopher handed Euphanel some money. "I want you to have it for the children. Deborah and I talked, and we're putting off the wedding trip."

Euphanel shook her head. "I wouldn't hear of it, Christopher. We're getting by just fine. We've been remaking old clothes and using up material on hand to see to their needs. The garden is producing in abundance, and G.W. and Arjan killed two hogs just last week and you brought in food not long ago. We have plenty to feed them and they're earning their keep—believe me." She threw him a broad smile. "You hang on to this money in case you need something."

"But you bought them new shoes. Those didn't come free. I

should have seen that they needed them, but it didn't even cross my mind."

Euphanel led him to a chair. The summer kitchen was hot and steamy from cooking, but Christopher barely noticed. He had far more on his mind. He'd tried everything he could to get a nice sum of money together, but folks were bad off. Those who could pay usually did so in trade—a chicken here, a sack of pecans there.

"You seem worried." Euphanel went back to the oven and peeked at her bread.

Christopher wasn't sure how to broach the subject of his fears with this woman. She would be his mother-in-law soon—at least he hoped she would—but Euphanel Vandermark was also strong and capable. She'd endured far more than taking on someone's orphaned children.

"There isn't much money to be made in this area," he finally said. "If the mill were back up and running, and if Albright hired me on to be the company doctor, then things would be better. Still, I can't see that happening."

Euphanel listened and nodded. "And it's hard to take on a wife and family without an income."

"Exactly. Deborah loves it here and I know she would hate to move, but it might be necessary."

"It happened that way for me, as well. I loved Georgia, and the last thing I wanted to do was move to Texas. Still, it was necessary for many reasons." She lifted a pot lid. Steam roiled from the pan and filled the air with the undeniable scent of molasses and brown sugar.

"Smells good," he told her.

"It's my special beans." She gave the pot a stir, then replaced the lid. "Secret recipe." She smiled and sat beside Christopher.

"Deborah will do what has to be done. My daughter is strong and knows that life is unpredictable. She is also determined to overcome obstacles."

"I know, but I don't want to be the one to take her from her family and all that she loves. It's bad enough I'd be saddling her with an instant family. She worries about how that will affect her ability to help me."

"I know. We talked. Christopher, you and I both know that life doesn't always look the way we think it should, especially when you're out of step with the times. Deborah has always been that way. She wants to be the Proverbs thirty-one woman—doing it all—working hard—providing for her family—using her mind. Yet society today puts many obstacles in her way."

Christopher worried the brim of his straw hat. "I want to give her a good life. I want to make her dreams come true. I know she longs to practice medicine and that she loves helping people. We talked about this the other day, and I was confident things would work out."

"But now you're not?"

"Well, there isn't enough work to keep me busy. If I can't earn a living here . . . well . . . we'll have to move to a bigger town."

Euphanel reached over and patted his arm. "I'd hate to see you go, but you have to do what's right for you and your family."

"But you don't understand. If we moved to a bigger town, then I'd definitely need Deborah to take care of the younger children. I had a solution in mind if we stayed here, and part of that depended on having family nearby. I knew you and Lizzie would help Deborah out if we were to have children—especially if Deborah continued to practice medicine. Moving away wouldn't allow for that."

"I see your point." Euphanel leaned back and wiped her face with the hem of her apron. "Have you prayed about this?"

"Until I'm all out of words." He turned to face her. "I love your daughter."

Euphanel smiled. "I know that full well."

"But I cannot condemn her to a life that she would hate, just to marry her. That would be a more selfish act than I could live with."

"Christopher, you need to let her be the judge of that. Lay out the situation and let her know what has to be. If she decides to walk away, then that's her choice."

He shook his head and dropped his gaze to the floor. "I just don't know if I can live without her."

∞

On Saturday evening, when everyone was gathered informally in the living room, Jimmy announced that he'd arranged with Mr. Huebner to take a test to show that he qualified to graduate from high school. The discussion about the week had already been lively, but when Jimmy told them about his plans, the conversation took on a whole new enthusiasm.

"Your folks would no doubt be mighty proud," Arjan said.

Jimmy nodded. "Ma wanted me to go on with my studies like Christopher did." He looked to his brother and grinned. "Of course, I don't have plans to deal with blood and guts."

"Can we go outside and play with the puppies?" Jonah asked.

"Please? It's still light," Emma added.

Mother checked the clock on the wall. "You can go for just a few minutes. I'll send Darcy to come get you when your bath water is ready. Remember, tomorrow is church, and we need to look our best."

"I hate havin' a bath," Jonah said, shaking his head as he stalked toward the door. "I'm not that dirty."

Mother and Lizzie exchanged a smile with Deborah. The boy was so covered in dust he might very well turn the bath water to mud.

"Have you thought about what you want to study if you go on to college?" G.W. asked Jimmy once the younger children were gone.

"I love numbers. Anything to do with mathematics," he replied.

"And you just have to pass a test in order to move ahead?" Arjan asked.

"Yes. It'll show that I've learned all that I need to know in order to go to the university. Mr. Huebner said he's more than confident I'll pass. Especially in mathematics. He says I'm well ahead of him in that." Jimmy's smile revealed his pride. "He said if the test shows I've done just as well in my other subjects, I can attend a university next fall. Of course, dependin' on the college, I'll probably have to take a test for them, too, but Mr. Huebner said if I pass one, I can prob'ly pass the other."

"That's wonderful news," Deborah said. "I am so happy for you. I know you'll enjoy college—I certainly did, and the test I had to take was not all that difficult."

"Mr. Huebner says there are some great schools here in Texas, but I think I'd like to go back East. Those schools have been around for a lot longer and have more to offer. I want to teach college one day."

"That's an admirable career," Mother said.

Christopher remained silent, and Deborah found that strange. "What do you think of all of this?" she asked him.

All attention turned to the doctor. Christopher looked almost startled by the question. "I am very happy that Jimmy is of a mind to follow his dreams." He looked to Tommy. "I'm proud of what Tommy has accomplished, as well."

"I sure don't want to go to college. I just want to work in logging. I like working outside—it's so much better than the work we had in town. In fact, I don't want to go back to school at all. I was told that here, I don't have to. Besides, with a job I can help take care of the family."

"We will discuss that later," Christopher told him. Tommy shrugged but said nothing more.

Deborah knew Tommy's idea wouldn't bode well with Christopher. The younger Kelleher had spent only a short time in the logging industry and had no idea of the dangers involved. Christopher, on the other hand, knew them only too well. She tried to give Christopher a smile, but he wasn't looking at her. In fact, despite the fact he was sitting beside her, Christopher was quite far away. He seemed troubled; maybe he was worried about Jimmy leaving. Maybe he thought his brother wasn't ready to face the world.

Mother got to her feet. "I'm going to get the bath water ready. Darcy, would you please go call Jonah and Emma back to the house?"

Darcy had stretched out on the rug to study an atlas. She glanced up with a yawn. "Yes, ma'am," she answered and closed the book. She got to her feet, mindful of the new skirt she'd actually helped to make. "But they won't like it."

Everyone chuckled. Deborah knew the girl was right.

"Christopher, why don't you spend the night here? Use the cabin. I know you prefer to go back to town and keep an eye on what's yours, but one night surely won't be too great a risk," Arjan told him. "We could all head in to church together in the mornin'." He smiled at Deborah. "And if you had a mind to do a little spoonin' on the front porch, well, we'd make sure to keep the lights down low."

Lizzie giggled and G.W. nudged her. "If they don't take up the offer, we just might. Since the twins are already asleep, we could use a little spoonin'."

Deborah got to her feet and held her hand out to Christopher. "Oh, no you don't. The porch is ours. Go find another place to court your wife."

One by one, the family dispersed. Deborah waited until the silence hummed in her ears. "Are you coming?"

He looked up and nodded. Without a word, he got to his feet and took hold of her hand. Deborah drew him out to the porch. "Are you going to tell me what's wrong?"

Christopher looked at her for a moment, then let go his hold. Walking away a few paces, he planted his hands on the porch rail and stared off into the growing darkness.

Deborah followed. "Christopher, what's going on? Why are you so distraught?"

He heaved a heavy sigh. "I just don't know how to make it all work."

"What are you talking about?"

"Jimmy and school. The family . . . us."

She grasped his arms and forced Christopher to face her. He didn't resist, but she could see by the look on his face his reluctance to discuss the matter.

"I'm not sure I understand, but I do know that secrets between us are no good."

He nodded. "I know, and maybe that's why this is so hard."

"Please sit with me. No harm can come from discussion."

Christopher allowed her to lead the way again and took a

seat beside her on the swing. "I'm afraid harm might come from this one. Or at least disappointment."

Deborah shuddered and rubbed her hands against her arms. Christopher didn't seem to notice, however, and for that she was glad. Was he upset with her? Was he only now really thinking about what she'd said regarding children and her desire to be a doctor? Did he regret having asked her to marry him?

She tried to ease into the conversation. "Jimmy seemed quite excited about attending a university."

He nodded. "But I don't know how I could ever afford to send him—and yet, I promised."

"That's what this is all about?" she asked, trying not to sound too hopeful.

"Partly." He leaned back against the wooden frame of the swing. "I can't seem to make any money. Folks around here— what few there are—want to trade goods for doctoring. They're as bad off as the rest of us because of the mill being destroyed."

"But I thought you were having a better time of it, riding out to the surrounding areas."

He shook his head. "Folks are suffering, Deborah. The bad winter up north helped some of the cattlemen to sell their stock, but many did so either in trade or selling on agreement. Not much cash actually changed hands."

A sinking feeling came over Deborah. He wanted to leave this area—to move elsewhere. He knew she wouldn't like it, and he was anticipating the conflict. For a moment, she felt guilty. This was because of her, not Jimmy. She was the one who'd made it clear she didn't want to leave Perkinsville again. She was the one who wanted to practice at his side when there wasn't enough work for one doctor, much less two.

"And now Jimmy wants to go to school back East. How

could I ever help him with that when I can't even afford to take care of food and clothes—or put a roof over their heads? I was almost relieved that Tommy wanted nothing more than to go to work and help with expenses."

Questions wormed their way to the front of her thoughts, but she dared not give them voice: Was he going to tell her they needed to leave Perkinsville? Would he suggest they all move east so that he could practice medicine and Jimmy could attend school? Did he want to forget about the wedding—put aside their love until the financial issues could be resolved?

She longed for answers and feared them at the same time.

"I don't know what we're to do, Deborah. I can't rely upon your folks' charity forever. The children seem happy—happier than I figured they'd be having just lost Ma and Da." He shook his head. "I know that has to do with the love your mother has given them. They need someone like her—not me."

"Are you actually thinking of giving them up to be adopted? You would send them to an orphanage?" Deborah asked. While she didn't particularly relish the idea of the responsibility right now, she certainly didn't want the family split up or sent to strangers.

"I don't know. I don't know what they need."

"They need you. They need each other. You can't send them away," she said, sounding harsher than she'd intended. She reached out to touch him, but he surprised her by pulling back and getting to his feet.

"That's the problem. Don't you see? There is no answer here. Nothing that will satisfy everyone. You don't want to move away. The children don't want to be separated. Jimmy wants to go to college, and there is nothing here to help with any of our needs.

Tommy is only fifteen, yet he has better chances at making a living than I do!"

He stormed off the porch, leaving Deborah to stare after him, her mouth open. She'd never known Christopher to act in such a fashion. She wanted to run after him, but perhaps it would be better to wait until he cooled off. He probably just wanted to take a walk and think through matters.

Instead, she was shocked a few minutes later when Christopher came riding past the house, headed for town. He was leaving. Without saying a word to her or anyone else, Christopher was going back to Perkinsville.

Was he giving up? Did he just need to be alone?

Deborah walked to the edge of the porch and hugged her arms close. What was happening to her perfect dream—the dream of practicing medicine at her husband's side? The dream of living in this community and helping the people she loved? Hope flickered like a dying ember.

She felt rather ill as answers crept into her mind. She had deluded herself. There was no dream. Her desires were too many, and she could not have them all.

Foolish woman, a voice condemned from within. *You refused to stay in your place and do what was expected. You had to have an education and take on more responsibility than anyone wanted you to have. People tried to advise you, but you wouldn't hear them, and now you'll have no chance for happiness unless you are willing to give up your own way.*

"But can I be happy in compromising what I believe to be so very important?"

She stared into the darkness, her gaze still fixed on the road. There was a slim chance that Christopher might come back. But even if he did, what could she say? What could either of them do to make this right?

CHAPTER 17

Although Stuart and Jael were in attendance at church the following morning, Deborah had no chance to speak to her friend. Stuart ushered Jael in after the singing began, and as soon as Pastor Shattuck said the last amen, the Albrights quickly walked from the building. Deborah found it curious that they should even be there. After all, neither were particularly interested in church, and Stuart even boasted of despising religious practices. Their presence had taken Deborah's focus all morning, along with her worries about Christopher. He hadn't even shown up for the service.

"Where's Christopher?" Darcy asked as they left the building.

"I don't know," Deborah admitted. "I thought he would be here."

"Maybe he's sick. You should go check on him," the astute thirteen-year-old suggested.

Deborah wanted to do just that, but thought better of it. "I'll have Jimmy and Tommy go see if he's at the house. Could be he was called out to attend to someone who's sick."

Darcy nodded. "I'll get the boys." She took off before Deborah could change her mind.

Fanning herself against the growing heat of the day, Deborah watched Zed Perkins talk in low hushed tones with her brother and stepfather in the shade of a tree. His brows were knit together and his head downcast. Arjan put his arm around the older man's shoulders. No doubt this had to do with Stuart and his plans to buy out Perkins's interest in the sawmill town.

"Here they are," Darcy said, pointing to Jimmy and Tommy. "I told them we were afraid Christopher might be sick."

Deborah looked to Jimmy and smiled. "Could you two just go over to his house and check? He might have gone out on a call, but if he's not feeling well, then I want to be able to help him."

"Sure. We'll go," Jimmy declared. "Come on, Tom." They made their way through the folks lingering in the churchyard.

Looking up, Deborah saw G.W. motion her over. Deborah crossed the space and joined her brother and the other men. "What's wrong?" she asked at the sight of their somber faces.

"Albright is forcing Zed out," Arjan said in a whisper. "It's worse than we figured."

Deborah could imagine that anything having to do with Stuart would only benefit one person—Stuart. "How so?"

Zed shook his head. "Albright says I owe more than I have assets to support. He says there's not much I bring to the table anymore." He looked to the ground. "He says he's taking over the business affairs, the buildings and inventory that's remaining, and that he'll give me only a small amount of money in return. This is because of all the money I owe him for the loan on the mill."

"But I thought," Deborah interjected, "that he had insurance on the mill and had already been reimbursed for the costs involved. He should have paid the loan off with that money."

"It was his insurance though," Arjan replied. "Not Zed's. He can do with it as he pleases."

"But surely the bank would expect him to repay them," Deborah countered.

"The loan wasn't through the bank," Zed explained. "It was a personal loan between me and them—Albright and Longstreet. They took on the amount I owed the bank and paid it off. That's why they have the controllin' say over what happens now."

Deborah looked to her brother. "We should get ahold of Lizzie's father and let him know what's happening."

Zed shook his head sadly. "I already talked to a lawyer in Lufkin. He said that Albright has some big city lawyers handlin' things for him and that they've got folks runnin' scared—seems politics are involved. It's pretty well figured that he's got some of the judges in his pockets, too. That's why he's not afraid to do whatever he wants. It's why he's treatin' you folks like he is—he ain't afraid of being told no."

"I can believe that just from what he said when I mentioned the idea of us suing him for breach of contract," G.W. affirmed. "He made it clear that we'd be the ones regrettin' it."

Deborah fanned herself all the more furiously. "It's not right. This state used to be better than that. You could count on folks to do what was decent and lawful."

"Money makes folks whistle a different tune," Arjan said in disgust.

"And not havin' money leaves you with no choice but to

dance to the song bein' whistled," Zed said with great sorrow in his voice. "I never thought I'd see this day. Rachel and me . . . well, we figured we'd be passin' the business on to our boys about now. We figured that we'd be takin' life a little easier. That's not even possible now. We'll have to move, and I'll have to find work. Sawmilling is all I know."

"What about startin' up again?" Arjan asked. "If you're free of Albright, then you could put your own business together, and he'd have no say in the matter."

"I don't have the money for it. Once Albright is done with me, I'll be lucky to have the clothes on my back."

Deborah felt consumed by sadness and guilt. Her stomach tightened. If she hadn't encouraged Lizzie to leave Stuart, none of this would be happening. "I'm so sorry, Mr. Perkins. I still say we need to talk to Lizzie's father. He might have some suggestions."

"You can talk to him if you'd like," Zed said, "but I figure the answer will be the same. Now, if you'll excuse me, I reckon I'd best collect Rachel and head home. We need to spend some time in prayer about what to do next." The man headed for his wife after shaking hands with G.W. and Arjan, shoulders slumped forward in defeat and his head down.

"That poor man. I cannot believe Stuart will be allowed to get away with this," Deborah said, pushing down her anger. "Can't we do something?"

"You know we can't. Our hands are tied," her brother replied. "Albright knows that better than anyone 'cause he's the one who tied 'em."

"But surely we know some honest people who could help. Not everyone can be bought."

"Christopher isn't at the house," Jimmy said from behind

her. Deborah turned and met the boy's shrug. "Guess he's out doctoring like you said."

Deborah hoped that was all he was doing. She had a bad feeling about the way things had been left between them. It wasn't like Christopher to lose his temper and leave without a word.

She thanked Jimmy and made her way out of the church. Outside, the slight breeze made things marginally cooler than inside. Deborah was grateful she'd worn her lightest gown. The yellow gingham had been sewn into a fetching creation that brought many compliments, but at this moment Deborah would have just as soon jumped into the millpond—dress and all.

"Goodness, but if it's this warm in May," Olivia Huebner said as she joined Deborah, "imagine what the rest of the summer will hold in store."

"I'd rather not," Deborah replied. "I was just thinking of how nice it would be to go swimming."

Mrs. Huebner nodded. "I remember days when I was just a girl. We would slip off—just me and my sisters—and strip down to our unmentionables and go swimming in the creek by our place." She gave a nervous laugh. "I don't suppose I would want to share that with just anyone."

Deborah smiled. Mrs. Huebner was the epitome of propriety and, no doubt, figured such a comment might ruin her reputation. "Your secret is safe with me. I've been guilty of the very same thing, only it was girlfriends instead of sisters."

Over by the wagon, Mother laughed and chased after Jonah. Olivia and Deborah seemed to catch sight of her at the same time. Mother had never seemed happier—at least she hadn't laughed this much in a long time.

"You know, I think those children have taken twenty years of longing off your mother's age."

"What do you mean?" Deborah asked. She had never thought of her mother as longing for anything.

"Well, you know she always wanted more children. She could only have the three of you—oh, there was the other baby that died before you were born."

Deborah nodded. "Yes, our sister Janna." The infant had been stillborn, and Mother seldom talked about her. In fact, it wasn't until Lizzie found out that she had been the twin of a stillborn child that Mother spoke openly of the matter.

"Well, she couldn't bear any more children after you were born, and I know it bothered her a great deal. She wanted a large family, and for many years, it tormented her. I suppose now with Dr. Kelleher's siblings, she can enjoy mothering young ones again."

Deborah turned her attention back to where her mother was now swinging Jonah by the arms. She twirled in a circle; both of them laughed.

"I never knew," Deborah murmured.

Mrs. Huebner waggled her finger at Deborah's face. "Well, don't you be tellin' her that I told you. I wouldn't want her to think I was gossiping."

"No, ma'am. I won't mention it."

"She does seem mighty happy," Mrs. Huebner added. "Oh, there's Curtis. I must run along now. Try to stay cool."

"You, too, Miz Huebner."

Deborah watched Mr. Huebner take his wife by the arm and walk down the road toward their house. She then returned her attention to Mother. She wasn't that old. *Goodness*, Deborah thought. *Mother will be but forty-five at the end of June.*

"You looks to be ponderin' deep thoughts," Sissy said, coming to stand beside Deborah.

"I was just thinking about Mama and how she'll be forty-five next month."

Sissy nodded. "Have to have a nice party for her. 'Course, I was reckonin' we'd have a weddin' in June."

"I don't know if that's going to happen."

"Is there troubles betwixt you and the doc?" Sissy asked.

With a sigh, Deborah found herself explaining to the older woman what had happened. "I think he's more worried about my feelings than anything. He knows I have no desire to leave this place."

"Women go where they men go. That be the way of things. Iffen you ain't of a mind to be a wife and let him lead, you best not marry."

Her words hit Deborah hard. "I suppose I'm afraid," she said honestly. Speaking the truth aloud didn't come easy. "I love him so much, but I worry that I won't be a good wife. Especially since I'm such an unconventional woman."

"Bah! You follow the Lord, and you be good 'nuf. It be God's way what matters—not ours. The good Lord ne'r said you couldn't work with your hands; fact is, He 'spects you to. But He 'spects you to trust Him first."

"I know you're right," Deborah said. She gave Sissy a brief hug. "You always seem to know the right thing to say. Sometimes I feel so foolish. Here I have all this book knowledge and yet I struggle."

"Book-knowing and heart-knowing be two different things, Miss Deborah. Bein' smart ain't the same as usin' your smarts." Sissy gave her a big smile. "I had to learn that the hard way— sounds like it be the same for you."

Deborah nodded. "I guess so, but I'm hoping to change for the better."

"The good Lord be all about that." Sissy pointed. "Looks like your mama is loadin' up."

"Deborah!" Mara called, making her way from the church. "Hold up, please."

"You go ahead, Sissy. I'll be right there." She crossed the distance to meet Mara. "What's wrong?"

"Nothing. I just wondered if it would be all right to pay you all a visit tomorrow and discuss the plans for Rob's birthday party."

"Mother is just over there at the wagon. Why don't we go ask her?"

Mara leaned closer as they walked. "I saw that Mr. Albright pulled his wife out of church before she could speak to anyone. Such a pity he's so harsh with her."

"I know. I'm praying things might change for the better. Jael wants a divorce, and you know what kind of ostracizing that could bring. She doesn't even care, she's so miserable," Deborah said, careful to make sure no one else overheard. "Please pray for her. I don't know for sure what God would have her do, but she's so very unhappy."

"We're nearly ready," Mother announced as Arjan helped her into the wagon. "Are you riding with us or G.W. and Lizzie?"

"I'll come with you," Deborah replied. "However, we have a question for you. Mara wants to know if she might visit us tomorrow and discuss ideas for throwing Rob a surprise birthday party."

Mother beamed. "I would like that very much. Please do come whenever is convenient."

"Thank you, Mrs. Vandermark. I'll speak to Father and see when he might be available to bring me out."

"You are both more than welcome to join us for dinner. We'll eat around noon."

"I'll tell him. I'm sure he'd enjoy that," Mara said. "Until tomorrow."

Deborah gave her a brief hug, then climbed into the back of the wagon unassisted and took a seat beside Darcy. "God go with you," Deborah told Mara.

"And with you."

Darcy looked up at Deborah. "Do you really think God goes with us when we say that?"

The question was simple enough, but it took Deborah by surprise. "I do," she said as the wagon began to move out. "In fact, I think He goes with us whether we say it or not. Don't you?"

Shrugging, the girl looked away. "Who can say? We can't order God around like that."

Deborah smiled. "I don't think I've ever considered it ordering God around, but I can understand why you might. Truly, we're just reminding each other to walk in God's ways, and if we do that—we know He's with us."

CHAPTER 18

Christopher looked at the note left at his door. He had presumed it would be from Deborah; instead, he found it a summons from Stuart Albright. Christopher figured Albright was going to demand he clear out. Zed had warned him to expect it, and so Christopher had already been hard at work, crating up his personal effects. Nevertheless, he left his horse hitched outside the office and made his way to hear what the man had to say.

As he arrived at the Albright house, Christopher found Stuart sitting on the front porch. He appeared to be engrossed in a handful of papers. He glanced up and greeted Christopher with an expression void of emotion.

"Dr. Kelleher, I'm glad you could finally make it over."

"Had to set a broken arm. What did you want to see me about?"

"I would like you out of the infirmary by tomorrow evening."

"All right."

Stuart's face pinched, as though he sought to identify a foreign odor. "All right? No questions? No complaints?"

Christopher shrugged. "Would it help if I did?"

Laughing, Stuart shook his head. "No. It wouldn't change my mind, if that's what you wonder."

"Is that all you wanted?" Christopher asked, turning to move back down the steps.

"As a matter of fact, it's not. I have something else to discuss—an offer, actually."

Christopher could hardly imagine what Albright would want to propose. "What did you have in mind?"

Stuart gave a smug smile. "Why don't you take a seat and I'll get right to the point."

Apprehension washed over Christopher. He briefly reconsidered. But the worries of the future compelled him to weigh all possibilities. All night and morning he had prayed that God would show him an answer. He tried not to look too eager, however, and ambled casually over to where Albright sat.

Sitting, Christopher raised a brow in question. "So?"

"I have in mind to give you a great deal of money." Stuart put his papers on the table between their chairs. "Does that surprise you?"

"Do you have to ask? Of course it surprises me," Christopher replied. "You give me twenty-four hours to vacate my residence, and now you want to give me money. Why shouldn't I be surprised?"

"Well put," Stuart said. "I like a man who isn't afraid to

speak his mind. My proposal will make you as wealthy as you are forthright. Given that you have five other people dependent upon you for their well-being, I think you'll find this most lucrative. Perhaps one could even say an answer to prayer."

Suspicion tensed Christopher's muscles. Stuart Albright had proven himself to be a man who did nothing out of the goodness of his heart. Albright wanted something—wanted it badly enough to subject himself to this conversation.

"What is it you want, Albright?"

"It's very simple, really. I will pay you two thousand dollars to do exactly as I say."

Christopher couldn't imagine ever having that much money in his hand at one time. He knew the deed Albright would request for that amount would, no doubt, be dear. "Get to the point. What is it you want?"

Stuart gave a small chuckle. "Leave this area and never return."

The demand confused Christopher. Albright had to know that with no steady work to be had, such an idea would have already surfaced in the doctor's mind. Christopher needed to make a living now more than ever.

"And where did you have in mind that I should go?"

"I don't care," Stuart replied. "Take your siblings and go back to Kansas City, for all it matters."

"And if I do that, you'll give me two thousand dollars? Just for taking my family away from here?"

"Well, there is one other requirement."

Of course. Christopher nodded and looked Albright in the eye. "And that would be what?"

"Break your engagement with Deborah Vandermark. Leave her and agree to never marry her."

The words fell like a lead weight, crushing any hope that

Christopher might have taken the man up on his offer. Christopher rose and walked down the porch steps. He had reached the walkway when Stuart finally called out to him.

"Two thousand dollars cash is a lot to walk away from."

Christopher turned. "You're quite mad, Albright. If you honestly think to buy me off so that you can perpetuate your vengeance on the Vandermark family, you have another think coming."

"Three thousand." Stuart's voice bore no hint of anxiety.

"No." Christopher started walking toward home.

Albright came to the side of the porch. "Five thousand dollars. That's my final offer."

It was a great deal of money, more than Christopher could ever have imagined. He looked hard at Albright and shook his head. "I'm glad it's your last offer, because my honor and love aren't for sale."

∞

Deborah had returned from swimming with the children only a few moments earlier and was still trying to fix her wet hair into a long single plait. Her heart leapt and sank when she saw Christopher ride into the yard, two large carpetbags hanging over his saddle horn. With nimble twists and tucks, she finally secured the braid and got to her feet to go to him.

Arjan greeted Christopher first and offered to take the horse to the barn for him. Deborah was glad when Christopher agreed. He took the bags from the saddle and dropped them on the ground. She wanted to ask about them immediately, but she remained silent.

He turned and gave her a sheepish smile. "I'm back."

"I see that," she said, returning his grin. "I missed you at church."

"Had a broken arm to set."

Deborah nodded and cast a glance at the bags, then back to his face. Christopher shrugged. "Albright kicked me out. I'm supposed to vacate the property by tomorrow."

"Oh, Christopher, I am sorry. G.W. is more than willing for you to take over the cabin. You can let folks know that you're setting up there. We'll get the word out."

He stepped forward and reached up to touch her cheek. "I'm sorry for the way I behaved."

"I know. I'm sorry, too. You've been carrying the weight of all this responsibility and I've done nothing to relieve your mind. I haven't been a very good example."

"In what way?"

She sighed. "I haven't exactly been allowing you to lead in our courtship. A wife should be obedient and let her husband direct their plans. I didn't do that."

"You aren't yet a wife," he replied.

"Are you rescinding your offer?" she asked, surprising herself.

Christopher appeared just as surprised. In fact, he looked almost like he'd been caught doing something wrong. Was he contemplating that very idea? Had she forced him to comment on it before he was ready?

"I see I've perhaps touched on a nerve." She started to go, but he took hold of her arm.

"Don't go. If I seem awkward in dealing with your question, it's just that . . . well, Stuart Albright asked me to do just that not even an hour ago."

"What?" Deborah could scarcely believe her ears. "Stuart asked you to end our engagement?"

"He did. In fact, he offered me five thousand dollars," Christopher said, grinning. "I should have thanked him, because, frankly, it put me in a much better frame of mind."

Deborah didn't know whether to be offended or happy. She looked at him and shook her head. "Five thousand dollars?"

Goodness, but that would resolve a world of problems. It would be enough to set up house elsewhere and establish his medical clinic. Why, with that much money, he could afford to send Jimmy to the university of his choice.

"He must really hate me."

"Not as much as I love you," Christopher said. "He helped me to realize that my moping about money was foolish. Money certainly isn't anything compared to love. Oh, a person still needs to make a wage and support his family. But I can do that without worrying about the amount of cash it yields."

"But that's a great deal of money, Christopher." What if they married and he later regretted not having taken it? Dread snaked through her veins like ice water. It left her feeling rather cold and clammy. She wasn't a woman given to fainting, but suddenly it seemed like a possibility.

As if reading her mind, he steadied her shoulders. "Deborah Vandermark. You surprise me. You're the one who has been trying to get me to see how God handles all things—even our financial needs."

She drew a deep breath to clear her head. "I know. I suppose it's just that . . . well, you were so angry at me last night."

"No I wasn't. You had nothing to do with it—well, very little. I was upset with myself. I was frustrated that I couldn't seem to find a way out of this. I spent most of the night praying and asking God to reveal the truth to me—and when Stuart Albright gave me his proposal, it was like God had done just that.

"I could see the matter clearly, Deborah. It was such a freeing moment. I was wrestling with the wrong things. Remember those verses in Ephesians? The ones Pastor Shattuck preached on here a while back?"

She remembered them very well. "Ephesians six."

"Yes, it says we aren't wrestling with flesh and blood, but with the powers of darkness." He shook his head. "I don't remember the exact words, but the principle is fixed in my mind—at least it is after dealing with Albright. My battle isn't for money or patients or a nice place to set up an office. It's about putting the future in God's hands and trusting that He will supply our needs."

Deborah knew that what he said was right, but she couldn't shake the feeling that she was keeping Christopher from a much-needed answer to his prayers. She looked at the ground to hide the tears that came to her eyes.

He put his arm around her. "Besides, five thousand dollars would never come close to the value of the love I feel for you. Now, if he'd offered ten . . ."

Deborah snapped her head up to meet his grin. How could he tease about something so important? Albright offered no mere pittance. Five thousand dollars was more money than most folks ever saw.

"How can you—" she started, but Christopher put his finger to her lips.

"Nothing equals the love I feel for you. I'm sorry I ever acted in a way that suggested otherwise."

It wasn't easy to remind herself that she'd been the one who'd had misgivings about their love—all based upon her fear of how children might interfere with her plans. What a fool she'd been.

"I love you, Deborah. I want you to be my wife—to share my life," he said, tracing the line of her jaw.

"I want that more than anything," she replied, finally knowing that it was the absolute truth. "I love you, too. I guess we've both allowed our fears to cast a shadow on our love. Oh, Christopher, I am so sorry for the way I've behaved."

He kissed her with such tenderness that Deborah felt light-headed and swayed in his arms. Perhaps it was just the heat, but there was no denying this man had power over her.

∞

"Mama Euphanel, can I have another piece of chocolate cake?" Emma asked.

Jonah nodded in a most enthusiastic manner. "Me too, Mama Yoonell. With lots of gravy on top."

"It's not gravy," Emma corrected. "It's toffee sauce. And her name is Yoo-fan-el—Mama Euphanel."

Mother looked at the children and then to Christopher. "I . . . uh . . . I don't know what to say. I never . . ." She stammered into silence and a dark shade of crimson flooded her cheeks.

Deborah thought it charming that Emma had addressed her in such a manner, but she could understand her mother's surprise. Christopher, too, seemed to understand.

"I would suggest just a little piece—perhaps they could share another piece of cake." He gave Mother a wink. "That way, Mama Euphanel, I can have another whole piece to myself."

"Me too," Jimmy chimed in.

"Well, you don't get it all," Tommy declared. "I want more, too."

It was wonderful how easily the situation resolved itself. Mother got up without another word and brought the cake plate into the dining room. She began slicing additional helpings while the others passed their plates to her.

Deborah reached over to squeeze Christopher's hand, but got his thigh instead.

"What!" he fairly yelled, and gave a start as if he'd sat on a hot coal. The plate he was planning to hand to Mother was all but thrown into the air.

Deborah nearly upended her chair in backing away. Now everyone turned to look at them, only making matters worse. She stared in silent horror that they should all know what had just taken place.

"What's wrong?" Arjan asked.

Christopher quickly recovered. "It's nothing. I was just startled. Thought maybe a spider had come to share my cake."

"You scared of spiders, *too*?" Jonah asked. "Just like me?"

"And me," Emma said, shuddering for emphasis.

"Not me," Darcy declared. "I think they're amazing. I saw a really big one the other day in the barn."

"Well, you need to be careful," Mother chided. "There are a great many poisonous insects and snakes here in Texas. I wouldn't want you to get sick from a bite."

"She's right. Spiders can be very dangerous," Christopher said, catching a sidelong glance at Deborah. "Often they appear without warning."

Deborah thought she might well die of embarrassment. She stared at her hand, still feeling the touch of his thigh beneath her fingers.

"Did you get bit?" Emma asked. "You keep looking at your hand."

Snapping her head up to meet everyone's intent stare, Deborah shook her head. "No. No, it's fine."

"I should probably check it," Christopher said, reaching over to take hold of her.

He was only making this that much harder. Deborah squirmed in her seat, but Christopher refused to let go of her.

"There are jumping spiders," Tommy offered. "I heard about them at school last year."

Christopher nodded. "Perhaps that was what I was thinking of just now."

Deborah wished she could find some excuse to leave. Of course, that would only serve to bring more unwanted attention.

"So when are you two gonna get around to havin' that weddin'?" G.W. asked, putting his arm casually around Lizzie's shoulders.

"That's a very good question. In fact, it's one that I was kind of hoping to resolve myself." Christopher turned to Deborah. "Why don't we take a little walk—check out my new home?"

"Be sure and look for spiders," Jonah instructed.

Christopher gave Deborah a wicked grin. "I would very much like to look for spiders."

Deborah felt her eyes widen and her throat tighten. Goodness, but would he ever stop teasing her about this?

Mother gave the final piece of cake to Arjan. "The cabin is all aired out, and I took fresh linens and bedding out there. I doubt you'll see any spiders. You, of course, will take your meals with us, Christopher."

"I'd like to see anyone stop me," he said, finishing the last bit of cake on his plate.

Deborah had never seen anyone gulp down food so fast, but even now, Christopher was pushing back his chair. "Will you accompany me? We can pick our wedding date."

"Now, I don't want to sound harsh," Arjan said, picking up his fork, "but if she's not back here in fifteen minutes, I'm gonna send the children over to see what's keepin' her."

"If there are spiders," Darcy said, "I can help you kill them. Just come and get me."

"I will do that, sister of mine." Christopher got to his feet and extended his hand to Deborah. "Fifteen minutes is more than enough time. If she can't make up her mind on a date in that span, I'll fix it myself."

Arjan laughed and nodded. "Go on, then."

Deborah had no chance to refuse. Christopher quickly hurried them out of the dining room and into the kitchen. From there, they slipped out the side door. By the time they cleared the back of the house and were half way to the cabin, Christopher burst into laughter and lifted Deborah to whirl her in a circle.

"You are quite the catch, Miss Vandermark."

Deborah felt her cheeks grow hot again as Christopher returned her to her feet and pulled her close. "I think you are the most charming woman I've ever met."

"Because I grabbed your leg instead of your hand?"

He laughed again and kissed her nose. "No, because you were so embarrassed by it. For a physician well acquainted with the anatomy, I am rather surprised, however, that you should mistake one part for the other."

"You moved your hand to pick up your plate. It's a wonder you didn't drop it," she said, clinging to what little self-respect she had left. "And then you start speaking about spiders, of all things."

"Would you rather I had pointed out your firm hold on my thigh? Of course, I could have told the family that you couldn't help yourself—that you were quite overpowered by your attraction to me." He put his finger to his chin. "No, I don't suppose that would have gone over all that well. Your brother would probably have refused to let me stay anywhere on this property if he'd thought that was the case."

"Oh, you are impossible," she said, moving away from him to head back to the house.

Christopher moved quickly, however, and pulled her back against him. "Darling, you need never be embarrassed around me. I might tease you, and I might correct your medical skills, but I would fight to the death to defend you and keep you from shame."

Deborah felt his arms tighten around her and leaned back against him with a sigh. How she loved this man. "June the eleventh," she said in a barely audible voice.

"June eleventh? What about it?"

"That will be our wedding day."

He loosened his hold and turned her to face him. "But that's over three weeks away. Do we have to wait so long?"

She smiled and gently brushed his lips with her finger. "The time will fly by. You'll see."

He sighed and nodded. "I suppose if that's the way it must be." He paused and cocked his head toward the cabin. "In the meantime, we could look for spiders."

Deborah pulled away and started back for the house. "I'll get Darcy to help you." His laughter rang in her ears, and Deborah couldn't help but smile.

CHAPTER 19

D eborah stood back as Zed and Pastor Shattuck loaded the last crate of Christopher's books onto the wagon. Mara strolled out of the house with a heavy brown coat and came to Deborah.

"Dr. Kelleher asked that you pack this in the wagon. He doubts he'll ever need it down here, but figures it's too good of a coat to leave behind."

Deborah laughed and took the piece. "Is that everything?"

"It's just down to a bit of cleaning now, and I told Dr. Kelleher I would handle that for him."

"How kind. You certainly don't have to, though. I offered to stay behind and handle it." Deborah tucked the coat into an open crate half filled with books. "There, that ought to ride all right."

Mara nodded. "I didn't have anything special going on today and figured you would have plenty to do at the other end, setting things up."

Deborah considered the idea for a moment. "You're probably right. I suppose if Christopher is all right with it, then I certainly will not argue." She smiled. "Have you heard that we set the wedding date—again?"

"I was going to ask."

"June the eleventh," Deborah said without further prompting. "I figure Rob will be home and that will make it all the more special."

"Oh, that is wonderful. Do you suppose . . . I mean . . . would you be offended if we also celebrated his birthday that day—after the wedding sometime?" Mara toyed with a single long black braid of hair. "I suppose that was really brash of me to ask."

"Not at all. I think that would be great fun. Folks will already be gathered," Deborah said. "You wanted it to be a surprise, so how about this—we will have the wedding and then I can turn to the congregation and announce that we're celebrating Rob's twenty-fifth birthday a few days early. That will be such a shock to him."

"You don't think he'll mind, do you?" Mara questioned. "I feel like I know him better and better with each letter he writes, but I also realize there is much to learn."

"I think he'll be quite embarrassed and unsure what to do. But I figure that's what will make it the most fun. Look, you get the word out to anyone and everyone that we're going to do things this way. Your father is going to announce the wedding date at church on Sunday, so you can let other folks know then."

Mara smiled and hugged Deborah. "Oh, this will be so much fun!"

"What will?" Christopher asked, coming up behind Deborah.

She let go of Mara and turned to him. "I'll tell you on the way home. Mara tells me she's going to clean up for us here."

"Yes, she said she would like to do it for us, and I yielded to her persuasion."

Deborah nodded. "As did I, but I've also arranged to compensate her in another way. That's what I have to explain on the way home."

"Are you two ready?" Arjan asked as he and G.W. climbed into the first wagon.

Jimmy and Tommy jumped onto the back of Deborah's wagon since it held less, and Deborah allowed Christopher to help her up. She took her place on the seat and waited for him to join her.

"I think we're set to go," he told Arjan.

"Thanks again for the help, Pastor. You, too, Zed."

"Glad to do it; sorry about having to do it under these conditions," Zed replied.

"God will work it all out," Christopher said.

His confidence made Deborah smile. She found strength in his words. God would work it all out—of this, she was certain.

∞

Euphanel finished sewing a sleeve onto the dress she'd made for Darcy. Sissy was working feverishly on hemming Emma's smaller matching gown.

"I think this sprigged muslin is perfect for the girls. The light blue will go perfectly with Lizzie's gown. Her dress is the color of a brilliant summer sky and has that lovely white lace and ribbon. It will look like we planned it all along." Euphanel held the gown up to better see the bodice. "I'm glad they'll have a part in the wedding. That will help them to feel a part of their brother's new life."

"I reckon so," Sissy said, stopping her labor. " 'Course, maybe it don' matter much to them one way or t'other. Young'uns always have their own notions 'bout such things."

"Yes, I'm sure you're right about that." Euphanel looked at her friend. "I've sure become quite attached to the children."

Sissy nodded. "I reckon you have."

Smiling, Euphanel could see the unspoken question in Sissy's face. The woman's dark brown eyes seemed to demand an answer. "I haven't mentioned it to Arjan, if that's what you're wondering."

"Don't you reckon it's time?"

"I do. I had planned to talk to him today, since I knew he'd be home to help Christopher get his things. The only problem is, he's been gone all day." She shrugged. "Maybe tonight."

"You best get it talked out afore the weddin'."

"I will," Euphanel promised. At the sound of the wagons pulling into the yard, she smiled at Sissy. "I'll see if I can't manage some time with him before supper."

Euphanel gave the men a half hour before she went in search of Arjan. She had practiced what she wanted to say and hoped— prayed—that he would understand and agree. Of course, he could be dead set against it, too, but she wouldn't know until she told him what was on her mind.

When she reached the cabin, she found Arjan getting ready to lead the first team back to the barn. "May I accompany you? There's something I'd like to discuss."

"I can take the horses," G.W. announced. "Why don't you two go ahead."

Arjan seemed surprised, but made no objection. "What did you have in mind?"

"How about a little time by the creek," she said, taking his hand.

They walked down the path toward the water, where Euphanel knew it would be cooler under the thick shade of the pines and hickory.

"Have a seat first," she said once they'd reached their favorite spot. "This might take a little explaining."

He raised a brow. "You been plottin' somethin', Wife?"

She smiled and allowed him to help her to sit on the grass. "You could say that, I suppose. Truth is, it's not so much plotting as . . . longing."

Arjan joined her on the ground and leaned on his elbow as he reclined. "All right, let's hear it."

Euphanel felt a rush of doubt. What if this wasn't a good idea? What if Christopher objected? What if Arjan thought her senseless? *Now I sound like Deborah. I should just follow my own advice*, she told herself.

"I want . . . well . . . let me start at the beginning." She twisted her hands in her apron. "As you know, I couldn't have any more children after Deborah. The doctors weren't really sure why, but it just never happened."

He nodded. "I know that grieved you. Grieved me, because of the hurt it caused you."

She smiled at his tenderness. "I know. Anyway, it's just that I've very much enjoyed having Christopher's little brothers and sisters here. I've enjoyed being a mother again."

"You never stopped being one of those," he replied. Then his voice filled with regret. "Wish I could have given you a child."

She reached over and touched his face. "I wish I could have done the same for you."

"I sure hope you know that I'm not holdin' that against you," he said, sitting up. "Were you thinkin' that?"

"Of course not. You've never made me feel that way. It's just me. I've always wanted more children, and having Christopher's family here only served to remind me of how much I love caring for a child."

"I've grown pretty fond of Jimmy and Tommy, to tell you the truth. Tommy and I actually had a long talk out at the camp a few days back. He told me he'd learned more from me than he'd ever learned from his pa."

"Then maybe it won't come as a shock to you."

"What won't?"

"What I'm about to say." She smoothed her apron on her lap. "I'd like to talk to Christopher about letting us adopt the children. My sister has even mentioned being willing to let Jimmy come stay with her like she did Deborah. He could attend the university there in Philadelphia."

He grinned. "I see you've given this some thought."

She felt her cheeks flush. "I have. It's been on my mind—day and night of late. Ever since the youngest children started calling me Mama Euphanel, I just felt a tug to give them my full time and attention."

"What if the boys aren't of a mind to go changin' their name to Vandermark? They may not have gotten to learn much from their pa these last years, but he was still the one to give them the Kelleher name."

"I thought of that, too," Euphanel said. "I guess what I mean by adopting is that we would take on the responsibility of seeing that they're raised right. A guardianship might be a better way to suggest it. It would also free Christopher and Deborah from having to deal with a ready-made family."

"What if they want that responsibility?"

"Then we just offer our support and perhaps we could look at finding some children to adopt elsewhere." She looked at him with a questioning gaze. "Would you consider that?"

"Nell, there isn't much I wouldn't consider for you. God knows I've wanted to give you a much better life than we've known these last couple of years."

"Oh, go on with you, Arjan Vandermark. We've had a good life and don't you go forgetting that. God has given us many blessings. Sure, things are rough right now, but God has made a way even in that. I'm truly a happy woman." She paused and gave him a smile. "I've just been thinking that I could be happier."

He laughed. "Well, I suggest we pray about this and then talk to Christopher and the others. If the children aren't of a mind to be cared for by us, then we sure don't wanna go imposin' such a thing on them."

"No indeed. I would not want that." She leaned over and kissed him lightly on the lips. "Thank you for your understanding."

He surprised her by pulling her down on the grass beside him. Wrapping her in his arms, Euphanel lost herself in the moment and the warmth of his touch.

∞

Jael looked across the table at her father. "I'm so sorry, Father. I never wanted to shame you like Justine did." She could see him wince at her sister's name.

"I was wrong, Jael. I was wrong for how I treated her. I was a proud and boastful man, and the price was the life of my child."

"No, Father. Justine's death was her own choice. Certainly she was saddened by the things that happened, but the responsibility was hers. She loved the wrong man and he was a scoundrel for deserting her."

He shook his head and dabbed the napkin to his lips. "That much is true, but I acted wrongly. And now you're telling me you married a man you did not love—one who has left you to fear what he might do."

"I asked him for a divorce." She bowed her head. "Not just for that, but . . . well . . . there were other women. I've never confronted him about it, but I knew that he'd had his way with my lady's maid back in Philadelphia. It was one of the reasons I didn't want servants when we came here. He insisted, however. I don't know if he's bothered any of them or not, but it wouldn't surprise me."

"This is outrageous," her father said, slamming his fist on the table. "No daughter of mine deserves to be treated in such a fashion. How can I help you?"

Jael breathed a sigh of relief. Her father understood. He loved her enough to put aside his fears of scandal and offer his support. "I don't exactly know. I cannot abide how Stuart has treated the Vandermarks. I wish you could do something about that before we even consider what I need. They are good people, Father. The very best, in fact. Deborah says it is because God guides their steps. I'm thinking perhaps it's time I considered His place in my own life."

"Well past time for the both of us. When your mother died, I did you girls a great injustice in turning away from God." Remorse rang in his words and echoed in his sorrowful expression.

"I don't know what can be done," Jael continued. "But I know you are a thoughtful and wealthy man in your own right. Since you are in partnership with Stuart, I thought perhaps you could influence him to do better by the Vandermarks."

"He's determined to have his revenge. I don't know what I could do. However, I will look over the contract we have with Vandermark Logging, and I will ask my lawyers to do the same. Perhaps there is a way to nullify it and start over."

Jael looked at the food on her plate and pushed it back. She was still uncertain as to whether or not she was pregnant, but just discussing her poor choices and husband's hard heart was enough to leave her unable to eat.

"If you don't mind, I believe I'll retire for the evening. This conversation has robbed me of my strength."

Her father nodded. "By all means. And Jael . . . please promise me that you won't keep such things from me in the future. I want to make a better life for us, but I need the truth to be spoken."

She gazed across the table to see his eyes were filled with tears. "I promise. I will be truthful with you, even if it's painful."

CHAPTER 20

Rob arrived home on a sweltering Sunday evening, the twenty-second day of May. Mara had already been invited to spend the evening at the Vandermark home, just in case Rob arrived. He had actually planned to be home on Saturday, but something forced the delay, though Deborah hadn't yet heard what that something was. She smiled at the way her brother had changed as she observed him and the rest of the family relaxing on the lawn. He no longer swaggered like a young dandy seeking female companionship, but rather walked with the confident air that their father once used. Still, his whimsy popped up from time to time, like when he teased Mara or told stories of when he and G.W. had been young. His eyes would almost twinkle in delight as he confessed his childish adventures.

"They make such a nice couple," Deborah murmured. She looked at Christopher and smiled. "Do you suppose folks look at us and think the same thing?"

He chuckled and put his arm around her shoulder as they enjoyed the porch swing. "No, they probably say, 'What in the world does that sensible Vandermark woman see in that Irishman?'"

She elbowed him ever so slightly. "You know that no one around here cares about that. And those who pay a mind to such things are too busy hating the black folks to worry over an Irishman or two."

"Or six," he said, motioning toward his brothers and sisters.

Deborah nodded. "Or six."

"Wouldn't you agree to that, Deborah?" her mother called from the yard below.

"What was that?" she asked. "I didn't hear your question."

"I was just saying it would certainly be a shame if Rob couldn't be here for the wedding, and that perhaps you would agree to move up the date."

"To when?" she asked. "And why can't Rob be here on the eleventh? I thought he was staying several weeks."

Rob clasped Mara's hand. "I wanted to do just that, but in order to finish my studies sooner, I agreed to take on some work this summer. I reckon I'll have to head back to Houston by the first."

"But that's just a little over a week," Deborah said, looking to Mara, then to Christopher and back to her mother. "Are you suggesting we move the wedding up to this Saturday—the twenty-eighth?"

"Well, why not? Everything is ready, and Pastor Shattuck has no other plans."

The pastor nodded. "It's true. I'm as free as a man can be."

Deborah turned to Christopher. He was already grinning from ear to ear. "So I take it that you like the idea?"

"I didn't want to wait until the eleventh anyway, if you'll recall. Six days from now suits me just fine. Fact is, the pastor's here now—we could just get the formalities out of the way."

The men laughed, but feminine sensibilities prevailed. Mother was the one to put everyone in their place. "Deborah deserves a nice wedding. We'll move it up to Saturday. That will be soon enough."

A million butterflies seemed to release at once in Deborah's stomach. She put her hand to her waist to try to vanquish the feeling. Christopher didn't help matters at all when he leaned forward and whispered in her ear, "Just six days and you'll be mine."

"You should give a maniacal laugh and twist your mustache when you say that," Deborah teased, trying not to show how nervous she felt. "I remember the villain doing that once in a play I saw in Philadelphia."

Christopher feigned distress. "I'm the villain?"

Deborah put the back of her hand to her forehead. In the voice of a pathetic damsel in distress, she stood and pleaded, "Oh please, sir! Do me no harm."

"You are mine, dear lady. No one can save you now," Christopher declared, jumping to his feet to pull her close.

Her family laughed at their antics and Rob even clapped. "You two really should work on the stage."

Deborah shot him a scowl. "Don't encourage him. Next thing I know, he'll have some plan for us to perform scenes for patients."

"Well, we have a full day ahead of us tomorrow," Arjan said, nodding to Jimmy and Tommy. The trio got to their feet and

Arjan continued. "I asked Jack to stop the train here in the morning at five. We'll head up to the camp and get done what we can." He looked to Rob. "Don't suppose you'd like to dirty your hands."

Rob didn't get a chance to speak. "If you don't mind, Mr. Vandermark," Mara interceded, "I have plans for him."

The men chuckled and whistled, but Mother quickly agreed. "Rob is resting this week. We will let him court his girl and enjoy our celebrations and food, but he will not work."

"Wish somebody would let *me* rest for a week," G.W. said, getting to his feet. He rubbed his thigh gently. " 'Course, my leg would really stiffen up if I just sat around—like that could ever happen. These rowdies of mine keep me busy day and night." He hoisted a child under each arm and turned to Lizzie. "What say we clean these two up and get them to bed?" The twins squealed in protest.

"Yes, it's well past their bedtime. I should have had Sissy take them inside earlier."

"Oh, it did them good to be up, and who knows? Maybe they'll let us sleep past five-thirty."

"If they do, then you'll have cold breakfast," Mother threw out.

"There truly is no rest for the weary," G.W. said. "I reckon we'll be to breakfast on time."

"They sure are a precious pair," Rob said as the little family started for the house. "I'll enjoy being an uncle and spoilin' ever' last one of your children."

"You do, and you'll answer to me," G.W. called over his shoulder. "My children ain't gonna be spoiled. They're gonna be well behaved and brought up in the way they should go—just like we were."

"Whoever said you two were well behaved?" Deborah asked.

G.W. grinned as the twins giggled in his arms. "There are some things a fella just knows."

Now it was the women who laughed. Mother, in particular, seemed amused as she came up behind Lizzie and G.W. "Come along," she told Lizzie. "I shall tell you a few stories about your well-behaved husband."

"Now, Ma, that ain't exactly fair," G.W. protested as the women sidestepped him and headed for the door.

"We're heading to bed," Jimmy announced, giving Tommy a poke. "He's already half asleep."

Tommy yawned and nodded. "Been a long day. Even for a Sunday." The boys headed for the house.

"Well, I should be getting back," Pastor Shattuck told Arjan.

"Are you sure you don't want to just stay the night? Awful dark without the moon to lead you back."

"I'll be fine, Arjan. Thanks for the invitation. I'd actually like the time to just pray and think on the Lord."

Arjan got to his feet. "Well, let me bring your buggy around."

"Much obliged," the pastor told him.

Deborah came to the rail of the porch. "So when are you two going to tie the knot?" she asked Rob and Mara.

Rob grinned. "Well, if I have my way, it'll be as soon as I get this schoolin' out of the way. I'm just as anxious to marry my gal as you are to marry your fella." He put his arm around Mara's shoulder. "I reckon the time can't pass fast enough for either of us. Now, if you'll excuse Miss Shattuck and me, we're gonna go see what's left to eat. I'm starvin'."

"You just had supper three hours ago," Deborah reminded him.

"No wonder I can feel my stomach pressin' against my backbone," he replied. "We'd best hurry, Mara, before I plumb fade away."

"Mara, before you go, did you have some special time I needed to pick you up tomorrow?" her father asked.

Rob answered for her. "If you'll allow me, sir, I'll bring her home in the afternoon."

"I think that would work out all right."

"I was also hopin' you and I could spend some time discussin' a few things," Rob told him. "Things regarding ministry work. I'd like to have your opinion on my future plans."

Pastor Shattuck appeared quite pleased. "I would like that very much."

"And I'll fix supper for us," Mara declared.

"Maybe you can get my brother to talk serious about marriage," Deborah said, smiling.

Rob turned. "Whoever said I wasn't serious about marriage? Mara knows exactly how I feel. She's also got more sense than to go marryin' a man who doesn't even have a job or home of his own."

Christopher stiffened beside her, and Deborah put her hand on his arm. "Maybe she's just heard from Lizzie and Mother how difficult it is to be married to a Vandermark man."

Pastor Shattuck surprised them all. "I've actually been meaning to talk to young Rob about how stubborn and ornery we Shattucks can be. Especially the womenfolk."

Everyone laughed at this. Mara gave a slight rise of a dark brow and batted her eyelashes. "Why, Papa, whatever do you mean?" She took hold of Rob's arm in a possessive manner. "We Shattuck women are docile, reserved, and obedient."

The pastor gazed heavenward. "I'll say nothing further on the matter."

Deborah loved the merriment and wished it could go on and on. Just then, however, Arjan led the horse and buggy around the corner of the house. The dapple gray gelding seemed almost ghostly in the pale light of the lantern Arjan had hung from the frame.

Pastor Shattuck climbed up and bid them good-night. "I shall see you both tomorrow, then. Arjan, please thank Mrs. Vandermark for another delicious meal." He snapped the reins lightly and the horse moved forward.

"Well, I reckon I'd best get to bed. You sweethearts behave yourselves," he directed. "I don't want to have to come lookin' for you."

"We have patients to see in the morning," Deborah stated, "so we won't be out here for long. Besides, the mosquitoes are biting something fierce."

"Is that what it was?" Arjan teased. "I thought it was your mother pokin' me with her knittin' needles." He opened the screen door. "See you in the morning."

"Good night," Deborah and Christopher said in unison. Rob and Mara were already well on their way to the kitchen.

Turning to face Christopher, Deborah gazed deep into his eyes. "Six days. Are you sure you don't mind?"

"I told you, woman—I would have married you long ago if you'd just said the word." He bent his head to touch his lips to hers. "I would still marry you tonight. All we have to do is catch up to the pastor."

Deborah felt a delicious shiver run up her spine. The thought was tempting, and no doubt, Christopher would have had the preacher back before she could so much as tell the others. But reason and sense surfaced.

"Saturday is soon enough," she told him. "It's only six days."

"Only?"

The look in his eyes—the desire in his expression—caused

Deborah to take a step backwards. "Yes . . . only." She felt her backside come in contact with the porch rail.

Christopher stepped forward like an animal cornering its prey. "God created the world in six days. That's a long time, as far as I'm concerned."

Deborah's breath caught in her throat. Christopher wrapped her in his embrace and began kissing her. His lips first touched her forehead, then trailed down to her eyelids. Deborah sighed and sank against him. He kissed her nose, her cheeks, and earlobes. Deborah raised her mouth to meet his, but instead Christopher began to kiss her neck. She couldn't help the gasp that escaped or the trembling that began in her knees and ran up her body.

Christopher moaned softly against her ear just before claiming her mouth in a hungry kiss. Deborah had never known such passion. She felt as if her skin were afire under Christopher's consuming touch.

"Oh, Deborah." He spoke her name as if it were a secret.

All rational thought lost, she tightened her hold on his neck, encouraging his lips once again to take hers. He eagerly complied; then without warning, Christopher stepped back and dropped his hold. Deborah thought she very well might have sunk to the floor had she not quickly grasped the porch railing. She looked at him in question and saw the burning desire in his eyes.

"I think six days will be very long," he said, turning to leave. "I'm going to the cabin. Good night."

Deborah fought the urge to follow him. "He's right," she said rather breathlessly to the night. "Six days is going to seem like an eternity."

"You do look thinner," Mara told Rob as he cut himself a hunk of ham.

"I don't eat as well there as here. Of course, no one there cooks as well as the ladies of Angelina County. And besides, I don't do anywhere near the amount of physical labor. Although I have become quite handy at tending the grounds and gardens."

Mara poured him some buttermilk. "I can scarcely allow myself to believe you're really here." She handed him the glass. "I've missed you."

He grinned and put the ham aside. Rob took the buttermilk and placed it with the ham. "I missed you, too. I haven't had a chance to tell you that you're the prettiest gal in all of Texas." He touched a curl of her ebony hair. "I think about you nearly as much as I ponder the Scriptures."

She smiled. "I don't suppose the teachers appreciate that."

Rob shrugged. "They don't seem to mind. I get my work done, and that's what matters. One of my instructors reckons I have a unique way of lookin' at life. He said I have a way of talkin' and thinkin' that reaches the common man. He thinks I'll do well in small towns with everyday folk."

Mara couldn't help but nod. "I agree. That's one of your charms."

Laughing, Rob picked up the glass and downed about half of the buttermilk. "I didn't reckon I had any charms."

"Oh, you have them all right. I have to say, I've heard plenty of stories about you from some of the other young women in the area. You were quite the charming suitor, as I hear it told."

Rob sobered and shook his head. "Those times seem like a long ways back. Fact is, sometimes I can't rightly believe that was me. I'm not that man anymore."

"Thank God for that," Mara said most sincerely. "I could not have loved that man as I love you."

He studied her face for a moment. "I know. I'm just glad God showed me in time. I can't imagine my life without you in it."

She smiled and gave him a nod. "Just don't be reckoning it any other way, because I don't intend to let you get away."

Grinning, Rob picked up the ham. "Honey, you'd be hard-pressed to get rid of me now."

∞

"Mama Yoonell?" a faint voice questioned from the doorway.

Euphanel bounded out of bed as if it were afire. "What's wrong?" she asked, finding Jonah standing in the hall.

"Emma's crying," he told her. "I think she needs you." His voice trembled as if he, too, might start in with tears.

"Let me get my robe." She hurried back to the end of the bed as quietly as she could. Arjan's steady snoring let her know she'd not disturbed his sleep.

Making her way back into the hall, Euphanel pulled on her cotton robe and tied the sash. Jonah looked at her and motioned to her head. "You sure got pretty hair, Mama Yoonell."

She smiled. "Why, thank you, Jonah. What a kind thing to say. I'll bet your mama had pretty hair, too."

"It was real long. She would braid it and wrap it around her head sometimes. I liked it that way." His voice dropped. "I don't like to think about her. It makes me sad."

"Well, that's all right. I'm sure that God understands how you feel."

"God? He knows how I feel?"

Euphanel heard the longing in his voice. "He truly does,

Jonah. He loves you. He knows that you're sad to lose your mama. He knows each tear you cry."

"And Emma?"

Euphanel paused as they reached the upstairs. "God knows how each of you feels. He wants you to remember that you are never alone. He is with you always."

"Truly?"

She smiled. "Truly."

Jonah surprised her by wrapping his arms around her legs. "I love you, Mama Yoonell."

Her heart swelled with joy. "I love you, Jonah. I love you very much."

ed. G.W." Bertram Wallace extended his hand and took a seat opposite the two men. "Thanks for the invitation to breakfast. Seems like a long time since I've seen you, Zed. It'll be good to catch up."

G.W. motioned to the table. "We knew that you'd want coffee, but they have two specials and we didn't know what you'd like to eat."

"Hello, Bert," the middle-aged waitress said as she brought platter-sized plates of food to Zed and G.W. "You want the regular?"

"Yes, ma'am," he said, grinning. "Cheesy grits and ham."

"Comin' right up." She looked to G.W. and Zed. "And do you gentlemen have everything you need?"

G.W. looked at the mound of scrambled eggs, potatoes, and bacon. "Yes, ma'am. I reckon we've got enough and then some."

"That's for sure," Zed said, digging into the pile of fluffy eggs.

She wasn't gone but a few minutes before returning with another large plate for Bert. "I had Cook give you a nice thick slice of ham."

"You're mighty good to me, Mabel." He gave his coffee a sample. "Strong . . . just the way I like it."

Mabel smiled. "You boys let me know if you need anything. I'm gonna go clean up a couple of tables."

G.W. glanced across the room. Several of the tables were in need of her attention. He figured it would give them plenty of time to talk without interruption.

"Zed, I heard what Albright has been up to," Bert began. "Your son told me he plans on buyin' you out."

"You can't exactly call it 'buying him out,'" G.W. interjected. "More like stealin' him blind."

"Do tell." Bert sliced into the ham. "Why don't you explain it to me?"

Zed nodded. "I'm much obliged to you for listenin'."

Bert listened patiently, and G.W. focused on his food. He knew Zed was proud, and begging a job wasn't easy for him. G.W. finished his coffee and lifted the cup to motion to Mabel. She was there without a word, filling mugs and scanning the table like a watchful mother. Seeing nothing amiss, she moved on.

"Seems like there ought to be a law against what he's doing," Bert said, shaking his head. "Have you signed any papers yet?"

"No, but it won't be long. Albright plans to have his father-in-law handle the matter in Houston and then bring the papers back to Perkinsville once everything is finalized," G.W. declared. "We've got good lawyers lookin' into it, but apparently Albright's put money in the right hands. So far he's managed to get folks doin' things his way."

"I'm mighty tired of them Easterners comin' in here, makin' changes," Bert growled. "I've seen it happen more times than I care to say. You know the old Carreston cotton plantation northeast of here?" The men nodded in unison and Bert continued. "Easterners bought 'em out and ruined the place. It's happened all across the South—I don't reckon I should be surprised by your news."

"You can see why I brought him here," G.W. said, lowering his voice. "You were good to help us in our time of trouble. We just wondered if you could recommend someone who might hire Zed on for a time."

"You're lookin' for a job?" Bert asked in surprise. "Well, I'll be. This must be what my wife would call one of them fortuitous moments."

G.W. shook his head. "How so?"

"My mill foreman up and quit yesterday. I've been tryin' to figure out who to put in his place. Zed, the job is yours for as long as you want it."

Zed reached out his hand. "I'll take it."

"We can discuss the particulars over at the mill," Bert said, pushing back his plate. "Why don't you come on over with me, and I'll show you around."

"Thank you kindly, Bert." Zed shook his head. "Don't know what I'd've done otherwise. I haven't even told the boys yet. They knew things were bad—just didn't know I'd gone and lost their inheritance."

"Things have a way of workin' out," Bert said as he got to his feet. "Breakfast is on me, boys." He fished out several coins. "Come on now. Let's make us a plan."

∽

"Father," Jael said, holding out a recently delivered telegram. "Deborah's wedding has been moved up to this Saturday. I must be there. I can't allow Stuart to force me to stay here in Houston when my dearest friend is getting married."

"I will accompany you," he said, looking over the message. "I have some business to discuss with Stuart, and I'm sure he wouldn't like you being left alone in the city anyway. If the wedding is Saturday, we would be wise to get up there as soon as possible."

"The housekeeper can have me packed up in twenty minutes," Jael said with a smile. "Can your butler do the same for you?"

Her father seemed more than a little amused. "I'm sure he can." He put the telegram aside and rose. "I'll send the driver around to the train station to see when the next train will be heading north."

Jael wasted little time making her way upstairs. Her father's house wasn't all that big, though there was certainly enough room for the two of them. She felt a sense of relief knowing Father would accompany her to Perkinsville; she had grown quite close to him since her arrival in Houston. They had talked about the past—about her sisters and the death of their mother. Jael had never known her father to be so free with his thoughts, and it truly blessed her to hear his heart. It blessed her even more to have learned the week prior that she was not with child. There was nothing holding her back from doing what needed to be done.

"Mrs. Lee," Jael called, spying the woman dusting at the end of the upstairs hall, "I need your assistance."

"Yes, Miz Albright?" the sturdily-built woman asked.

"Father and I are traveling to Perkinsville as soon as he can arrange passage. My dear friend is getting married on Saturday," Jael explained. "I'll need for you to help me pack."

The woman put her dusting rag in her apron pocket. Following Jael into the bedroom, Mrs. Lee went to the window and raised the sash. "It's going to be another hot day," she said, as if Jael had asked after her actions. "The weather will most likely make things miserable for travel."

"I won't take a great deal with me," Jael said, trying to think through her plan. She would love nothing more than to tell Stuart she was leaving him, but she didn't want to ruin Deborah's wedding. It would be bad enough to have her sulking husband at her side during the wedding. Of course, he might yield and allow Jael to be accompanied by her father. That would be much better.

Mrs. Lee opened the armoire, then went to the dresser. "I'd advise you take only your lightest gowns. The cottons and muslins will serve you better than silk. The silks tend not to breathe as well."

"That's quite true." Jael began sorting through the dresses. "Of course, I can't wear cotton to the wedding. I shall have to take at least one silk gown."

Just then, the butler appeared with Jael's trunk. "Mr. Longstreet said you would have need of this."

"Oh, thank you, Mr. Adams." The man was older than her father, yet seemed to have the strength of someone half his age. He placed the trunk at the foot of the bed and straightened. "I must now help your father to pack, but should you need anything, simply send Mrs. Lee to find me."

Jael nodded. Adams had been with her father for over twenty years. The two had a wonderful relationship that sometimes mimicked father and son, with Adams offering her father advice or comfort. Other times, they seemed like two friends. Never did they really appear as employee and employer.

Mrs. Lee came to the armoire. "You look lovely in blue, Miz Albright. It goes so nice with your red hair. I knew a redheaded woman who attended our church long ago. She would never wear any color but brown. Such a pity."

"Then we shall take this one," Jael said, pulling out a peacock-blue silk. "I've always been partial to this gown, even though it has to be cinched up extra tight. I think it will be perfect for the wedding, and it does have the removable sleeves."

"What about this one, as well?" Mrs. Lee asked, holding out a creation of white sprigged muslin.

"Yes, that one is definitely good for the heat. So is this green batiste." Jael held up the gown of pale sage. "Have you seen the underdress that goes with it?"

"I believe so." Mrs. Lee moved to the dresser. After several minutes of rummaging through the drawers, she managed to locate it. "You'll have to have it pressed."

Jael nodded. "We can round things off with several blouses and the plum-colored skirt. That should suffice."

"I'll put in two nightgowns. That way if one gets too dirty, you can use the other while it's being washed." The housekeeper pulled the nightclothes from the bottom drawer. "I'll see to it you have an extra corset and other undergarments."

"I will put some personal items in my small carpetbag," Jael said, pulling the luggage out from under the bed.

"It won't be pleasant traveling in this heat. Miz Buckley—the neighbor two doors down—fainted dead away in the middle of the street." Mrs. Lee was already packing the peacock-blue silk between paper. "You'd best make sure to take extra fans, and your smelling salts, of course. And what do you plan to wear?"

Jael looked down at her simple day dress. "I suppose I should change." She rummaged through the ensembles available to her.

"Why not just wear a muslin gown," Mrs. Lee asked. "No one's gonna mind. Your lilac one is plenty modest and will afford you the benefit of keeping cool. At least, as cool as is possible."

Jael pulled the gown from the armoire, held it up, and nodded. "It seems rather informal, but I think you're right. I have never cared all that much for what is said about me. If they post an article in the paper about my risqué attire, you will simply have to cut it out and show me later."

"Goodness, if they post an article on that, I'm bettin' they'll hear an earful. Newspapers ought to be for more important things than what a lady wears on a hot day."

"I think you look quite lovely," Mrs. Lee announced after she'd helped Jael change into the lilac-colored gown and arranged her hair. She went back to the trunk and closed the lid. "Everything is ready. I'll summon the groomsmen to come fetch this."

Jael glanced at the ring on her finger and couldn't help but think of Stuart. What would he say when she told him she intended to see Deborah wed?

He would forbid it, of course. But she refused to be intimidated. He would threaten to reveal the shameful impetus of their marriage to her father, but now the upper hand belonged to Jael. The truth had set her free.

"He could threaten Deborah again," she said aloud without thinking. She glanced up, relieved to see that Mrs. Lee had already gone from the room. It wouldn't be good to have the older woman asking questions. Mrs. Lee was a woman who thought it her business to know everything about everybody. Especially if the people involved were other than Texans themselves.

Jael walked to the open window. The air sagged with moisture.

The stifling heat was not unlike that which she'd known during Philadelphia summers, but this was only late May. What would July and August be like?

"Jael?"

She turned to find her father standing in the open doorway. "Did you manage to get us tickets?"

He nodded. "But we will have to hurry. There isn't much time before the train will arrive and be ready to depart."

She pointed to the trunk. "I'm ready to go. Mrs. Lee has gone to bring the groomsman to carry my things to the carriage. I have only to secure my bonnet and take up my parasol." She beamed him a smile. "Stuart won't be happy to see me, but with you by my side, I feel I can face just about anything."

"A letter for Stuart arrived just this morning. It's on the front table. You might want to take it with you. It's from his father, and perhaps that will put him in a better state of mind upon seeing you again."

Jael doubted that anything would cause Stuart to approve of her, but it was worth a try. "I'll get it before we leave."

∞

Rob strode up to the pastor's door and rapped on it. He gave Mara a lazy grin when she opened the door. "You get prettier every time I lay eyes on you."

"You've just been in the heat of the sun too long, Mr. Vandermark." She looked past him to the wagon. "I see you've brought some of the wedding food. Why don't you drive the wagon around back so we can unload it easier?"

"I reckon I can do that," he said. "I hear tell you're makin' the weddin' cake."

She nodded. "I am. I'll bake it today, and tomorrow I'll

decorate it before the service. I have a garden full of budding roses, and I plan to use them on the cake."

He frowned. "Can't eat roses."

"Well, actually you can," she chided, "but these will simply be for show. I plan to sugar them so they'll sparkle."

"You gals sure dream up a lot of work for yourselves. Sparkly roses aren't exactly what I call worth the effort."

She giggled. "Then I suppose you won't be wanting them on our wedding cake?"

"I don't even care if we have a cake, to tell you the truth. And I'm mighty fond of cake." He leaned down to whisper in her ear. "But I'm even fonder of you. Perhaps you could share a kiss with me before I get to work."

She let him give her a brief kiss before stepping back. "You, Mr. Vandermark, are becoming quite talented in the art of persuasion. They must be training you well in the seminary."

He laughed. "I was always good at talkin' folks into things. It's just now, I'm using it for the Lord."

Mara looked past Rob and frowned. "What does *he* want?"

Rob turned and found Stuart Albright approaching the house. Rob positioned himself between Albright and Mara. From the stories he'd heard of late, this man's appearance could only spell trouble.

"Mr. Vandermark," Stuart said as he came up the steps. "Miss Shattuck. I'm here to see the pastor."

"He's not at home, but I expect him back soon," Mara replied. "He went to see a family across the tracks. I'm sure you could locate him there."

Albright glanced over his shoulder and then back to the couple. Rob didn't care for the look in the man's eyes. With the pastor out, Rob felt quite protective of the woman he loved.

"I would just as soon leave a message. Tell your father that I am closing the church, effective immediately."

"What?" Mara exclaimed, coming out from behind Rob. "You can't do that. We're having a wedding tomorrow."

"So my wife tells me. She insists she attend the wedding, but I have no intention of setting foot at such an affair." Stuart pretended to dust something off of his tan linen coat. "But the fact of the matter is, I can close the church. It's my property. There will be no wedding held there on Saturday or any other day. Nor will there be Sunday services. In fact, you can tell your father that I want the two of you to vacate this property by Monday."

"How very generous," Mara said. "You only gave Dr. Kelleher a day."

Stuart shrugged. "I have a soft spot for beautiful ladies."

Rob restrained his urge to punch Albright in his smug face. "You sure you wouldn't like to reconsider?" he asked, taking a step toward the smaller man.

Albright backed up but didn't retreat in full. "If you think to threaten me—"

"I haven't threatened anything, Albright. I just asked if you wouldn't like to rethink this. What's it gonna hurt you to allow for the weddin' to take place as planned?"

"Hurt?" He shook his head. "I don't imagine it would hurt anyone if I allowed the wedding to go on, and that's the problem. I *intend* to hurt you and your family. I intend to make you all as miserable as you have made me. After all, this ordeal started with a wedding." He turned to leave and called over his shoulder, "Good day, Miss Shattuck, and thank you for relaying my message to your father."

Rob started to go after the man, but Mara took hold of his fisted hand. "Don't. It will serve no purpose. He's hoping to make people miserable—it feeds his evil nature. Let's not allow him any foothold in our happiness."

"What do you propose we do about the weddin'?"

She smiled. "You Vandermarks have the most beautiful grounds around. Why not hold the wedding there? Father and I will come out and help you set up. When Father returns, I'll explain the situation. We'll pack our things and"—she shrugged—"who knows? Maybe we'll move to Houston."

Rob glanced around for a moment, then pulled her into his arms. "I've probably just ruined your reputation, but you, Miss Shattuck, are a very smart young woman and you deserve to be kissed properly."

He kissed her with as much restraint as possible, then put her an arm's length away. "Maybe we should plan a double weddin'."

"That would not hurt my feelings in the least, Mr. Vandermark," Mara said, grinning. "Not even the tiniest bit; however, your sister has worked hard to bring this day about. I say we let her have her moment to shine."

"I suppose if you reckon that's for the best." Rob shook his head. "I don't know, though. Seems to me it would only make sense to take care of two birds with one weddin'."

"That phrase is 'to kill two birds with one stone,' Mr. Vandermark, and frankly, I'd just as soon not have my marriage to you associated with such a thing."

He laughed and jumped from the porch, not even bothering with the steps. "Mara Shattuck, I am crazy about you. I hope you know that."

She laughed. "I do, Mr. Vandermark, and I'm just as crazy about you."

CHAPTER 22

"O h good, it looks like Rob is back from town," Mother said, heading to the door. "I'll get him to take the smoked pork and corn bread along with the dishes on his next trip."

Deborah wiped the sweat from her forehead with the back of her hand. She had insisted on helping prepare the food for their wedding feast, deciding it would be better to keep herself occupied. Christopher requested she stay home these last two days while he rode off to make his rounds. Today he would visit the Vandermark logging camp, and he didn't want her to have any last-minute upsets with Jake Wyeth. Deborah had supposed it really was for the best. While Jake hadn't tried to see her or send her any other letters, Christopher had told her that a man like that would hold out hope to the bitter end when it came to loving someone.

"Ma, we've got problems," Rob said as he bounded into the summer kitchen. "Whew, it's hotter in here than out there."

"That tends to happen when you light a stove," Mother replied. "Now, what's this about problems?"

Rob turned to Deborah. "I'm sorry to be the one to tell you this, but the weddin' can't take place at the church."

Deborah looked at him in disbelief. "But why?"

"Albright." Rob let the word linger on the air a moment before explaining. "He's closed down the church and said it wasn't to be used anymore. He's also demanded that Mara and her pa get out of their house by Monday."

"The very idea," Mother said, shaking her head. "That man is heartless. What could it possibly hurt to at least allow them to remain in their home?"

Lizzie stepped forward. "Stuart is about causing pain, not preventing it."

"Funny, he said very nearly the same thing," Rob said. "So I brought the food back here. Mara suggested something, and I think it's a good solution. She said we ought to hold the weddin' here in our yard. What with the flowers and newly painted fence and porch, it ought to be a right perfect place for a weddin'."

"You're the bride," Mother said to Deborah. "What do you say?"

"Well, it's not exactly like Mr. Albright gave us a choice." Deborah shook her head and looked at Lizzie. "I'm so glad you didn't marry him. I feel so sorry for Jael."

"Speakin' of which, she's back in town. Albright made a comment about that and how she's insisted on bein' at the weddin', but that he doesn't want any part of it. I saw her pa on the porch of Albrights' house as I headed home. Maybe he'll bring her."

"Well, if we don't get this matter resolved, there won't be

any wedding to attend," Mother said. "Deborah, we can make a lovely wedding for you here. Will that be all right?"

She was angry that Stuart Albright should have any chance to disrupt her wedding. Angry, too, that he should force Mara and her father out of their home. When would this madness stop? She looked to Lizzie and could see that she was close to tears. Forcing a smile, Deborah turned to her mother.

"I think it's a wonderful idea. I wish I'd thought of it first. A wedding here will be all the more special. We'll need to get word out to folks."

Mother looked to Sissy. "Later today, you and I will go to town and spread the news about the change of location. For now, let's get the food inside."

Deborah let her mother and the others head to the wagon. She was surprised that Rob waited behind.

"I'm really sorry, Deborah," he told her. "I tried to reason with him, but Albright wouldn't listen."

"I don't doubt it. Thank you for trying to help."

"I never said this about anyone before, but I'm inclined to believe the man is just pure evil. He seems to be full of demons."

Deborah leaned back against the wall and sighed. "Rob, he's not going to stop until he destroys everything and everyone I love."

"Now, Sis, you know God is stronger than the devil. He won't let Albright win—at least not for long."

"I wish I could believe that, but as Lizzie has said over and over, the world is evil and bad things happen all the time. I know one day God will put everything in order, but for now we must endure the misery caused by Satan."

Rob nodded. "I know it seems that way, but you know the Bible says we aren't to fear those who can only kill the body.

Albright can take all we have, and it won't matter. Not truly. Pa started with little of nothin' and if need be, we can, too."

"I just can't believe one man can be so completely controlled by the devil."

"You know, I saw a puppet show in Houston. It was very entertaining, but the one thing that I thought about most was how those puppets couldn't do anything without the puppeteer controllin' them." Rob mimed having a puppet on each hand. "Folks who do evil are just like that. They wouldn't do a thing on their own, but when the devil gets to controllin' them—pullin' the strings—they come to life, doin' his work for him.

"Albright's no different. He's allowed the devil to harden his heart and pull the puppet strings that control his thinkin' and feelin's. There will always be folks who give the enemy power over them, and yet we don't need to be afraid of those folks. God will see to us. His love is more powerful."

Deborah reached out and embraced her brother. "You certainly have gotten a whole lot smarter since you went to Houston."

He hugged her and kissed the top of her head. "It's amazin' what happens when a man is willin' to listen to God."

Deborah considered his words and nodded. Stepping away, she drew a deep breath. "We'd best help the others, and maybe while we're at it, I'll work at listening to God at the same time."

∽∾∿

After supper, Euphanel shooed Deborah and Christopher from the dining room. G.W. and Rob took Jimmy and Tommy to play horseshoes while it was still light.

"All right, whose night is it to clear the table?"

Emma and Jonah held up their hands. Euphanel smiled. "Then let's get to it."

Jonah jumped up and started picking up silverware while Emma reached for the plates.

"Don't forget to save the scrapes for the dogs," Euphanel instructed. She leaned forward to retrieve an empty platter.

"What do you want me to do?" Darcy questioned.

"Darcy, if you wouldn't mind watching the twins," Lizzie said, "I'll help Sissy wash."

"Oh yes! I'd *much* rather play with the babies," Darcy said, jumping up. She went to where Rutger and Annie were straining to be set free from their chairs. "Come on, you two. Let's go wash up and play."

Annie clapped her hands and Rutger fought a little harder to get loose. Euphanel had to laugh. How she loved her little family.

"Mrs. Vandermark, if you wouldn't mind," Arjan said, coming to Euphanel's side, "I'd like a word in private."

Euphanel nodded eagerly, hoping he'd brought some good news.

They moved through the house to their bedroom, and Euphanel quickly closed the door behind them. "So, what did he say?"

Arjan laughed. "I'm amazed you could sit through dinner without asking."

"Don't tease me. What did he say?"

"He was surprised to begin with."

Euphanel pulled him to where two chairs flanked the fireplace. "Come sit and tell me everything."

She settled into the seat on the right and waited for Arjan to speak. Her stomach felt as if it were doing flips.

"Well, Christopher seemed open to the idea. 'Course, he said it was ultimately up to the children. He planned to talk to the boys later tonight—well, at least Jimmy and Tommy. He wants to see how they feel about it first. Then he suggested we could talk to the others together."

"So he said yes?" she asked, clasping her hands to her chin.

Arjan held up his hand. "In a manner of speakin'. But he said that while he felt we could offer the children a more beneficial home, he would leave it up to them. He didn't want them—'specially the younger ones—to feel yet another sense of loss."

"But surely you told him that he and Deborah could stay on here for as long as they liked. That way, no one need feel a loss of any sort."

"Of course, but Christopher also knows that various issues of parenting and discipline will come up. He don't want there to be any confusion on that."

"But if we explain to the children, they will understand," Euphanel replied. "They are very smart."

"Yes, but they're still children, Nell. We don't want to hurt them no more. We've shown them love and kindness, but we ain't their blood kin."

Euphanel smiled. "There are ways to be family that have nothing to do with blood." She felt so very hopeful. "Love knows no boundary of blood or location. This will work. I know it will."

∞

"So the wedding will be here tomorrow instead of the church," Christopher said. "Are you sure you won't regret that?"

"The building doesn't matter to me. What matters is that my family and friends will be with us, and God will join us together. What more could any bride want?"

Christopher looked at Deborah and thought she'd never been more beautiful. He loved the way her dark eyes seemed to dance. She was both little girl and woman grown, but most of all, she was his.

"Tomorrow you will become my wife."

She sobered and fixed him with a gaze. "You aren't having second thoughts, are you?"

"Good grief, no, woman. I'm beside myself with anxiety that you will change your mind."

Deborah looked surprised at his comment, then gave a brief laugh. "You needn't worry, my dear doctor. I am most assuredly yours." She leaned forward and rose up on tiptoe to touch his lips with her own. Christopher didn't move. He didn't so much as twitch.

"I will always be yours."

Christopher felt her breath against his lips. He wanted nothing more than to lose himself in her gaze, her touch. His heart quickened, and he knew that if he wasn't careful, he'd soon find Deborah back in his arms. He took hold of her shoulders.

"Wait, there's something I wanted to say."

She looked at him with her dark passionate eyes. "Is something wrong?"

He wanted to explain Deborah's mother's and Arjan's plans to take on his siblings. He wanted to tell her about his desire to give them a better life—a family. He hoped that she would agree and approve.

"Christopher! Come quick!" It was Darcy, and she sounded frantic. "Jonah cut his hand!"

Christopher and Deborah both turned at the same time and hurried for the house. Christopher beat her to the kitchen by only a step.

"What happened?" he asked, hurrying to where his brother sat crying on Euphanel's lap.

"He broke one of the dishes."

"It . . . it . . . cut me bad," Jonah said, sobbing.

"Let me see," Christopher said, taking hold of the little boy's hand. He examined the wound on Jonah's palm.

Deborah brought a warm wet cloth and gave it to Christopher. "I'll get your bag from the cabin."

"Thank you." He looked back to Jonah and smiled. "Now, I'll just wipe the blood away."

Jonah began to howl again, and Euphanel whispered in his ear. The boy immediately calmed.

"Are you sure?" he asked.

"Quite sure. Your brother would never hurt you. He needs to clean the cut so he can see how deep it is. When he's done, I'll give you a cookie."

Christopher wiped at the cut and could see it wasn't all that bad. "You're very lucky, Jonah. I won't need to stitch it up."

Deborah soon returned with his bag. Handing him the carbolic acid, she waited patiently at his side. Christopher appreciated the ease with which they worked together.

"This might sting just a bit, but don't worry—it won't last long."

Jonah leaned his head against Euphanel's shoulder. "I'll be brave."

Before Jonah could fret too much, the task was done. It touched him the way Euphanel comforted the boy. His brother obviously felt reassured in her arms. It made him all the more certain his siblings would be well cared for by Euphanel and Arjan. Perhaps he should forget about discussing the matter with the children and simply announce that the Vandermarks were going to raise them as their own.

"All done," he announced.

"There, you see," Euphanel told the boy, "it wasn't so bad."

"No," Jonah said, smiling. "Now can I have a cookie?"

Euphanel laughed and helped the boy from her lap. "Yes, indeed. Let's go right now and get you one."

Christopher gathered his things as Euphanel led the others from the summer kitchen. Only Deborah remained. He pulled his pocket watch and glanced at the time. Nearly nine. In fourteen hours, they would marry.

She looked up and smiled. "You seem very deep in thought."

He gazed into her eyes. "I am. I'm thinking of tomorrow."

Deborah stopped and put her hand on Christopher's chest. He took hold of her hand and pressed it to his lips. "I can hardly believe the day is almost here. When I first arrived in Perkinsville, I wasn't at all sure that I was doing the right thing. I knew my family needed support and felt that this was the best I could do for them. Now I see it was really the best for me—God's very best for me."

CHAPTER 23

ob could hardly believe his eyes when he found Mara at the breakfast table with his family on the day of Deborah's wedding. She looked radiant—angelic, even—all dressed in a pale pink gown. He smiled and took a seat beside her.

"I gotta say, this is quite a surprise." He looked to his mother. "Sorry I'm late. Guess I overslept."

"We just went ahead and started without you," she replied. "I figured you could use the rest."

"I was perty tuckered, to be sure." He turned to greet Mara. "Nice surprise to find you already here. I figured I wouldn't see you until closer to the time for the weddin'."

She squeezed his hand. "I had to come early so I could take

care of the cake. I just brought everything with me and Father delivered me."

Rob looked around for the pastor, but Mara quickly added, "He'll be back in time for the wedding."

"I should hope so," Arjan said with a wink at Deborah. "So are you gonna eat or just stare at the food?"

Deborah shook her head. "I'm not hungry. I'm too nervous." The clock chimed half past five and her eyes widened. "Five and a half hours are all I have to get ready."

"Goodness, child," her mother said, patting her back, "why don't you go back upstairs and try to relax. I'll bring you a tray in a little while."

Rob heard his sister protest and his mother respond, but it was Mara who held his attention.

"Is there anything I can do to help?" Rob asked.

"You can help me by carrying the cake once it's finished," Mara said. Rob found himself mesmerized by her lips as she spoke. "And you may keep me company while I work—if you like."

"I have plenty for the boys to do," Arjan interjected. "I know we said no work for Rob, since he just got home and all, but this is just for an hour or two. We have to build a few benches so our weddin' guests won't have to stand. We're just gonna use simple planks of wood and supports, but they'll do the job. And then we'll need to haul them up from the barn."

"Of course I'll help. I'll do whatever needs to be done to help make this day special for Deborah." He looked for his sister only to find that she'd slipped from the room.

"She's got the jitters somethin' fierce," G.W. said, laughing.

"As I recall, Mr. Vandermark, you were none too calm yourself on our wedding day," Lizzie said, wiping Annie's face.

G.W. shrugged. "I figured grooms were always nervous.

Brides, on the other hand, have planned out all the details. They're the ones in charge, so I reckoned they weren't that jittery."

Lizzie rolled her eyes and picked up her fork. "I was so nervous I could hardly make sense of anything."

"You sure didn't seem like it," he said, grinning. "I figured you were completely at ease, havin' caught me and all."

"Me? Caught *you*?" she asked in surprise. "It was really the other way around."

Arjan laughed. "Ladies always figure to let us chase them until they want to be caught. By then, it's too late for us to do anythin' else. We're completely taken in by their beauty and charm." He winked at Mother and shrugged. "I don't reckon I minded bein' caught in your spell."

"Me neither," G.W. said, locking his gaze on Lizzie.

Rob couldn't help but turn back to Mara. He lowered his voice. "I know I don't mind." She blushed, and Rob thought it only added to her beauty.

After breakfast Rob followed Mara to the summer kitchen and watched in silence as she went to work. He marveled at her ability to create a thing of beauty out of cake and icing. She was skilled in so many things, and it only served to remind Rob of what a good wife she'd make.

"You're mighty good at that. 'Course, I haven't seen much you ain't good at."

Mara looked up and smiled. "I have my flaws same as everyone. I just happen to enjoy baking and decorating cakes."

She squeezed some icing in a scalloped pattern. "Say, aren't you supposed to be helping with the benches?"

"Yeah, I'll get out there to help soon enough."

The time seemed to fly by and before he knew it, Rob realized she was finishing up. And as she did, he knew it was time for what he'd truly come home for. He'd thought about this moment for a long time—and truth be told, he hadn't figured it would happen over sugared roses and icing. But his mind was made up. Pulling a ring from his pocket, he took hold of her hand and pulled her away from the cake. Dropping to one knee, he held up the ring like an offering.

"Mara Shattuck, will you marry me?"

Her mouth dropped open in stunned amazement. He couldn't help but chuckle at the look on her face. "Didn't you think I meant it when I said I love you?"

She nodded and tears filled her eyes. "I knew you meant it. It's just . . . well . . . I wasn't expecting this. Not today. Certainly not here."

He frowned. "I hope I didn't disappoint you. I just couldn't wait any longer. I've been wantin' to make it official ever since I came home. It's the reason I was late gettin' in. I was buyin' this ring and missed the train." He stood and placed the ring on her finger. Drawing her hand to his lips, he kissed the ring in place. "I pray you'll never take this off."

Mara stared at her hand for a moment. Without warning she hugged Rob close. "I'm so happy. Of course I'll marry you. I've always known I would marry you."

He laughed and lifted her face to his. "I'm glad God let you in on it first. If He'd told me, I'm sure I would've just made a mess of things." He kissed her ever so gently.

"I have work to do," she said, pulling back just a bit. "It's nearly eight o'clock. I have to finish up here and then change my clothes for the wedding."

"What do you mean change? You're beautiful, and that gown is quite fetching."

She laughed. "And dotted with bits of frosting and sugar. I

have something else to wear to the wedding. First, however, I need to put the last of the roses in place."

With great reluctance, Rob released her with a sigh.

She gazed down at the ring on her finger. "Leave me. Go help the men. I can't seem to concentrate while you're in the same room."

Rob laughed, but nevertheless headed for the door. "I reckon that's only fair. You distract me all the time when you're not even in the same room. When I'm reading the Bible, I think of you and how blessed I am that God gave you to me. When I'm studying how to help folks, I can only think of how much you've helped me. You're never far from my thoughts—even when we're in chapel, singing—"

"Robrecht Vandermark, you need to go . . . now." She pointed to the door. "This minute."

"I'm goin'. Mercy, but you sure can be bossy." He turned at the door and grinned. "I reckon we'll need to think about settin' a date for our weddin'."

She glared at him and picked up a wooden spoon and hurled it at him. Rob only laughed and quickly ducked from the room. Yes, sir—this was shaping up to be a fine, fine day.

∞

Deborah could scarcely breathe as Lizzie finished cinching her corset. "Not too tight," Mother admonished. "We don't want her swooning before she says 'I do.' "

Lizzie let the ties release just a bit, then secured them. "Besides, she doesn't need much corseting. I think she's lost weight since this dress was first made," her friend declared. "Probably just in this last week. I don't think I've seen you take more than a few bites of food at any given meal." Lizzie brought the bustle and quickly tied it around Deborah's waist.

Deborah's head was spinning with concerns. "Oh, Lizzie, Mother—I pray I'm doing the right thing. I'm so anxious that I won't be the wife Christopher needs. I don't know anything about raising children, and Jonah and Emma are still so young."

Lizzie continued dressing her while Mother took hold of her shoulders. "Deborah, I want you to listen to me. God has a future—a wonderful future—for you and Christopher. Never doubt it, and don't bring it grief by worrying about what might or might not be. I had hoped Christopher would mention this to you first, but I think I'd better say something to put your mind at ease."

"What?" Deborah asked hesitantly.

"Arjan and I asked Christopher if we could take over guardianship of the children. He was very positive about the idea. He knows how attached Emma and Jonah have become—especially to me. The older boys are very fond of Arjan, and whether they want to be formally adopted or not, we want to raise them. I've even shared letters with your aunt Wilhelmina. She is open to the idea of Jimmy coming to stay with her and attend university. That just leaves Darcy. She's a mighty independent little miss, much as you were, but I have a soft spot in my heart for her, as well."

Deborah looked at her mother in disbelief. "I don't know what to say. I can hardly . . . well . . . I presumed in marrying Christopher that I would also . . . well, in a fashion, marry his siblings, as well. I figured mothering them was a part of my promise for better or worse."

Mother put her hand to Deborah's cheek. "There will be time enough for you to be a mother. Be a wife first."

"If we don't get her in this dress," Lizzie said, holding up the wedding gown, "she's going to have to get married in her undergarments."

Both Deborah and Mother giggled at the thought. Deborah savored the release of tension as she imagined walking down the aisle in her petticoat and chemise. That would definitely get tongues wagging for years to come.

Raising her arms, she let Mother and Lizzie settle the gown over her head. Deborah was surprised by the coolness of the fabric. The morning had dawned bright and beautiful, but the air felt dryer than it had in days and the silk slid against her skin like a breeze. Perhaps the mild temperatures were a wedding gift from the Lord.

Lizzie did up the thirty-some tiny back buttons and stepped aside when Mother brought the veil and headpiece. There hadn't been time to get waxed orange blossoms, but Deborah didn't care. Her mother had fashioned a circular crown of white roses and ribbon, and the dress was perfect even without the extra adornment. After carefully arranging the veil on Deborah's beautifully styled ebony hair, Mother leaned forward and kissed her on the cheek.

"Your father would be so proud. You are a beautiful bride."

"I wish he could have seen this day," Deborah whispered.

"I do, too. He would have loved Christopher. He's just the kind of man your father would have hoped for you to have as a husband."

Deborah grasped her mother's hands. "I love him so."

Mother smiled and nodded. "I know you do. And I know that he loves you. Just remember that with God, there is nothing you cannot overcome. Don't let the sun go down on your anger, and always be willing to forgive and try again."

"I will do my best," Deborah replied. "I promise I will."

A knock sounded on the door, and Lizzie went to open it. "We're nearly ready," she told Arjan.

Deborah looked to her uncle-stepfather. Dressed in his only suit, he looked very dapper. He'd seemed quite honored when she'd asked him, instead of G.W., to give her away.

"I reckon it's time," he told the ladies. "The bridegroom is gettin' mighty antsy."

"He's waited this long," Lizzie chided. "He can cool his heels just a little longer." She smiled at Deborah. "Best he learn how to wait patiently, eh?"

Deborah had never known a man with more patience than Christopher. She couldn't imagine that he was all that concerned with the time. He knew she would be his by the end of the day, and that they would have the rest of their lives together.

Mother pulled Deborah's veil in place to cover her face, then Lizzie helped Deborah into delicate white lace gloves. With this accomplished, Lizzie handed Deborah a bouquet of pink and white flowers that Sissy had put together.

"Sissy said she prayed over each flower as she picked and arranged them," Lizzie said. "She said to tell you that you should let these flowers remind you never to fret about what you'll wear or eat. Consider the lilies of the field and the birds of the air. God doesn't forget them, and He certainly won't forget you."

Deborah looked at the flowers in a new light. What a precious blessing. Mother pressed a fine white lace handkerchief into Deborah's gloved palm.

"This belonged to my mother and her mother before her. We've each carried it on our wedding day, and I'm hopeful you will continue the tradition. My mother told me that this handkerchief is for tears of joy and sorrow. The two mixed together represent all that a good life offers—for without the times of struggle, we cannot truly appreciate the times of rest. Without the moments of pain, we do not realize the blessing of its absence."

Deborah nodded. She was afraid to speak for fear she might cry. She caught her reflection in the mirror and was startled. She couldn't help remembering that she'd felt this same way on that day, two months earlier, when they'd been making the final adjustments to the gown. She felt like a queen, all garbed in silk. It was all the more special because this was the gown, albeit remade, that her mother had worn to wed her father. It was more precious to Deborah than she could ever express.

Arjan came to her side. "You make a beautiful bride, Deborah. I'm right proud to give you away."

Deborah tucked the handkerchief around the flower stems and placed her hand in the crook of his arm. "Thank you. I'm so blessed." She looked to her mother and then to Lizzie. Drawing a deep breath, she smiled and gave a nod. "I'm ready."

They made their way downstairs and out the side door. When she'd dreamed of this day, the wedding service had always been in a church with hundreds of people in attendance. But instead, it was in her mother's own beautifully cultivated yard with just a few friends and family. Yet Deborah forgot all about that when they rounded the corner and she saw Christopher standing beside Pastor Shattuck.

She felt light-headed as G.W. nudged him and Christopher caught sight of her for the first time that day. The look on his face told her everything she needed to know. He loved her. It was all she could do to keep from running to cross the distance. A nervous giggle escaped her at the thought. What would they all say if she hiked her skirts and dashed for the porch steps?

"Are you all right?" Arjan whispered.

"I'm fine. I'm just fine."

Deborah caught a whiff of honeysuckle from the bush near the porch. In a flash of blue and white, Emma and Darcy came rushing around the corner of the house. They looked quite dainty and stylish in their new gowns.

"Is it time?" Darcy asked, looking up expectantly. "Emma and I are all ready."

"It's time," Lizzie told them.

♦

Jacob Wythe stood at a distance, obscured from view by the trunks of longleaf pines. He'd told himself he wouldn't come to the wedding. He'd convinced himself that it wasn't something he should do—that he would only regret it and cause others pain. And still, he couldn't help himself.

He'd very nearly convinced himself to leave when he caught sight of Deborah coming from the side of the house. He couldn't take his gaze from her.

She might have been mine, he thought. He watched Lizzie and Mrs. Vandermark fuss with the skirts of Deborah's wedding gown while Arjan patiently waited until the women finished.

Two young girls came bounding up as the wedding party reached the front yard. Jake supposed they were the doc's sisters that he'd heard so much about from Jimmy and Tommy. They danced around Deborah in their excitement.

He remembered days long past when he had known a family's joy and celebration. Everything had changed with the drought and his father's decision to sell the ranch. If he'd only been able to hold on a little while longer, he might have found himself in a good position after the horrendous loss of the previous winter. Many Texas ranchers were making good deals on their cattle because of the thousands of head lost to the blizzards.

Jake watched Deborah for a few more minutes and realized that his sense of loss wasn't in her—but in her family. He wanted to be a part of something. When his family headed to California, it was as if he'd lost his history.

"Why did I stay?" he questioned, shaking his head. He remembered the anger he'd held toward his father. He'd argued with the man for not having the courage to stand fast through the drought. Jake sighed. He'd put up a wall of separation with the only two people he truly needed in his life. Maybe, he thought, it was time to apologize. He could send a telegram to California. The idea encouraged him. He cast one final glance at Deborah and smiled. She was beautiful. Kind and loving. She'd make a good wife—just not his. And for the first time in many, many months, Jake felt that he could accept and live with that fact.

CHAPTER 24

Do you, Deborah, take this man, Christopher, to be your lawfully wedded husband—" Pastor Shattuck threw her a smile—"to have and to hold from this day forward, for better or for worse, for richer, for poorer, in sickness and in health, to love and to cherish?"

Deborah looked through the fine netting of her veil and nodded. "I do."

Christopher, having already agreed to the same, took hold of her hand. He carefully removed the glove and slipped a simple gold band onto her finger. "With this ring, I thee wed." His gaze rose to meet hers, and he tightened his hold on her hand. "May it be a symbol of all that we've pledged today."

She fought back tears of joy and managed a nod. Pastor

Shattuck closed the Bible. "It is my joy to pronounce you husband and wife. You may kiss your bride."

Christopher lifted the veil. He smiled at her. "We finally managed to see it through," he teased. Then with great tenderness, he drew Deborah into his arms and kissed her.

Deborah heard the applause and shouts of congratulations, but it was Christopher who held her attention. "I love you," she whispered as he pulled away.

"Good thing, too, for I love you with all my heart."

"I think this was the perfect setting for your wedding," Lizzie said, handing Deborah back her bouquet.

"I agree," Pastor Shattuck said. "Perhaps my next church will have some lovely gardens in which I can marry folk."

"I'm hopin' your next wedding will be mine and Mara's," Rob declared, coming to congratulate Deborah. He looked to Mara's father. "Thank you for giving us your blessing."

"So it's official now?" Deborah asked.

Mara held up her hand and revealed the small pearl that adorned a simple gold band. "He asked me this morning."

Mother seemed nearly ready to dance at the news. "And have you set the date?"

Rob and Mara exchanged a glance. "No, but we'll work on it," Mara replied. She motioned to the table where Sissy and Mrs. Perkins were already helping to ready the food. "A great deal of work went into this feast, and I suggest we celebrate."

"I couldn't agree more," Arjan declared. "I'm very patient, but that roasted pork is hard to ignore. The aroma just about caused me to make a scene."

The gathered well-wishers laughed at this comment. Christopher, however, appeared to feel the same way. "Let us lead by example, Wife." Mara came to Deborah's side and whispered in her ear. Deborah smiled and nodded.

"Ladies and Gentlemen, I have an announcement to make. Today we are not only celebrating my wedding, we are also celebrating my brother's birthday." She looked at Rob and her smile broadened. "Surprise!"

His expression was one of confusion. Glancing to Mara and his mother, Rob shook his head. "But it isn't my birthday."

"It will be soon enough," Mara declared. "You're the one who forced us to move up the date."

Deborah crossed to where Rob stood. "And if we'd waited until the actual day, it wouldn't have been a surprise. Now come along and let us celebrate."

Christopher joined his wife and gave her a wink. "I'm gonna waste away if we don't get to eating soon."

Everyone laughed, but Deborah's expression was serious. "I suppose you only married me for this feast."

He chuckled and leaned close to her ear. "If you would allow me some privacy, I'd explain in great detail why I married you."

"Dr. Kelleher!" she exclaimed, pulling back. "Mind your manners."

He only laughed and took hold of her arm. Deborah allowed him to guide her to the main table. Arjan and the others had put together several tables to accompany the newly made benches. Mother and Lizzie had, in turn, covered those with tablecloths.

"I'd much prefer privacy . . . with or without food," Christopher whispered in her ear.

Deborah felt her face flush. She looked toward the ground to avoid anyone seeing her embarrassment. Christopher hugged her close, then assisted her onto the bench. She worried that her wedding gown would be snagged by the wood, but someone had thoughtfully put a small covering on her seat. Her bustle neatly collapsed as she took her place. Deborah carefully arranged the skirt of her gown to allow Christopher room to sit at her side.

The party spirit grew as the minutes passed by. Zed Perkins shared stories about his wedding day, including his last-minute stop on the way to the church to shoot a ten-point buck.

"Grandest deer you ever saw," he said, laughing. " 'Course, I doubt Rachel saw it the same way. She was less than impressed when I told her we'd be cleaning it later that night."

"How awful, Zed," Mother said, shaking her head. "That's no way to treat your bride."

"Well, as luck would have it, our friends took pity on me," Zed replied. "They told me they'd gut it and hang it, in return for a dance with Rachel. Of course, I complied."

"He knew better than not to," Rachel countered. "Otherwise, that deer would have been his only companion that night."

Laughter filled the air, and Deborah said, "I was afraid my new husband would be off delivering babies or setting bones."

"The day's still young," her uncle declared. "You can never tell what might happen."

∞

Jake had taken his time lumbering down the road to town, planning in his mind exactly what he would say in the telegram. He didn't have a lot of ready cash, so it would have to be short, but he wanted to apologize and let them know that he wished to come back to live with them. Of course, there was the possibility that his folks wouldn't want him to come to California. They might hold him a grudge.

Jake shook his head, as if trying to dislodge the fear. He wouldn't know the truth until he sent the telegram and heard back from his folks. It didn't make sense to give credence to such ideas before their time.

A sound caught his attention and he paused at the side of the road. Riders were approaching. A good many riders, from the sound of it. They were headed north toward the Vandermarks'. He didn't know why, but something told him to head back into the woods. He slipped behind several hardwoods and waited to see what was going on.

The sound grew louder and now he could hear voices. Horses and riders came into view, and Jake's blood ran cold at the sight of them. Flour or gunny sacks covered every head. Holes had been cut out for the eyes, but otherwise, nothing hinted as to who they were. There wasn't any need. Jake clearly recognized the uniform of the White Hand of God.

The horses slowed as the man in the lead held up his hands. "Reload. We don't wanna get caught on empty chambers."

The men allowed the horses to walk on at a slow pace while they loaded their pistols and rifles. Jake walked quietly through the trees, pacing the riders—backtracking toward the Vandermark place. He had to strain to make out what they were saying.

Jake edged back toward the road to see if he could figure out how many there were. Looked to be at least fifteen, and the one in front appeared to be the leader.

"You done good back there, boys. Now we'll take care of this last little bit of business and head home."

"I heard there was a weddin' goin' on at their place," someone said.

"I heard that, too," the leader answered. "I figure it's the best place to lay down the law. Every white man and woman in the area 'ceptin' us is gathered there to watch that Vandermark gal get hitched. I figure it makes the job all the easier. We go there and tell them all how it's gonna be. I don't wanna hurt no white man, but I guarantee we'll get their attention. Sometimes you have to discipline a wayward child."

That was all Jake needed to hear. He knew that if the men moved into a full gallop he'd never be able to reach the Vandermarks first. Unconcerned with whether the men heard him, Jake lit out through the forest, praying that they would be far too consumed by their plans to even notice him.

He felt a burning in his legs but pressed on. His lungs were aching from the exertion of running, but Jake couldn't slow. He knew if he did, the others would reach Deborah first. He saw the cutoff that would bring him around to the railroad tracks and decided to take it. The horses and riders would no doubt stick to the main road. The Vandermark place was more easily reached that way on horseback. Jake angled off toward the tracks, and only when he was certain the road was clear of any possible observer did he dare to dash across the open path.

Plunging into the woods that ran alongside the tracks, Jake was grateful that the forest ground had been burned off earlier in the year. The distance was fairly easy to cover, and he knew he'd soon approach the Vandermarks' southern property line.

All he could think of was that those men meant to cause harm. Harm to Deborah and anyone else who got in their way. He prayed, pleading with God to protect the woman he loved and the family and friends she cherished.

He was completely exhausted by the time he reached the clearing. Jake could hear the laughter and joy of the celebrators. They would, no doubt, be surprised by his intrusion, but they'd be grateful, too.

The guests were sitting at tables, enjoying dinner, and waiting for Rob to cut a large cake, when Jake stumbled out across the yard. G.W. and Arjan were first to get to their feet, but it didn't take long for the others to gather round him.

"Riders . . . White Hand riders . . . comin' this way." He gasped for air and Arjan directed Rob to bring water. He dropped the knife and grabbed a pitcher.

"Take it easy, son. Get your wind and then tell us what's goin' on," Arjan instructed.

"No. No time. Riders comin'." Jake pointed toward the road. "There's . . . gonna . . . be trouble."

He sank to his knees and took the water Rob offered him. Gulping it down, Jake struggled to control his breathing. They didn't understand. They just stood there, looking at him like he was crazy.

Just then, however, the sound of horses moving in at a full gallop drew G.W.'s attention. "He's right—someone's coming."

"They're armed," Jake said, getting back on his feet.

"Well, we can be, too," G.W. said, running for the side of the house. "Christopher! Rob! Help me out."

The men bounded up the porch stairs. Arjan motioned to Deborah and her mother. "Nell, you and Deborah get the women and children inside."

But it was too late. The first of the riders could be seen on the road, and that was when guns started blazing. Jake did the only thing he could. He ran for Deborah and put himself between her and the gunmen.

Deborah could scarcely believe what was happening. The riders stormed the yard like soldiers taking a battlefield. Jake shoved her behind him, but she couldn't register the words he was saying over his shoulder. Shock made her deaf and nearly void of rational thought.

The riders circled them, upsetting the tables of food. They fired their guns into the air, and one particularly large man cocked the hammers of his shotgun as he aimed at the wedding cake Mara had made. Cake and sugared roses splattered out across the yard.

Deborah turned slightly to see her mother forcing the younger children and Lizzie into the house. There was no hope of making it there herself. She wondered where Christopher was—if he would know to sneak around from the back of the house rather than rush out through the front door. He would be worried about her, just as she was concerned about him.

Calm yourself. Calm down, or you'll be no use to anyone. G.W. and Rob will help him.

All at once, the riders came to a stop. It was very nearly like a well-planned dance. The horses settled and the shooting stopped, but the leader pressed forward and pointed his long barreled pistol directly at Jake and Deborah.

"I'm here on account of the bride," he declared. The masked men snickered, and Deborah couldn't help but look around Jake to get a better view. It wasn't like she could see their faces, but even so, she had to look.

Jake pushed Deborah back behind him again. "You'll have to shoot me to get to her."

"That doesn't bother me one bit." He lowered the gun to aim at Jake's chest.

"No!" Deborah shouted. "What do you want?" She sidestepped Jake, but he took hold of her arm.

"That's just what I was gonna ask," Arjan said, moving in front of Jake and Deborah.

The man on the lead horse stared in silence for several

minutes. The eerie face covering gave him a surreal appearance—not quite human, not quite apparition.

Arjan crossed his arms. "I asked what you wanted, mister."

"I heard you. I reckon I'll answer you when I'm good and ready."

"Well, get ready," G.W. called from the side of the house. "I have a rifle fixed right between your eyes."

"Well, ain't you the brave one," the man replied.

Deborah glanced across the yard to the other side of the house and saw Rob and Christopher. "We have a bit of a standoff here, fellas," Rob declared. "I'd suggest you put away your guns."

"I don't reckon I'll do that," the leader said. "And further, I don't figure you'll do anything about it. You might shoot me, but my men will kill this pretty bride deader than Mr. Lincoln."

"So tell us what you want and get off our property," Arjan demanded.

"Well now, I'm figurin' you already know full well what we want. After all, we paid you folks a little visit not so long ago. Y'all've been stirrin' up trouble and takin' up the cause of the colored folk. We've decided to put an end to that. First, we took care of the situation in town, and now we're takin' care of you. You Vandermarks need to realize that there are far more of us that hate the Negroes than those of you who appear to love 'em."

Deborah could see the strained expression on Christopher's face. She feared he might well charge across the yard to reach her. Shaking her head, she mouthed just one word: *No.*

"We aren't the kind of folks to run scared," Arjan said. He nodded to the pastor and some of their other friends. "We're Texans, and we don't take kindly to threats."

"This ain't just a threat, Mr. Vandermark." The man nudged his horse a little closer and pointed the pistol at Arjan. "This is a bona fide promise. Let our example speak for itself. If you don't stop tryin' to interfere, you and yours are gonna end up like the folks in Perkinsville. We'll burn this place to the ground—just like we did that shantytown."

"What?" Deborah found it impossible to remain silent. "You burned them out?" The breeze had been westerly all day and no doubt that was why they hadn't so much as smelled the burning wood.

The man laughed. "Burned 'em and beat 'em. There ain't much left, and there'll be even less of this place if you don't yield."

"You had no right!" Deborah started for the man, but Jake held her fast. It took only that action to cause Christopher to rush across the yard.

"Stay there, Doc. You don't wanna make her a widow before she gets a weddin' night. Worse yet, you don't wanna be a widower." He turned the pistol again on Deborah and Jake. The men around him laughed and threw out vulgar comments. "Now, I ain't in the habit of shootin' white folks, but I'll do what I need to do in order to get my point across."

"Please, Christopher, don't move." Deborah felt a sense of dread like she'd never experienced in her life.

Arjan shook his head and stepped forward as if to take hold of the leader's horse. "This has gone on long enough. I answer to a higher authority. God Almighty directs my steps."

The pistol rang out without warning. The man had moved his aim so quickly that Deborah actually found herself waiting to feel the bullet pierce her. Instead, she watched Arjan crumple to the ground. The horse reared up beside him, but miraculously missed coming down on the injured man by only inches.

"See if you can walk His way with a bullet in one leg." He repositioned the pistol on Jake and Deborah. "Now, unless you want the next one to cut down this heroic young man, and then the bride . . . I'd suggest you all put down your guns."

For several minutes, no one did anything. Deborah strained to see if Arjan was all right, but she couldn't tell.

"We're puttin' 'em down," G.W. announced, his words surprising Deborah.

"That's a wise choice. Now, like I said, today is your last warnin'. The law won't help you because *we* are the law—the new law of the land. You'd do well to understand that fact right now." He backed the horse up with the slightest pull of the reins.

"I want five of you boys up on the road, holding guns on these kind folks." Without questioning the request, five riders headed off toward the main road. The leader waited for them to be in position.

"I never intended to shoot you, Vandermark, but it's enough for you to know I'll do what I have to. The boys and I are gonna leave you to your weddin' party, but in the future, I'm hopin' you'll remember this and realize that the times have changed. Mr. Lincoln's war may be over, but Southerners everywhere are regaining their legs—we're gonna rise again, and that's a fact. Best you figure out which side you'll be on."

He reined the horse hard to the left and gave him a kick. "Yah," he cried and the other awaiting riders did likewise.

Deborah didn't wait for the men to clear the yard. She rushed to Arjan's side, mindless of her wedding dress. She reached out to steady the leg. "Hold still." She waited for Christopher to join her. He gave her a look that said far more than words.

"Let's get him inside."

G.W., Jake, and Rob came to help, as well as Jimmy and Tommy. Mother appeared at the door. "I saw it all," she said, biting her lower lip. "Is it grave?"

"I don't know yet," Christopher told her.

Sissy already had an oiled canvas atop the dining room table and the men lowered Arjan onto it. Christopher wasted no time tearing away the man's trouser leg. He assessed the wound and motioned to Deborah. "Get my bag."

She hurried through the kitchen and out the door. The shock of what had happened kept her from breaking into tears. She had to do what was needed. She had to help Arjan.

To her surprise, the cabin had been decorated for their wedding night. Someone had brought in flowers and candles. But there was no time to take any pleasure in the setting. Deborah went quickly to where Christopher had begun to set up a small examination room. She grabbed the bag, bandages, and several other items before heading back to the house.

"Oh, God, please help us. Please help Uncle Arjan."

"Is there anything I can do?" Jake asked, appearing on the path.

Deborah nodded. "Pray, Jake. Please pray."

CHAPTER 25

I t's not much more than a flesh wound, shot clean," Christopher told them. "It didn't hit the bone or major blood vessels. Take it easy for a while, and I think it will heal up nicely." He washed his hands and looked to where Deborah was applying the final bandages to Arjan's leg.

Euphanel shook her head. "I can't believe this has happened. What in the world are we going to do?"

"Well, Christopher and I are going to head into town and see how we can help the people there," Deborah announced.

Christopher glanced at the clock and nodded. It was just after one o'clock. "Can I borrow a wagon?"

"You know you can," Arjan said, struggling to sit up.

Deborah gripped him firmly at the shoulders. "You need to

rest. G.W. and the others can put you to bed for Mother. Then they should probably come help us."

Zed and Rachel headed for the door. "I think we'd all best get back to town."

"I'm so sorry for all that's happened," Jael said, coming to give Deborah a hug. "This certainly wasn't what any of us would have wished for your wedding day."

Deborah embraced her friend. "I didn't even have a chance to realize that you were here until we were gathering to eat. I'm sure Stuart was livid about your coming."

"He'll get over it, I assure you," Jael said with a weak smile. "You'd best go. We can talk later."

"Yes." She looked down at her clothes. "I need to go change."

When Deborah turned back from Jael, Christopher frowned. The front of her wedding gown was saturated with blood and dirt, ruined. There would be no passing it down to their children. No beautiful memento of their joyous day.

Some joy, he thought. He just couldn't shake the picture of that horseman holding a gun to her.

"Doc, you'd best change your clothes, too," Sissy said. She gestured to his instruments. "I can boil these things for you. I has the water hot on the stove."

"Thank you, Sissy. Boil them for exactly five minutes, then dry them and wrap them in a clean towel. We could also use any spare bandages or sheets."

Euphanel waited until her sons had carried Arjan from the room before moving. "Tommy, run upstairs to the attic. There's a stack of old blankets and sheets. If those men burned the town down as they said, then those folks will need all the extra supplies we can spare." She turned to Jimmy. "Take Darcy and the little ones and go to where we keep the canned food. Start packing crates with whatever you can."

Christopher shook his head and headed for the door. "I'll gather my things from the cabin. Perhaps we can talk Mr. Albright into sharing goods from the store." He doubted that Stuart would consider it, but it was worth a try.

Making his way to the cabin, Christopher felt a heaviness settle over him. As much as he longed to see an end to prejudices and negativity, he knew they would go on. People were people, with their own opinions and desires. Some were productive and useful to society. But with the hatred and bitterness of racism, the bad seemed to outweigh the good.

He rushed through the cabin, peeling off his wedding clothes. Like Deborah's, they were stained with blood. How much more blood would he have on him before the day was over? He gathered his things and headed back to the house, not even bothering to tuck his shirt in.

G.W. stood ready with the wagon and Christopher's horse, while Rob helped Mara into her father's carriage. "I'll head in with them," he told G.W. and jumped up to join the Shattucks.

Deborah and her mother were bringing out baskets of food. "I'll be here with Arjan and the children," she told Deborah. "Send word if you need anything."

"I want to help," Darcy said, coming to stand by the women. "Can't I go?"

Christopher couldn't help but think of the ugliness that awaited them. "You'd be more of a help here keeping the little ones busy. I'd like Sissy to come with us. Mama Euphanel won't have anyone else."

Darcy met his gaze and seemed to understand. "I'll stay."

"Thank you." He mounted his horse.

Sissy came from the house with the doctor's bag. She handed it up and motioned to where Jimmy and Tommy were climbing into the back of the wagon. "I figure to go along."

He nodded. "I hoped you would. I know you'll be a comfort and help."

The rest of the wedding guests had already headed back to Perkinsville. Christopher kicked his horse into action and headed down the road at a full gallop. He passed Jael and her father, giving only a nod as he rode on. His mind was on the tragedy at hand. How much time had passed? How bad would he find things? The men had said they burned out the shanties. Would any structure remain to shelter those who had survived?

ငှား

Deborah wasn't surprised to find Stuart Albright doing nothing. He was sitting on his porch, casually watching the chaos with disinterest. How could he be so heartless? Deborah wanted to climb from the wagon and rail at him for his lack of Christian charity toward the less fortunate. She wanted to call to mind that these people were, in every way that mattered, his responsibility.

Instead, she held her tongue. Stuart wouldn't care. In fact, he'd probably laugh at her, and that would only anger her more. As G.W. drove the wagon across the tracks, Deborah cast a brief backward glance and saw that Mr. Longstreet had brought the Albright carriage to a stop in front of the house. Perhaps as his business partner, he could talk some sense into Stuart.

The smoke hung heavy in the air, as some of the houses were still afire. The school for the colored children was now completely gutted, as were the houses nearest the railroad tracks. Men and women were struggling to pull bodies of the unconscious to safety.

"Oh, Lord, have mercy. Have mercy," Sissy said, weeping. She didn't wait for anyone to help her from the wagon and nearly fell as she jumped from the back. Hurrying across the ground, she came to where several women were heating kettles of water over fires. "Let me help you," she commanded.

Deborah looked out across the destruction. The charred, smoldering remains bore witness to the violence—the broken bodies, along with the screams and moans of the wounded, assaulted her like a slap across the face. What kind of monster did such things?

She knew the answer. She'd dealt with those monsters face-to-face. Well, not really. They hid behind masks, and she understood why. If she'd ever done something so heinous, she would hide her face, as well.

"Well, they did exactly as they said," Christopher said, helping her from the wagon. "Are you ready?"

"I don't really have a choice, do I? Helping the sick and injured is what I want to do—what God has called me to do."

He nodded. "We need to open the hospital. Do you suppose we can talk Stuart into that?"

"I don't plan to talk him into anything," Deborah declared. "We will simply tell him that's how it's going to be. After all, there are more of us." She crooked her finger to G.W. "We need to open the hospital," she told him as he approached.

"I'll take care of it."

Christopher reached for his bag. "I'll leave it in your capable hands. Come along, Deborah. We need to see whose injuries are the worst."

She started to follow him, then noticed the trees near the edge of the clearing. "Oh no!" Her gasp caused Christopher to take note.

Deborah thought she might vomit. At least seven swinging

bodies, lynched. A couple of young boys were struggling to bring down the dead. Several bodies were already on the ground.

"I'll take care of that," Rob said, coming alongside them. "I'll take Jimmy and Tommy. It's hard for a boy to become a man this way, but we have no choice."

"I'll help you," Pastor Shattuck declared.

Deborah and Christopher made their way to where the injured were gathered. Many had been shot. Some would make it; others were certain to die. Deborah watched as Christopher assessed each man, woman, and child.

One little girl had been shot in the face. It was a glancing blow, but she would be marked for life—if she lived.

G.W. came running—his limp hardly noticeable. "I've got the hospital ready."

Christopher looked from his patients to the wagon. "We need to get the worst of them to my examination room. Take these folks first. I'm going to have to operate. Arrange them as best you can in the front room. We'll move as quickly as possible."

"What do you want me to do?" Deborah asked her husband.

"I'll need you to assist me in surgery," he told her. "Sissy!" The black woman came running.

"Yessuh, Doc?"

"I need you to tend those whose wounds are less severe. Deborah and I are going to be operating over at the hospital."

"You jes' leave it to me," she assured him. "I'll get hot water to you, too."

He nodded and turned back to G.W. "Let's get the wagon unloaded at my place, then you can use it as an ambulance."

"Sounds good." The two men jumped into the wagon.

Deborah motioned them on. "I'll be there shortly. I'm going to see if Jael can help."

She crossed the tracks and made her way to the Albright house. Stuart and Mr. Longstreet seemed to be arguing. She didn't have to explain her presence, however. Jael bounded out of the house, her arms full of sheets. She had changed her clothes and now wore a full apron.

"What can I do?" she asked Deborah.

"You'll do nothing," Stuart said, coming between them. "I will not have my wife acting in such a manner."

"What manner, Stuart?" she asked. "That of a compassionate human being? No doubt that is foreign to you, but I will not be stopped." Jael looked to her father. "We could use help from both of you. After all, you're the ones who own this place. At least that's what you're always boasting. Have you no concern for your people?"

"They aren't *my* people. The land and the buildings that have been destroyed are mine, but the people were set free—or have you forgotten?"

She shook her head. "Sure doesn't look that way to me."

Deborah wanted to applaud her friend, but instead reached out to take some of the bedding from Jael's arms. "Come. We need to hurry. I hope you aren't squeamish."

Jael gave Deborah a look that said it all. "I'm stronger than you think."

ᨀ

As night closed in, Deborah had never known such exhaustion. She remembered briefly when Sissy had sent someone with food and instructions that Deborah and the others were to eat or she would come and feed them herself. Deborah paused long enough to grab a piece of bread and ham. She downed it without even tasting it. Christopher and Jael did likewise, and by then, Mrs. Perkins and Mrs. Huebner had come to assist in the infirmary. They had agreed to stay through the night and attend the wounded. As Christopher explained, there was little else he could do at this point but wait.

Most of the injured were treatable. Those who weren't had died fairly soon after being brought to the examination room. Deborah wept silently as she covered the body of a ten-year-old boy. Someone had bashed in his head. He had struggled to live, but he had lost too much blood. It was just as well, she supposed. His mother and father were both dead.

Christopher once spoke of a certain ability with which God blessed medical folks. It was a kind of separation—a numbness that allowed them to see the most horrific sights and still function. His words proved true this day. But now, as the urgency passed and the moments settled into routine, emotion overwhelmed Deborah. Scenes revisited her thoughts—gashed heads, gunshot wounds, burns, and the ever-present odor of burnt flesh and death. When Mr. and Mrs. Perkins came forward to tell them to go home, she nearly cried with relief.

"You've done all you can, Doc. Why don't you go on back home and get a good night's sleep. We can handle these folks tonight. Rachel here is quite good at nursing, and Sissy won't be far."

Christopher seemed torn in regard to his duty. "I can sleep in my old bed."

Zed led him to the door, taking Deborah along as he walked by. "We took that bed into the infirmary for a patient. You two were just married, and already you did more than anyone had a right to ask."

"He's right," Jael said, coming alongside Deborah. "You two need to rest or you'll be no good to us tomorrow."

Deborah looked to Christopher. He nodded and put his arm around her. "I suppose we can bring back more supplies in the morning."

"Take our carriage," Jael offered.

"That's all right. We can ride back with G.W." Deborah had seen her brother only ten minutes earlier. He and Rob were going to finish up the remaining burials and then head home.

"I'll go let them know," Christopher said, heading toward the railroad tracks.

"I hope your work here hasn't caused you too much trouble," Deborah said to Jael. "I know we couldn't have helped as many without you."

Jael smiled. "I will be fine. Sometimes God brings about answers we don't expect."

"So you're feeling less inclined to ignore the Lord?"

"I realized that doing things my way wasn't exactly accomplishing a whole lot of good." She smiled. "I'm new at this praying thing, but I asked God for His help and promised to do whatever I could to live a life He would find worthy of saving."

"Just remember that salvation is a free gift. We can't earn it, Jael. We aren't any of us worthy in and of ourselves. We only find value in God's eyes when we accept His Son as Savior."

"Then that's what I want," her friend assured her.

Deborah embraced Jael. "I'm so glad. You won't regret it."

Jael pulled away and nodded. "I have already had answered prayer."

The look on Jael's face piqued Deborah's curiosity, and apparently the question was fixed in her expression.

"I'll tell you all about it later. Your brothers and husband are coming back this way." She kissed Deborah's cheek. "I'll see you soon—I promise."

Jael looked at Stuart and crossed her arms against her chest. Her father had long since gone to bed, but she wasn't going anywhere until she had settled some issues.

"I do not intend to return to Houston until after I see this matter resolved with the Vandermarks."

"Do you suppose to order me around—tell me how it will be?"

Jael took a seat opposite Stuart's desk. "I had hoped we could work amicably together. Reach a compromise, if you would."

"What makes you think you have anything I want?" He sneered. "You satisfy my needs quite well already, and as my wife you will continue to do so. There is no compromise to be had."

"Ah, but there is."

"If this is about a divorce, I have already told you no. We are married and will stay that way."

"Not unless there are some changes." She fixed him with a hard look. "You see, I know the truth."

He looked around the room for a moment as if someone else had joined them. "What is this about?"

"I know you had to marry me to obtain your inheritance. We were both in need of marriage, and together we helped each other. I had hoped love would grow between us, Stuart, but I'm not sure that you are even capable of such emotion."

"This is nonsense, Jael. Of course you knew the situation when we married. Now, leave me be and stop with any further thought of making demands. Or have you forgotten my previous threats? Miss Vandermark—excuse me, Mrs. Kelleher—may be married, but she could still meet with an accident." He shrugged. "Things like that do happen." He appeared to focus on the ledger before him.

Jael refused to be moved. "Of course I knew that you needed a wife to obtain your inheritance." She waited until he raised his gaze to her before continuing. "What I didn't know then was that you needed to remain married for a certain time period or your father would fail to release the final fortune to you. He would also cut you from his will irrevocably."

Stuart tried to hide his surprise, but he was unable to mask his expression. "What are you talking about?"

Jael smiled and held up a letter. "I found this from your father. It was waiting for you in Houston."

"You had no right to open that." He pounded his fist against the desk. "No right."

She shrugged. "Be that as it may, I read the contents and must say, they were quite liberating. You need me to remain married to you."

Stuart appeared most uncomfortable. He pulled at the neck of his shirt and fell back against the chair. "What are you proposing?"

"I will stay with you, Stuart. I have spoken to my father about the matter, and while he is appalled at my being in a loveless marriage, I assured him that I could be content. We will live as man and wife in name only—perhaps even in the same residence, so long as we maintain separate living arrangements. You have your mistresses and liaisons anyway. I doubt you'll be that inconvenienced."

"And what must I do in return?" he asked, leaning forward.

She could see she had his utmost interest. "I think you already know the answer to that. Tear up your contract with the Vandermarks. Free them to do business elsewhere and stop this childish determination to get revenge. Do that and I will stay with you. Refuse and I will have lawyers draw up papers immediately for a divorce. My father will wire your father and explain, and your inheritance will be forfeited."

"You tramp. You think you have me where you want me."

Jael got to her feet. "No, because that place would be six feet under."

"Speaking of which, I could simply do away with you," he threatened.

She smiled. "But you won't. The proviso of your father's instructions stipulates that if I should die in any way other than during childbirth, he would immediately withdraw your funds until such time as you were able to remarry and remain that way for . . . what was it—ten years? Yes, I believe it was to be increased to ten." She narrowed her eyes. "Since I do not intend to bear your children or share your bed again, my death in childbirth is clearly not going to happen."

Stuart jumped to his feet. "I could force you! I could have my way with you here and now."

She stood her ground. "You dare to try, and our divorce will be imminent. You see? I now hold the winning cards. You have tormented and tortured my friends for long enough. Resolve this matter immediately or lose it all."

CHAPTER 26

JUNE 1887

Stuart was not pleased to see his wife and father-in-law enter his study. "I'm very busy." He looked at Longstreet. "It's been over a week since you arrived—don't you have business to attend to back in Houston?"

"I do, but I also have affairs that need my attention right here," Longstreet replied. He seated Jael and pulled up a second chair for himself. "As your partner, I figure we need to talk."

Stuart looked at Jael, and the rage brewing within him since her proclamations the week before threatened to boil over.

"With all that has happened," Longstreet began, "we need to figure out what is most beneficial and productive for this town. I have arranged to have the blacks moved into the houses on the north side of town."

"What? Those are quarters for whites. This isn't their side of town," Stuart protested.

"That was once the case, but now there is no other alternative. They cannot be expected to live without shelter. The thunderstorms of the past few days should prove that if nothing else. Then there are the sick to contend with."

"I already allowed the infirmary to be reopened. Dr. Kelleher has used up most of the inventoried supplies, and I haven't even charged the people for their care."

"Nor will you," Jael declared.

Stuart was not used to being ordered about—especially not by a woman. He glared at her. "I may have money, my dear wife, but I won't have it for long if I give charity to everyone."

"You are the reason this town is in ruins," she countered. "I've overheard your conversations with the insurance inspector. Whether you set the mill on fire yourself or hired it done, it was still your doing. You have a grudge against the Vandermarks and anyone who cares for them."

"You can never prove that," Stuart said without thinking. He fought to regain his composure, adding, "Because it isn't true."

Dwight Longstreet raised his hand. "It isn't important. We need to turn things around and see this town rebuilt. Until new quarters can be constructed to house the blacks, they will stay in the ones already in place."

"No white man will put his family in a house where former slaves have lived. Your knowledge of whites in this part of the country may be limited, but I've made it my duty to understand." Stuart crossed his arms. "We'll only end up having to tear those houses down or drag them to the other side of the tracks."

"If it comes to that, then we will do what must be done," Longstreet replied. "In the meanwhile, I intend to speak to Zed about setting up an outdoor mill. I'm going to instruct him to order the things he needs and get at least a minimal mill operation going. That will give people work to do and provide the needed lumber for the reconstruction."

Stuart jumped to his feet. "You overstep your bounds, Longstreet. You forget that I am the controlling partner in this business."

Jael stood to face her husband. "And you forget that I know full well about your father's requirements for your inheritance. Your days of revenge and control have come to an end. You are no longer going to do these people harm."

"Me? I didn't burn down the shanties. I didn't shoot up the town." He was annoyed that she should even imply such a thing. Certainly he'd done nothing to stop it, but he was only one man against fifteen or twenty. Lying low in the house was far wiser until he could learn to what extent the riders intended to cause damage.

"Have you torn up the Vandermark Logging contract yet?" she asked.

Stuart knew that he had to reclaim control over the conversation. He drew a deep breath. "I have considered it, but given what your father is demanding of me, I cannot." She frowned and he continued. "We must have logs in order to create lumber. I will let the Vandermarks know that we need to immediately resume deliveries."

Jael considered this for a moment, then retook her seat. Instead of looking to Stuart, however, she turned to her father. "Would that be helpful to them—to rebuilding?"

Stuart wanted to throw something at her. How dare she look to her father for answers? He held his tongue, however.

Longstreet was already assuring her that it would be a good arrangement.

"The Vandermarks will get paid, and we will have immediate product. Stuart has already had some lumber brought in, as well as milling equipment. I'm certain that if we get Zed Perkins back on the job, we can see progress within a matter of weeks."

Jael nodded. "And what of the people, Father? They've lost everything. They have no food or other necessities."

"I have already placed an order for the commissary to be restocked in full. We will give the people company tokens for working to help us clear the debris and rebuild the mill and houses. Women will be hired, as well as youngsters. I'll have Zed get word out that we need workers."

"You take too much upon yourself." Stuart all but growled out the words.

"When will you let the Vandermarks know about bringing in the logs?" Jael asked, turning back to Stuart. "Today?"

Stuart looked at the two people. Was it possible that he now hated this pair more than he did G.W. and Deborah?

A thought came to mind. Perhaps he could still have his revenge. If things went his way, he might even own Vandermark Logging before it was all done. Of course! Why hadn't he considered this before?

"I will go today," he told them. He searched around the desk and pulled up several pieces of paper. "I will see what we are entitled to and request it all. They will make a small fortune, and I will have the necessary wood to begin rebuilding."

Jael smiled. "That sounds wonderful. Come, Father. Let's go talk to Mr. and Mrs. Perkins."

"I thought they'd returned to Lufkin," her father replied.

She frowned. "I'd forgotten that. Let's send them a wire,

then. We need to get them back here immediately. They can bring others with them." She waited for him to get to his feet. Glancing at Stuart, she gave him a curt nod. "Thank you, Stuart. I'm glad you've decided to cooperate."

∞

"Deborah, you in here?" Arjan called from the cabin door.

Coming out from the small room they'd made into an examination area, Deborah smiled. "Goodness, you gave me a start. I was just putting away some supplies."

Arjan entered the house, cane in one hand and a very pale Jake helped along by the other. Jake held his left arm close to his body. Someone had wrapped his hand and forearm in a bandage, but blood was seeping through.

"What happened?" she asked. "Bring him in here."

Deborah led the way to the examination room. She motioned for her uncle to assist Jake while she lit the two bracketed wall lamps at the head of the table and angled their reflectors to give her maximum light.

"Christopher isn't here right now, so I'll have to take care of you," she said, looking at the solemn-faced Jake.

"I'm all right with that. I know you're good. I've seen you work."

His face was a pasty white, and Deborah feared he might well faint. "Why don't you lie down here on the table and tell me what happened."

Arjan leaned the cane against the wall, then helped ease Jake into position as best he could. "Saw slipped. He just happened to have his hand and arm in the way."

"Hurts like the devil," Jake said.

Deborah unwrapped the bandages. Caked blood and dirt

would need to be washed away before she could tell exactly how bad it was. "I'll need to clean it. This won't be pleasant, but you'll be glad for it in the long run."

"If you don't need me," Arjan told her, taking up his cane, "I'll go let your ma know what's happened."

"That's fine. Jake will hold still." She looked at him and smiled. "Won't you?"

Arjan laughed, but Jake only gritted his teeth as Deborah began to wash the wound. "I'll be back shortly to check in on you," her stepfather told her.

Taking a good look at the damage, Deborah could see that the wound was far deeper toward the center of the hand. The gash ran along the lower edge of the forearm and right between the line of tendons that connected to his thumb and index finger.

"I think that if an injury could be called lucky, this would be the one. If you'd been sliced the other way, you probably would never be able to use this hand again."

"Sure don't know why it had to happen."

"Who can say? I'm going to have to stitch you up between your finger and thumb, but the rest isn't so deep. I don't think this is going to give you too much grief. You'll have to take it easy for a while, though, and keep it clean so infection won't set in. I don't know that you can work."

Jake opened his eyes and smiled. "I was going to be quittin' at the end of the week anyway."

"Truly? But why?"

He grimaced as she examined the wound further. "I sent my folks a wire. I want to join them in California."

"That's wonderful, Jake. I'm so glad you felt you could."

"I came to realize something," he said, fixing his gaze on her face. "I do care about you, but I care just as much about your family. What I was lookin' for was that sense of belonging. I just figured it meant that I needed to take a wife and that she ought to be you."

Deborah was touched by his confession. "Jake, I'm so blessed to hear it. Thank you for telling me."

"I miss my folks. We were always close, but the drought and the loss of the ranch changed my father. Changed me, too. I wasn't kind to him. I was angry and I blamed him for losin' what had been in the family for some time." Jake's expression saddened. "I have a great deal of apologizin' to do."

She reached for her needle. "The important thing is that forgiveness is something we do for ourselves as well as the other person. If you forgive your father, you will feel better in your own soul. If your father forgives you—who knows? It may well set matters aright and find him able to move forward. I'm sure the loss of the ranch was hard on him, as well."

"I know it was," Jake said. "Knew it then, too, and I hate myself for being so heartless."

"But hate won't serve any good purpose. Look what it did in town. Look what it's done to this country. We won't ever be without it, but we can do our part to lessen it."

"I heard that Arjan talked to the law about the White Hand of God."

Deborah nodded. "Not that it will resolve the problems here, to be sure. Some folks will support ugliness as well as beauty. We talked long and hard with Pastor Shattuck, and he said that it will take time to change the hearts of folks who are steeped in such a desperate desire to punish others. I have to have hope that God can do it, though. If not, then I would truly be lost in despair."

Jake glanced down at his arm. "So you really gonna stitch me up or just sit there and jaw with me?"

299

She laughed. "Believe me, by the time I finish, you'll be beggin' me to just talk."

He drew a deep breath. "Well, give me something to bite down on. I don't want no one hearin' me holler."

Deborah glanced across the room for something to give him. She spied a towel and went to fetch it. Fixing it into a tight roll, she handed it to Jake. "This ought to help muffle your protests."

He took the towel and brought it to his mouth. "Let's get this over with, then."

∽

It was bad enough being forced to do something he'd never intended to do, but Stuart hated wasting his time even more. After making excuses for several days, he'd finally ridden up to the Vandermark logging camp only to find it deserted. Now it was late afternoon and he was finally reaching home, but he had no answers to give his nagging wife. He'd considered stopping at the Vandermark house on his return, but with the light fading and his mood definitely darkening, as well, he decided against it. If Jael asked him about it, he would simply let her know that he'd try again the next day.

It was clear they'd moved the camp, but Stuart had no idea where they'd gone to or why. He would ask around and see if anyone could tell him. If that failed, he'd have no choice but to go to the Vandermark house and inquire there. He didn't want to do that if he could help it. He despised seeing G.W. and Lizzie together. They were happy, in spite of the problems he'd created for them. It didn't make sense, but Stuart supposed it didn't have to. It frustrated him, nevertheless.

When he rode up to his house, Stuart could see that Jael was serving a guest on the front porch. He frowned. Who had come to plague them now? He dismounted and tied the horse off at the post near the front steps.

Jael came to the rail. "Mr. Jennings from Houston has come to see you," she said as any dutiful wife might. "Since it was cooler out here on the porch, I thought to serve him some chilled lemonade. Would you care for a glass, also?"

Stuart shook his head and tried to recall who Jennings was. The name was vaguely familiar. He climbed the steps and extended his hand to the older man. Getting to his feet, the man gave a hint of a bow.

"Mr. Albright, I'm from your bank in Houston. I have some business to discuss, if you can take the time."

He remembered the man then. He was one of the lesser bank officers who kept an eye on the Vandermark accounts for him. Stuart turned to Jael. "Thank you for seeing to our guest in Essie's absence. I do need to speak with him privately, however."

Jael nodded. "Then I will go check on supper." She smiled at Mr. Jennings. "I hope you'll find our guest room to your liking. I'll see to it that you have fresh water in the pitcher. We'll dine at six-thirty."

"Mrs. Albright, you are a delightful hostess. I'm certain that I will sleep like a babe in the arms of his mother," the man said, bowing lower than he had for Stuart. "And if the aroma of that food is any indication, supper will be a culinary delight."

"Thank you, Mr. Jennings. I will allow you to reserve judgment until you've sampled the meal."

The interaction irritated Stuart, but he said nothing. He waited until Jael had returned to the house before motioning the man back to his seat. Pulling up a chair to sit directly in front of the man, Stuart gave his guest a sober gaze. "So tell me what has caused you to come all this way."

୬୦

The last person G.W. had expected to see that Saturday morning was Stuart Albright. Even so, there the man stood, filling the office doorway with a scowl as dark as the growing clouds outside.

"What can I do for you, Mr. Albright?" Thunder rumbled in the distance, making the moment feel even more ominous to G.W.

Stuart's expression changed to one of smug control. "It's more what I can do for you. I tried to let you know about it yesterday. I made my way out to the logging camp but found it deserted."

"Camps move from time to time. You have to go where the trees are," G.W. replied, hoping he sounded convincing. "Turpentiners finished up in one section, so we wanted to get those trees down before a strong storm came along." He'd certainly not expected Albright to venture anywhere near the camp, but now that he had, it would be up to G.W. to make it seem irrelevant.

"And where are you now located?"

"Well, we have one camp up on the northern edge of our property. There's another we've started just east of here. Why do you ask?"

G.W. could sense that the man was up to something, but he was still uncertain as to what that was. Albright could not be trusted—that much G.W. knew.

"I'd enjoy seeing it sometime, especially now."

"Especially now?" G.W. questioned. "What's that supposed to mean?"

Albright laughed, but it sounded hollow and devoid of any real amusement. "It means that I have come to reinstate our logging contract. My father-in-law has convinced me that we can do better for ourselves by processing our own lumber for the rebuilding of the mill. Of course, that also means we must act fast."

G.W. found it hard to believe the man was serious. This couldn't be boding well with Albright. He meant to force Vandermark Logging out of business. He wouldn't do anything to benefit them.

"So when would you like delivery to start?"

"Immediately," Stuart replied. "Of course, I realize that may tax you somewhat."

"Tax us? I don't reckon I understand."

"Then perhaps I'd better explain," Stuart said, finally taking a seat in front of G.W.'s desk. "I want what is owed to the Perkinsville Sawmill, the full amount. Of course, I will also be paying you in full, you understand."

G.W. did understand. Albright wanted Vandermark Logging to supply them with the quota of logs that they'd agreed to under contract. That would entail thousands and thousands of board feet, but it would bring them a nice tidy sum and put the family business back on its feet.

"I reckon we can to do that." G.W. took up a piece of paper. He figured it would come to Albright as a surprise with what he was going to say next. "We can have the first delivery made on Monday. Do you want 'em dumped in the millpond like before or just stacked?"

"I want them stacked. I want all of them stacked and ready by June twentieth."

G.W. wasn't sure exactly what Albright meant. He looked at the man and shook his head. "I said I could have them on Monday. You want me to wait till the twentieth? That's two weeks from Monday."

"You're right," Stuart replied, pressing his fingers together.

"So you don't want a delivery on Monday?"

"I didn't say that. What I want is what is owed me—in full—in two weeks."

It began to dawn on G.W. exactly what Stuart was implying. "You want delivery of all the logs we would have brought into the mill since it burned down? And you want them in two weeks?"

"Exactly," Stuart said, his smug smile broadening.

"That's impossible," G.W. said, shaking his head. "We can't cut that fast."

Stuart shrugged. "You should have been cutting all along."

"We have been, but we can only stockpile so many logs. You wouldn't want the quality jeopardized."

Stuart didn't seem to even hear him. "It's legally owed me, and if you do not comply, then you will be in breach of contract. I will see to it that you are forced to forfeit your land in payment." Getting to his feet, Stuart headed for the door. "Perhaps if you'd seen fit not to go behind my back and arrange for your logs to go elsewhere, you'd have enough stockpiled to meet my needs."

He was gone before G.W. could respond—not that he knew what to say. G.W. thought of going after Albright and telling him they had done nothing illegal, but he figured Albright already knew that. In fact, it was probably the very reason he'd come with the demands he'd just made. He couldn't punish the Vandermarks for giving away their logs, but he could penalize them by forcing them to meet an impossible deadline.

G.W. glanced at the clock on the wall. His mother, Arjan, and the children were out checking on the black grapes. Mother always liked to get them picked early, and even though they mostly ripened in July and August, she kept a close vigil. Arjan could get around with a cane but Mother wouldn't yet let him return to the logging camp, so he busied himself the best he could by helping where she'd allow for it. Lizzie and the twins were out in the garden. His son and daughter would celebrate their first birthday on the sixteenth—just four days prior to Albright's newly imposed deadline.

He rubbed the long healed injury to his thigh and wondered how they could make it all work out. G.W. had never been as good with figures as he would've liked to be, but a fella didn't need a higher education to know that the logs they owed Albright were more than they could hope to cut with the small crew employed by Vandermark Logging.

"We're gonna need your help on this one, Lord," he said, looking to the ceiling. "And we're gonna need it by the twentieth."

CHAPTER 27

Deborah sat beside Christopher and listened as her brother and Arjan laid out their plans for the two weeks to come. She and Christopher had agreed to come and help at the logging camp. Christopher felt that with her there to tend the injured, as well as help with the cooking, he could lend a hand in the actual logging. The idea made Deborah smile. He had no idea what he was in for. Logging was not for the faint of heart, and while her husband had great stamina and strength, he was used to tending patients.

"We've got to get the word out that we'll take any and all workers," Arjan said. "I figure with my leg the way it is, I can at least take care of that much."

Mother shook her head. "You shouldn't even be up and

around, but like my mama used to say, 'You can't harness the wind.' "

Arjan laughed. "Is that your way of declarin' I'm full of hot air?" He smiled and continued. "I'll send out a wire, then head up to Lufkin and see if I can round up some men. We've got friends all around us, and hopefully they'll lend a hand."

"I'll help Deborah at the camp," Lizzie announced. "Mother has already agreed to keep the children here with her."

G.W. nodded. "Havin' you gals there to cook and clean up will be a great help. Those fellas are gonna need hardy helpin's of food. Jake, you sure you don't mind stayin' here to lend Ma a hand?"

"I don't mind at all. In fact, I'll come back to work if Mr. Vandermark will just let me."

"No, Son. Havin' you here will put my mind at ease."

"Mine too," Mother said, giving Jake a reassuring nod.

"I'll go to the commissary and see what can be had," Arjan promised. "I'll be headin' there to send the telegram anyway."

"I'll go with you," Deborah interjected. "There are cots at the infirmary. We could use them for the workers. Stuart Albright may not like it, but I don't intend to ask for his permission."

"Sounds good. I know any extra tents are bein' used to help shelter the folks who lost their homes," Arjan replied. "I'll see what's to be had later in Lufkin. We'll get what we can and get back here as soon as possible. By then, you oughta have the rest of the gear loaded and ready to go."

Mother nodded. "Sissy and I will pack the other wagon with dried beans and cornmeal." She looked to her friend. "We're running low after taking so much into town after the fire, but we'll get by."

"The garden is producing, and with game and such, we can

surely get by until Albright pays us on the twentieth," G.W. said. "We'll need to work around the clock at the camp, so we're gonna need a lot of lanterns and kerosene."

"I'll add that to the list," Arjan said.

"Can we really do this?" Mother asked.

Deborah hated the way her voice sounded—so uncertain, weary before they even attempted to accomplish the goal.

"It'll be close. We'll have to work every day," G.W. said.

"We aren't working on the Lord's Day," Arjan declared firmly. "Your pa and I had a long-standin' agreement that we would always honor the Lord by keepin' that day holy. I don't intend to break with that now."

Deborah looked at him in surprise. "But it's just this once, and the circumstances are critical."

"Either we believe God will see us through this or we don't," Arjan replied. "God certainly expects us to work and do our part, but He won't be replaced by a false idol—even one as honorable as meetin' our contract obligations."

"He's right," Mother said, glancing at her husband with a smile. "We put God first. He will provide what we need."

Deborah fully believed in having faith, but this surprised her. Surely God allowed for extenuating circumstances. Jesus was even confronted by the Pharisees about healing on the Sabbath. What was it He said?

" 'Wherefore it is lawful to do well on the Sabbath days,' " she murmured, remembering the twelfth chapter of Matthew.

Her stepfather met her gaze. "What was that?"

"I was just remembering that Jesus said it was lawful to do well on the Sabbath. He said it just before healing a man."

"And I suppose we must reckon what the Lord meant by doin' well," Arjan said. "Like healin'. I figure selfless acts that keep a fella or animal from starvin' or dyin' are doin' well. Earning a livin' can't hardly be the same difference."

Deborah knew she wouldn't convince him otherwise and only nodded. She supposed he made a good point. Their dilemma was one that, when resolved, would provide them with monetary gain.

"Don't fret, Deborah," her stepfather added. "God ain't forgotten about us in all this time. I don't reckon He's gonna start anytime soon."

She smiled, knowing he was right. She pushed back her fearful thoughts and settled on revisiting such issues at a later time. "Well, we'd best get to town. There's no tellin' what we'll find. Stuart Albright may well have shipped the commissary off to Houston by now." She got to her feet.

"Let's pray first," Arjan said, standing.

The others rose and joined hands. Deborah bowed her head and closed her eyes. *Father, this seems to be more than we can bear,* she prayed even as her stepfather began his petition. *Please go before us.*

☼

Deborah was surprised to find the commissary very nearly emptied. Arjan stood at the counter, shaking his head as Jude Greeley explained.

"Mr. Longstreet came in here with the black folks and set them up accounts to get the things they needed. He moved them over to the row of empty houses on the north side of town and said they could stay there until new places could be built. He figures to get the mill going mighty quick—even put in a big order of supplies to come up from Burke and any place else he could get 'em."

"Do tell," Arjan said, shaking his head. "Well, it would seem

Mr. Albright and Mr. Longstreet have had a change of heart in matters regardin' Perkinsville."

"It would seem that way," Jude admitted. "I still have some bags of beans and meal, though. Just not a great deal. I'll give you what I can and then you come back next week and we should be restocked. Mr. Longstreet wired for the new supplies to be sent right away."

"Guess that'll have to do us," Arjan replied. "How about kerosene and some lanterns?"

Jude shook his head. "I have some kerosene left, but they cleaned me out of lamps and lanterns. Why don't you take a look around and see what's left. If you can use it—take it. Say, you oughta check over at the livery. Maybe they could spare a few lanterns for you to borrow."

"It's worth askin' after," Arjan agreed. "We may just have to make some smudge pots."

"Or some good old-fashioned bonfires." Deborah touched his arm. "I'm going to go over to the infirmary and get the cots."

"I'm sorry, Miss Deborah—I mean Mrs. Kelleher," Jude interjected, "but they took those, as well."

She looked at him in disbelief. "All of them?"

" 'Fraid so. Those folks lost everything, as you know."

"Looks like we'll be sleeping out under the stars," she told Arjan.

"Reckon so. Guess we'd do well to finish up here and get on our way."

∽

G.W. loved being out in the woods again. He relished the smell of pine and earth. Watching the men at work, he found he even missed the hard labor of swinging an ax. His father had taught him at a very early age how to cut wood for the hearth. Later, he instructed G.W. how to cut a wedge to fell a tree. So many lessons he'd learned from his father. And in times like this, G.W. couldn't help but think of them. His father had been a good man—loving and generous. How he missed him.

An approaching wagon drew G.W.'s focus. He figured Arjan and Deborah were returning with the commissary purchases and left his things to go greet them. Not seeing any telltale evidence heaping the back of the wagon, he frowned.

"What happened?" He saw only a few bags of beans, cornmeal, sugar, and salt. There were also half a dozen other items, including some extra axes and saws and tins of kerosene.

"Apparently, Mr. Longstreet and Albright practiced generosity on the black folks. The commissary was pretty bare by the time we got there." Arjan climbed down, accepting G.W.'s offer of help. "The ride put me to achin', but don't tell your mother or she'll be fussin' over me."

G.W. nodded. "We can make do. I'll send a couple of the boys out to shoot a rabbit or two. Maybe a squirrel. We'll get by."

"They took all the hospital cots, as well," Deborah said, coming from the other side of the wagon. "I can't fault them for doing such a kindness, but it does change things for us a bit."

"Not to worry," Arjan said. "I'm gonna head right up to Lufkin. If I get a move on, I can get there by dark. I'll attend church with Bertram Wallace in the morning and return on Monday."

Deborah reached into the wagon bed and took up several small sacks of flour. Smiling at her stepfather, she said, "We'd best get you on your way."

Within a matter of minutes, Arjan was back in the wagon

seat. "I'll see you on Monday." He snapped the reins and moved the horses out.

G.W. turned to Deborah. "Lizzie has been workin' to expand the cooking area. I'm gonna send Jimmy and Tommy down to bring up the tables and benches we made for your weddin'. I reckon they'll serve us pretty well."

"Where's Christopher? I need to let him know that I couldn't bring much of anything from the old house. It was pretty well stripped."

"He's actually gettin' a lesson on the two-handed saw. I have a feelin' your husband is in for blistered hands and a sore back before this is all said and done."

"There are worse things," Deborah replied. "Where did he set up?"

"Right over there. We doubled the boys up in the other tents, and you and the doc are in the one by mine and Lizzie's." G.W. pointed to where two tents sat apart from the others. "You'll be closer to the creek that way. I told the boys to just figure on bringin' up two pails of water every mornin' to help you ladies get it heated for coffee and anything else you need. After that, you'll pretty much be on your own. The men are gonna be too busy."

She laughed. "Gijsbert Willem Vandermark, we are fully capable of doing our part. Hard work never hurt anyone."

"I beg to differ with you," he said, grinning. "Hard work just about kilt me when I fell out of a tree."

"I can see your point, but unfortunately there's no more time to chat. There's a lot of work to be done. I've got to get the beans soaking for tomorrow and help Lizzie figure out how we're going to manage everything."

"Oh, Sis?"

She turned back to face him. With a rise of her brow she questioned him without a word.

"You use my full name again, and I'm gonna tell doc about the time you tried to hatch that nest of eggs by sittin' on them. Then I'm gonna tell him about the time—"

She held up her hand. "Point taken, G.W. It won't happen again."

∞

Nearly a week later, Jael was happy to see a noticeable change in the town. The remaining debris from the mill site had been cleaned up and cleared away. Zed Perkins had returned to town, along with two of his sons, and with them came several other men from Lufkin. Apparently, Arjan Vandermark had found Zed before he and Rachel had even received the telegram Jael had sent. Zed was more than happy to return to town, and happier still when her father explained that he intended to take over Stuart's supervision of the town and send his son-in-law back to Houston. At least that was the plan.

Jael tried not to think about Stuart. She knew he was unhappy, being forced to adhere to the demands she and her father had given him. He'd barely said two words to her on any given day that week, although she'd heard more than one yelling match between her father and Stuart behind closed doors. He'd made it clear that he was enraged at being ordered about. He accused her father of going behind his back and spending money that should have been spent elsewhere. Jael had been proud of her father's willingness to stand his ground, however. He was no pauper, and in his own right, he could very nearly match Stuart's financial success. He, however, could boast that his money had been earned—something that was now more respected than it used to be. Stuart felt his wealth was more impressive because he'd inherited it, even if it came by deception and cruelty.

Jael made her way to the commissary and walked in to find several black women helping to put away supplies. Jude Greeley was telling one woman where to place the cast-iron pots while another waited patiently to be shown what to do with a box of thread.

"This is certainly a fine change," she said as Jude pointed the last woman in the right direction.

"It is indeed. Reminds me of when we first set up business, only then it was just the missus and me puttin' away stock. It's good to see the place up and runnin' again."

"There will be a great many more people coming back to Perkinsville," she told him. "My father and Mr. Perkins intend to see the mill operating, at least in part, by the middle of next week."

"I heard that, as well, Mrs. Albright. What was it that changed your husband's mind?"

Jael smiled. "I suppose he saw the value in moving forward."

"Jael!"

She turned to find Deborah rushing across the store. "I can scarce believe my good fortune. I had heard you were far to the north at the logging camp." She embraced Deborah. "Goodness, but you're thin as a rail."

"I don't think I've ever worked harder in my life," Deborah said with a laugh. "G.W. and I came down to the house to see how Mother and Sissy were doing. We heard the supplies had come into the store and thought to take a load back up with us."

"You look exhausted," Jael said, taking Deborah aside, "but how marvelous that Stuart finally honored his contract."

"He honored it all right. Honored it with his demand that

we meet an impossible goal by June twentieth or he'll sue us and take our land." Deborah frowned. "Hardly a victory."

Jael could hardly believe what she was hearing. "I don't understand."

Deborah cocked her head to one side. "Don't you know?"

"I can't imagine what you're talking about."

"Stuart demanded the full quota of logs owed him by Vandermark Logging—the amount we would have provided from the time the mill burned until now."

"How can that be legal?" she asked in disbelief.

"It's within his rights, despite the absurdity of his demands. As usual, he's found a way to manipulate the legal aspects to his benefit—and our detriment. Lizzie's father told us that Stuart apparently has several judges eating out of his hand. He has an entire team of lawyers who do his bidding, and apparently owns the bank—or at least some of their people where Vandermark Logging has borrowed."

Jael felt her ire rise. "I knew it was too good to be true. Stuart has been far too quiet. I demanded he tear up the contract with Vandermark Logging, but he said he had a better idea—he would get you back in business. My father even thought it sounded like a worthy idea."

"It would be, except for the deadline and quota of logs." Deborah shook her head. "We've hired on as many men as want work and have experience. The job is getting done, but we still don't know that we can meet Stuart's demands."

"Leave that to me."

"What can you possibly do?"

She wasn't exactly sure. She could only push Stuart so far, but given all that he'd done, Jael figured he still owed her. "I'll do what I can. When is the deadline?"

"Monday the twentieth. We're to have the logs stockpiled by the tracks or already delivered here to the mill. I'm not sure Stuart understands exactly how much ground that's going to take up, but I figure that's his concern."

"And it will be the least of them." Jael took hold of Deborah's arm. "I'll speak to Father. He may have additional ideas."

"Thank you. You have been a good friend to me." Deborah caught sight of the clock as it chimed two. "I need to run. G.W. and I have to get the wagon loaded and delivered yet this afternoon." She leaned forward and kissed Jael on the cheek.

Jael watched her friend head to the counter and contemplated what she should do. She thought about just confronting Stuart and decided against it. She would talk to her father first. He had proven himself more than capable of handling Stuart and the business of Perkinsville's rebirth.

∞

Deborah awoke Sunday morning to the sound of rain pelting the tent. Thunder rumbled overhead and left her feeling more discouraged than she'd thought possible. The summer storms were wreaking havoc on their ability to harvest trees. Ever since the week before when she'd run into Jael at the commissary, the weather had been unpredictable. There had been no word from Jael or her father, not to mention Stuart. Deborah had hoped that one of them would arrive to say the deadline was extended—especially since it had rained off and on most every day.

Christopher stirred, but he was still asleep. She smiled and scooted closer to her husband. What would they do if the deadline wasn't met? Would Stuart really find a way to take their land? She sighed. Why were there no answers?

Christopher opened his eyes and smiled. "What time is it?"

Lightning flashed and thunder boomed right behind it. Deborah wanted to bury herself in her husband's protective embrace. The storm was apparently right on top of them. "It doesn't matter. We can't leave the tent."

He held her tight. "Pity."

"That was exactly my thought," she said, giggling.

"I've got things pretty well figured out now," Christopher declared.

She looked at him oddly. "What things?"

"Well, I now know that I don't want to be a logger. I don't want to work with mules, and I definitely prefer houses to tents."

"I'm glad, because I'm of the same mind. My back is sore from sleeping on the ground."

He slid his hand down to the small of her back and rubbed it gently. "I found myself wishing for one of the infirmary cots."

The rain grew heavier and beat out a rhythmic beat on the canvas tent. "I'm glad I left the lids off all the pots. That rainwater will come in handy," Deborah said, snuggling close.

After a few moments of silence, Christopher sighed. "The deadline is tomorrow."

She leaned up on her elbow. Doubt and worry etched her husband's features. "I know. I was thinking about that before you woke up."

"We aren't doing too bad," he added.

"We don't have enough to meet the quota," she reminded him. "I doubt Stuart is going to give us an extension. Jael had thought she could help, but I'm guessing that was just wishful thinking. Otherwise we would surely have heard something by now."

The wind picked up and pummeled the tent walls. Deborah dropped again to the crook of Christopher's arm. "I hope the storm will pass quickly."

"Arjan said the storms have been unusual for this time of year."

"Well, at least this many in a row and this strong," Deborah agreed. The fury of the weather kept them from working in any consistent fashion. "Just when I thought we had a chance . . ."

"Hey, that doesn't sound like my ever-optimistic wife," Christopher said, gently stroking her cheek. "You aren't giving up, are you?"

"I don't want to give up, but . . . I feel depleted of hope." Lightning illuminated their tent. The thunder seemed to rumble the ground around them. Deborah shuddered. "I've never had to be out in a storm like this. I'm afraid."

"Don't be," he said. "We're going to make it through this." He grinned and placed a kiss on her nose. "I kind of like being here with you. It's not the wedding trip I would have planned for us, but I'm content. I think I will always be content, so long as you're at my side."

The storm inside Deborah began to abate, even as the one raging around them lessened. Nestling down in her husband's arms, she listened as the storm began to slowly move off. Little by little the rain diminished to a gentle rhythm as the storm played out. In the distance, she heard someone singing and smiled.

It was Lizzie. The tune was more than a little familiar, the words so very appropriate for the moment.

" 'The raging storms may round us beat,' " Lizzie sang, " 'a shelter in the time of storm. We'll never leave our safe retreat, a shelter in the time of storm.' " Deborah couldn't help but smile. It was a fairly new hymn that her mother had found for the sacred-harp singing. Deborah felt peace wash over her as Lizzie's voice lingered in the air.

" 'O Rock divine, O Refuge dear, a shelter in the time of storm. Be thou our helper ever near, a shelter in the time of storm.' "

CHAPTER 28

The storm dissipated and the warmth of summer returned. The sun steamed the air, making everything feel heavy and sticky. Since it was later than usual, Deborah decided to do what she could to hurry breakfast. Taking dry wood from the tent, she worked quickly to get the fire going. Despite having been sheltered, the wood was still rather damp and the fire didn't want to catch. Coaxing it with dried bits of pine straw, Deborah finally established a tiny, but growing, flame. She soon had the fire built up and burning nicely.

Lizzie brought two coffeepots to hang over the fire. "I'll get some water on to boil."

"Thanks. I'll start slicing the ham."

The others emerged from their tents, rather like she imagined

Noah and his family had from the ark. They looked hopeful, but hesitant.

"Breakfast will be ready in about twenty minutes," Deborah told them as Lizzie put a large kettle of water on beside the coffee and threw more logs onto the fire.

G.W. pulled up his suspenders as he walked toward the women. "Lizzie and I talked about it last night and plan to go home after the Sunday service. We're missin' the little ones, and I reckon Ma could use the rest. Woulda headed there last night, 'cept for that storm."

"I'm sure Mama didn't mind. She loves those babies," Deborah replied, focusing her attention back on cutting the ham. She figured there would be at least twenty of them for breakfast. When they'd finished working near eleven-thirty the night before, many of the men had decided to ride to Lufkin with what little pay Arjan could amass. Those who remained were mostly young men who had come west looking to make their fortune, only to find that life on the frontier didn't come easy. Arjan had promised each a bonus if he would willingly work for no pay until the twentieth. Most had originally agreed, but after a week of battling the weather, over half of the men had decided to head to where they could get a hot bath and a comfortable bed. Deborah could only wonder if they'd made it home ahead of the storm.

"I figure with the deadline loomin' over us tomorrow, Lizzie and you might as well stay home anyway. Either we'll make the number or we won't. No need to keep you gals workin' here," G.W. said. "The train will be haulin' in logs all day and there's nothin' you can do to help with that."

"We can still cook and clean," Deborah replied. "Lizzie can stay home and maybe Mama would like to join us here."

Lizzie returned to put two more coffeepots over the fire

before checking the water in the pot. "It won't be long before it's boiling."

"It would do us all some good to go home," Arjan declared, joining them. "We could enjoy a nice restful Sabbath there just as well as here."

"That would be fine by me," Deborah agreed. "But I plan to return in the morning. If Christopher's going to work here, then I am, too."

"I think that's just fine, but you'd both better be willin' to take your pay, just like the others." Arjan grinned and gave Deborah a wink.

Deborah heard movement behind her and saw that her husband had finally moved to join them. "What do you think?" she asked Christopher, who sort of duck walked out of the tent.

"About what?" He straightened and grimaced. "I think the ground is getting harder."

She laughed. "Arjan was just suggesting we all head home for the day after breakfast. So many of the men left last night for their homes in Lufkin. Those that remain can come to the house and enjoy some time in out of the rain." With the water finally boiling, Deborah stirred in grits and covered the pot with a heavy iron lid.

"I'd be happy to sleep in my own bed, even for a few winks." Christopher suppressed a yawn and stretched. "Coffee ready yet?"

"Not quite. Soon." Deborah collected the plates. She motioned everyone to the tables. Thunder rumbled from far away.

Deborah glanced at the skies overhead. The clouds churned and thickened once again. "Hopefully we can eat before the next storm moves in."

"We haven't had a run of weather like this for years," Arjan declared.

"It's actin' like spring instead of summer," G.W. threw in.

Lizzie brought out two jugs and plopped them down on the table. The men were notorious for eating their grits with equal amounts of the thick molasses sweetness. Hopefully two jugs would be enough. It wasn't long before Deborah was ladling the food into large serving bowls. Jimmy took the first one to the table, and Lizzie took the second. Tommy and Arjan took the next bowls, and G.W. and Christopher helped by taking the platters of ham and leftover corn bread. Lizzie and Deborah brought the coffee at long last, and Arjan offered the blessing.

"Lord, we thank you for your many blessin's. We ask that you would guide us on this, your Sabbath. Help us to remember that you gave us this day of rest to think on you and your goodness. Bless this food. Amen."

"Amen," the men murmured around the table.

Arjan stood and began to speak again as the food was passed. "You men are welcome to come back to our place for the day. Looks to me like it will rain and storm into the night. You can get in out of the weather, though you may be sleeping on the floor."

There were some chuckles over this. "Hard floor, hard ground—take your choice."

"One's dry and the other's wet," Jimmy added.

Deborah watched her stepfather nod and smile. "He speaks the truth. Still, you're welcome to it. We'll leave just after breakfast and return tomorrow mornin' to finish what we started."

"We haven't made the number yet, Mr. Vandermark," one of the men declared. "Won't make our goal for tomorrow iffen we don't keep workin' today."

Arjan nodded. "Son, as I've said before, this is God's day. I know we could work it, but I believe we'll honor it instead. God multiplied the loaves and fishes for the crowds of hungry folks in the Bible. I reckon He can multiply logs if need be."

In the end, about half the men decided to go home with the Vandermarks while the others decided to stay put. Arjan had led them all in prayer and Scripture reading before announcing that they could further their time with the Lord once they were safely inside with a roof overhead.

Sprinkles of rain had started to fall by the time they reached the house. It appeared, however, that the worst of the storm had passed them by. Deborah was certainly glad about this. The children and Mother came bounding out from the house as the wagons came to a stop near the barn.

"You boys help me turn the mules loose in the corral," Arjan instructed. "Tommy and Jimmy, you throw them some feed."

"We've got kittens!" Emma declared to the new arrivals.

"Truly?" Deborah smiled. "Who's the proud mama?"

Her mother held Jonah back to keep him out of the way of the mules. "It was the long-haired gray."

"And how many babies are there?" Deborah asked, getting down from the back of the wagon with Christopher's help.

"Five. There are five kittens and five of us children. Mama Euphanel said that's just like God to provide exactly what we need," Emma announced.

Deborah laughed. "I believe she's right."

"She also said we can't be pickin' them up yet," Jonah said. "Else their eyes won't open."

"That's very wise. The mama cat knows best what they need right now," Deborah told him. "Soon enough those kittens will be scampering all over the place. How are the puppies?"

"They're getting big," Darcy replied. She was dressed in her Sunday best and looked like quite the young lady.

"What are you all gussied up for, little gal?" Arjan asked. "You look right pretty."

"Pastor's coming for dinner," she told him. "He was here yesterday, and Mama Euphanel invited him and Miss Mara."

"I'm right glad she did. Maybe he'll preach us a sermon," Arjan said, taking Mother in his arms.

Deborah smiled as he gave her mother a big kiss. "I missed you, Wife."

"Not half so much as I missed you." Mother kissed him right back.

Deborah turned to Christopher. "I'm going to have a bath before the pastor arrives."

"I could use one, too."

Jonah pulled on his brother's coat. "You can't both take a bath at the same time. Mama Euphanel says it's not fittin' for girls and boys to take a bath at the same time, so I know she won't let you grown-up folks do that."

Deborah saw her mother's eyes widen in alarm while Arjan coughed and sputtered as he did his best to keep from laughing. Pretending she hadn't heard, Deborah left Christopher to handle the comment.

"I reckon I can wait until she takes her bath first," Christopher replied. "I don't want Mama Euphanel mad at me. I haven't had her dessert in nearly two weeks."

Jonah nodded. "That'd be good, 'cause today we're having pie."

Arjan regained control of his merriment and motioned to the family. "We'd best stop jawin' out here in the rain."

"It's barely a sprinkle, but I agree," Mother said. "Come along, little chickens, let's get in the house."

Deborah headed for the cabin, knowing that Christopher

was right behind her. She didn't say a word until they were inside with the door closed, then she burst out laughing.

"You . . . you nearly . . . caused a scene," she sputtered.

"I thought your ma would have kittens," he replied, grinning.

Tears came to her eyes as she fought to get her breath. She hadn't laughed this hard in years. She fought to sober herself as she listened to the rain begin to fall in earnest. "I guess I'll get a rainwater bath. The barrel is bound to be full."

"Why don't you light the stove, and I'll drag out the tub." He tossed his bag and coat onto a nearby chair. "Then I'll bring the water in for you. It shouldn't take too long to warm up."

Deborah nodded. It was just good to be home. Good to be able to soak in a tub and rest in bed. She hurried to light the stove. Time was a-wasting.

∞

After the evening meal, Pastor Shattuck stood to offer a reading from Psalm ninety-one. " 'He that dwelleth in the secret place of the most High shall abide under the shadow of the Almighty. I will say of the Lord, He is my refuge and my fortress: my God; in Him will I trust. Surely he shall deliver thee from the snare of the fowler, and from the noisome pestilence. He shall cover thee with his feathers, and under his wings shalt thou trust: his truth shall be thy shield and buckler.' "

"What's a buckler?" Jonah asked, a little louder than intended.

"That's a very good question," Pastor Shattuck declared before Mother could hush the boy. "In the old days, when men fought with swords instead of guns, a buckler was used as a small shield. But it was decidedly more than that."

Lightning lit the room, seeming to come out of nowhere.

Thunder cracked shortly thereafter, but Pastor Shattuck continued without concern.

"A buckler had five main uses. The warrior would hold it in the hand opposite his sword. It was often round and made of strong metal. It wasn't all that big, but it didn't need to be for what it was intended. You see, a buckler was a weapon of close combat. The kind of fight you would have face-to-face with your enemy."

Deborah could see that Jonah was completely captivated. So, too, were most of the young men who'd come home from the logging camp to share the Vandermark hospitality.

"A buckler's first job was to act as protection for the hand," Pastor Shattuck told them. "The grip that allowed the warrior to deflect the blows of his attacker. Thus, the second job—deflecting. Because it was lightweight and small, it was easier to use than a large shield.

"Third, a warrior could use his buckler as a blinder. He could hide his sword momentarily from view and strike his opponent unexpectedly. He could also reflect the sun into his opponent's eyes."

The pastor's words fascinated Deborah. She had always enjoyed learning the deeper meaning of scriptural details. Knowledge of God's word was precious to her, and this explanation made a most beloved psalm all the more meaningful.

"The buckler could also be used as a metal fist to the face or body of the enemy," Pastor Shattuck continued. "Soldiers punched at their opponents and drove them off balance while wielding their sword to strike.

"And lastly, the buckler was used as a binder. A soldier could trap a man's sword arm against him, binding him from further attack. It offered a means of controlling one's enemy." He smiled at Jonah. "Now, I can tell you something else about this. I once had a very learned friend who knew the language of the Old Testament—Hebrew. I learned that the word used here for 'shield' was *tsinnah*. This was a shield so large it covered a man's entire body. Only his head would be exposed. The word for 'buckler' in the Hebrew was *cocherah*. I'm told that this verse is the only place in the entire Bible where this word appears. Of course, I couldn't tell you for sure that this was true, but I've tried to explore that for myself and haven't yet seen it elsewhere.

"*Cocherah* actually means something that wraps up a person. So perhaps God desired to show us in this verse that His truth is a shield that surrounds us completely. A protection, as well as a weapon. You see, God has given you weapons to fight the devil, your enemy. The truth of God is your shield and buckler. You are not to fight without a means of defense *and* offense. God has provided for all our needs." Jonah nodded with great enthusiasm.

Pastor Shattuck picked up his Bible once again. As he spoke, the winds outside seemed to calm. " 'Thou shalt not be afraid for the terror by night; nor for the arrow that flieth by day; nor for the pestilence that walketh in darkness; nor for the destruction that wasteth at noonday. A thousand shall fall at thy side, and ten thousand at thy right hand; but it shall not come nigh thee. Only with thine eyes shalt thou behold and see the reward of the wicked. Because thou hast made the Lord, which is my refuge, even the most High, thy habitation; there shall no evil befall thee, neither shall any plague come nigh thy dwelling.' "

He paused and smiled. "It doesn't mean we won't face the enemy or that adversity won't threaten, but God has assured us that we *will* be delivered. We rest in His protection. He will completely surround us."

"Like a sucker-raw!" Jonah exclaimed.

Pastor Shattuck laughed and nodded. "Exactly right, young Jonah. And well pronounced."

Deborah heard the train approaching in the distance and frowned. If Jack had found it necessary to put the old engine in motion today, it could only mean some problem. Perhaps someone needed the doctor. She glanced toward the door and decided to see for herself. She slipped out of the room and pushed back the screen door.

The air suffocated her with moisture and warmth. Arjan joined Deborah on the porch as the sound of the train grew louder.

"I wonder why Jack's coming," she said looking toward the track. "You don't suppose there's been another attack by the White Hand?"

Arjan's eyes suddenly widened as the wind once again began to pick up. "It's not Jack or the train. It's a twister. Get inside—we have to take cover!"

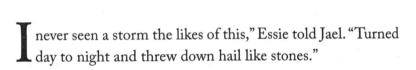

CHAPTER 29

never seen a storm the likes of this," Essie told Jael. "Turned day to night and threw down hail like stones."

Jael was still battling her rattled nerves. The wind had blown so hard that she'd feared the walls would come down. "Do you suppose there has been a lot of damage?"

"I figure there is, iffen a tornado dropped out of them clouds."

"We had a few bad storms in Philadelphia, but nothing like that." Jael walked to the porch to survey the surroundings. Tree limbs littered the tracks, making it look as though the workers had never gathered up the White Hand's debris. Where were Stuart and her father? When the clouds rolled in, thick and black, they had headed over to get Zed Perkins and help secure the mill supplies. They hadn't returned.

The skies overhead cleared, making it appear as if nothing had happened. An eerie calm settled over the world. Only a short while ago, Jael had feared they could lose their lives; now, everything seemed again at peace.

She saw her father coming down the street and hurried to meet him. "Where is Stuart?"

"He and Mr. Perkins are checking out the mill. I wanted to make sure you were safe."

Jael hugged her father close. "It was terrifying."

"I know. I'm so sorry you were here alone."

"Essie was with me," Jael said, pulling back. "She knew exactly what to do. We hid in the hall at the very back when we heard the hail."

"We did the same at the commissary. We never even made it over to Zed's place until after the storm."

"Has there been a lot of damage?"

Her father shook his head. "I don't know. I only wanted to make sure you were all right."

She smiled. "Too bad my husband didn't feel the same." She walked away, telling herself that it didn't matter. Though she held no affection for Stuart, she did care if he'd made it through the storm. Stuart only cared about his investment.

"Essie said there may have been a tornado," Jael said, heading back to the house.

Her father reached out to stop her. "Do you suppose the Vandermarks were in the path of the storm?"

Jael felt as if she'd been slapped. She looked at her father in horror. "I . . . I don't know." She knew that Deborah and the others had been working at the logging camp. Living in tents, they wouldn't have had any place to take refuge from the violent winds.

"We need to go to them," Jael told her father. "We can at least go to the house."

"I'll get the carriage."

Grateful that he didn't question her suggestion, Jael hurried into the house. "Essie!" The young woman appeared with a quizzical expression. "Father and I are going to drive out to the Vandermarks'. Will you let Mr. Albright know where I've gone, if and when he comes home?"

"Sure will, Miz Albright." Essie looked at the clock. "Gettin' late . . . will you be back tonight?"

"I don't know." Jael took up her parasol. "I suppose we'll know better after we make certain the Vandermarks are safe." She didn't want to think what she'd do if they weren't. The house might have been directly in the path of the storm, and the logging camp might have been destroyed, as well.

Her new faith in God was being sorely tested. What was she supposed to do at a time like this? Jael looked at Essie.

"Are you . . . do you . . ." She wasn't even sure what she wanted to say. "Essie, I'm worried about Deborah and the others. I haven't learned very much about praying, but I'm sure we should pray."

"Oh, absolutely, Miz Albright. I been prayin' all along."

༄

Stuart watched his father-in-law drive the carriage around to the front of the house. Where were they headed at this hour of the day? He crossed the road, his boots sinking deep in the muck. He'd had just about all he could take of this town. Nothing was going right. Now that Jael had let her father know about her reasons for marrying him, Longstreet treated him with contempt. The man no longer regarded Stuart as being in charge. He'd taken many decisions into his own hands without so much as a discussion. Just like now.

"Where are you going?" he asked as Longstreet got down to help Jael into the carriage.

"To check on my friends," Jael declared. "Essie said there may have been a tornado, and I intend to make sure that Deborah and her family are all right."

"But they're up at the logging camp. You can't possibly hope to make it up there before the light is gone. And even if you did, you'd still have to drive back in the dark. The roads are certain to be difficult, if not impassable, from the heavy rain."

"We only intend to get as far as the house. Hopefully they will have gotten word to Mrs. Vandermark and she can let me know. Then Father and I can simply return."

"Not before the light is gone. I won't have you out there on the road given the problems we've had in the area."

Jael looked at him oddly. "Why, Stuart, you almost sound as if you care about our well-being."

Her sarcasm irritated Stuart to no end. "I don't need the expense of a funeral."

To his surprise, she laughed and settled into her seat. Longstreet looked at Stuart and shook his head. "This is a most unholy union. If I can convince my daughter to leave you, I will."

"We're partners, you and I. Or have you forgotten?" Stuart fixed the man with a scowl. "We stand to lose a great deal of money and land because of your daughter's interference."

"You know, I never came here to seek revenge on anyone. That's probably why I feel capable of walking away from this ordeal without making a profit. I would rather lose money than friends."

"Then you're a fool!"

Longstreet shrugged and climbed into the carriage. "At least I realize my foolish doings. You seem blind to yours."

Stuart watched the carriage pull away and cursed them both. The same kind of helplessness he'd known the day Elizabeth had married G. W. Vandermark crept upon him. She had ruined all his plans, and now Jael and Longstreet were attempting to do the same thing.

He stormed into the house, mindless of the mud he tracked throughout. Stomping out his frustrations on the stairs, he made his way to the bedroom he'd once shared with Jael and began tearing at his clothes. They were filthy and he hated being dirty. Dirty like a common laborer.

"The world will judge you by your appearance," his father had always declared. *"You can hide what you're really thinking—what you plan to do in order to have your way—but you cannot hide your appearance."*

Stuart threw his shirt aside. Such advice had served him well over the years. Pleasing his father by keeping a well-dressed, fashionably groomed appearance had allowed Stuart to conceal his true feelings of hatred toward the man who had never shown him the slightest consideration.

"Essie!" He bellowed from the door and waited for some response. There was none. Jael had probably let the woman leave.

He railed at the air, cursing his wife and everything around him. Nothing was going his way. Not even something as simple as a bath.

∽

Deborah felt Christopher loosen his hold on her as the winds died down and the rains ceased. She had scarcely been able to draw a breath at the height of the storm, and now she gasped to fill her lungs.

Jonah cried in Mother's arms while Emma and Darcy clung to either side of her. Deborah felt a sense of relief and regret. She prayed that she would one day be able to offer such love and peace to her own children.

"We'd best check out the damage," G.W. said, pulling Lizzie to her feet. They each reached down to pick up one of the sleeping twins. "I swear these guys could sleep through anything."

Mother smiled. "They felt safe in your arms."

Deborah remembered the comfort of Christopher's arms around her. Better still, their time of prayer through the storm and the sense of being wrapped in God's protection. Just like the cocherah Brother Shattuck had mentioned.

"I'll take that boy," Sissy said. She lifted Rutger from his father's arms. "Me and Miz Lizzie can tend them."

Lizzie nodded. "You probably have more than enough to deal with outside."

They had taken refuge down the main hall and under the stairs, far away from any windows. A good idea, too—Deborah had heard glass shattering through the wind's roar.

The family slowly made their way outside to survey the destruction. The house, except for some missing shingles and broken panes, had come through the storm without much noticeable damage. Deborah noted with relief that the barn was untouched.

"I ain't never been this close to a twister's path," Arjan said, looking across the vast cut of destruction.

The tornado had taken a sharp turn to the north after narrowly missing their house. Downed and twisted trees were left in its wake. Worse still was all the debris slung across the railroad tracks.

"The train ain't gonna be able to get us to the camp," G.W. said, following his stepfather's gaze.

"If there's a camp left to get to," Arjan said, shaking his head. "Unless that twister took another turn, it looks to have headed straight on to our site."

"Surely it would have lifted by then," Deborah said. But in her heart, she couldn't help but fear they were right. Why had God let this happen? They had honored Him by resting on the Sabbath. They had blessed His name for the safety and harvest. They had kept their faith. And still, they'd suffered the storm.

Mother came alongside them. "We are so blessed that it didn't hit our house or the barn and outbuildings. The animals all seem fine. We're all safe."

Deborah didn't have the heart to remind them that it might be only a temporary blessing. If the storm had destroyed the logging camp, they would lose it all on the morrow.

Arjan put his arm around Mother's shoulders. "We are blessed. Indeed, we are. We're alive, and no one was hurt."

"Do you suppose it hit town?" Mother asked.

"Can't say for sure. Looks like it was hoppin' and skippin' around. See over there? No damage. But then it touched down over here, just beyond the tracks, and cut a path as far as you can see."

Pastor Shattuck and Mara walked over with Jake. "We can stay and help," the pastor declared. "Since Mrs. Albright managed to get her husband calmed down about forcing us to move, we haven't a care in the world." He grinned. "Just tell us what we need to do."

"We'll have to clear the tracks," Arjan said, leaning hard on his cane.

Deborah knew her stepfather was probably in pain, but he refused to let on. It wasn't the Dutch way to make a fuss.

"It's the Sabbath," G.W. reminded them. "There's time enough to work tomorrow."

"But we won't be able to get the logs down to the mill unless the tracks are clear," Mother reminded him.

G.W. nodded. "True enough, but I reckon God will work all of this to His good. Ain't never seen Him fail us yet."

But Deborah knew he didn't feel as convinced as his words indicated. Maybe God didn't want them to supply Stuart Albright with logs. Maybe God didn't want Perkinsville to revive. Who could say for sure?

Pastor Shattuck rolled up his sleeves. "I believe we can honor God even in our labor. Miz Euphanel, why don't you start us in some hymns of praise?"

⋙⋘

Jael had been more than a little frustrated that wreckage on the road kept them from reaching Deborah's house. She and her father had turned back only a mile or so down the road. Stuart looked pleased at their return. He said finally something was going his way.

On Monday morning, Jael tried again. This time she donned her riding habit. Without sitting down to breakfast, she announced to her father and husband her intention to ride out to the Vandermark place.

"I'll take the black gelding from the stable. He'll be able to jump anything too big to ride around."

"You shouldn't go alone," her father said, getting to his feet. "Stuart, why don't we both accompany her. Today is, after all, your deadline for the logs. It would do you well to see if that quota has been met."

Jael frowned. She wasn't at all sure why her father had said such a thing. It would have been far better to say nothing and hope that Stuart would just let the matter go. Of course, now he wouldn't.

"I suppose you are right," Stuart said.

Jael looked at her husband and then to her father. "I'll let the stableman know to saddle three horses."

She wasn't surprised to see most of the townsfolk out working to clear the yards and streets. The wind had done some damage, but upon further inspection in the light of morning, Jael could see that the town hadn't suffered too greatly.

The horses were saddled and ready to go by the time her father and husband finally made their way to the stable. Jael sat impatiently atop her mount. She saw that her husband held something in his hand.

"What have you there?" she asked.

Stuart gave her a smug smile. "The Vandermark contract." He folded it and put it in his pocket. "I intend to see that they live up to every word."

Maybe it wasn't such a good idea to head out to the Vandermarks' after all. Stuart would show no mercy whatsoever if things were bad. That could only lead to problems. But she had been the one to insist on the journey; it would only cause him more reason to be ruthless should she suggest they forgo the venture.

The road was far from easy to manage. From time to time large branches blocked the main part of the path, forcing her father and Stuart to get down and move the ones they couldn't jump. It took nearly an hour to cover what should have taken less than half that time.

"The house is still standing!" Jael announced, urging her horse past her father and Stuart. She thought for a moment the place was deserted, but then heard the sound of mules, somewhere beyond the house.

She maneuvered her horse toward the railroad tracks, where she found the entire Vandermark family working to uncover the tracks. Deborah pulled a long, skinny branch to one side and let it drop. Straightening, she noticed Jael and waved.

"Oh, you are all right!" Jael declared, quickly jumping from the gelding's back. "I was so worried." She dropped the reins and ran to embrace her friend.

"We worried about you, as well. How are things in town?" Deborah asked.

"Nothing quite this bad." Jael looked at the path the twister had eaten. "Oh, it must have been quite frightful."

"It was," Deborah admitted. "I suppose Stuart has come to see about his logs."

"Oh, bother," Jael said. "He surely can't expect you to provide logs when the tracks aren't even passable."

"He has a way of expecting a great many things."

Jael's father and Stuart came to join them. Deborah turned. "G.W., we've got company."

Every last person, including Pastor Shattuck and Mara, congregated to where Deborah and Jael stood with the two men. Jael knew the questioning looks were all for her husband.

"Mr. Albright, Mr. Longstreet," Arjan said. He turned and tipped his hat to Jael. "Ma'am."

"I'm come to find out if my logs will be delivered in time to meet the deadline," Stuart said in an almost amused fashion. "But I can see for myself that things do not look hopeful for that."

"No, I s'pose not," Arjan said. "We made a trip up to the

camp, and truth is . . . the storm destroyed most of the waiting logs up at the camp. At least it disbursed them. I imagine your logs are all over Angelina County."

"Well, that's a pity. It would seem you have broken our agreement."

"Now, just a minute," Jael's father said. "Do you mean to tell me that you are going to hold the Vandermarks to every point of the contract?"

Stuart smiled and gave Jael a smug look of satisfaction. "I do."

Her father then turned to Mr. Vandermark. Jael saw Mrs. Vandermark grasp her husband's hand in support. Deborah went to stand beside her mother, and Jael felt tears come to her own eyes at the sight of them offering each other comfort.

"You cannot do this," Jael told Stuart. "You are being cruel in their time of need."

He said nothing, and Jael's father continued. "Mr. Vandermark, has it been your intention to honor the contract in full?"

"It has."

The simple statement seemed to boom across the short span of space. Jael was surprised to see her father smile. "Mrs. Kelleher, I wonder if you would be so kind as to read the last paragraph of the contract."

Deborah frowned but stepped away from her mother. "I'll have to go retrieve it from the office."

"Oh, don't bother," Jael's father said. "I believe my son-in-law brought his copy along."

Stuart pulled the folded papers from his pocket and handed them to the older man. "I did, indeed. I wanted to make certain that you would not attempt to dupe me with a different contract."

"Of all the low-down—" G.W. was silenced as his stepfather put his hand out to hold him back.

"We are men of honor," Mr. Vandermark declared.

"I'm quite glad to hear you say that," Jael's father said. He handed the contract to Deborah. "Please, read it aloud for us—just the last paragraph."

Deborah seemed none too happy to do so, but nodded. " 'The terms of this contract are to be strictly met and fulfilled until the termination date given. However, the contract will be set aside should any act of God cause either party to forfeit their responsibilities to the other.' " She looked up and smiled. Turning back to her mother and stepfather, she repeated one phrase. "Any act of God."

"Well, there's no denying the destruction of our product was at the hands of the storm, which I believe would be deemed an act of God," Jael's father said, turning back to his son-in-law. "Just as you claimed the fire that burned the mill to be such an act. As I recall, the judge allowed you to set aside the contract terms until the insurance company could assess and determine the cause."

"I . . . that isn't . . ." Stuart narrowed his eyes. "It doesn't change anything."

"Oh, but it does," Mr. Longstreet countered. "Read the final line, Mrs. Kelleher."

Deborah looked back to the contract. " 'Should said "act of God" interfere with the continuation of the agreed upon terms, such terms will be open for renegotiation and new dates of delivery and quotas set.' "

"But you couldn't possibly have met the terms to begin with," Stuart declared. "It would have been impossible for you to supply me with what you owed my mill."

"I hardly believe that is the issue now," Jael's father said, taking the contract back from Deborah. "The fact of the matter is, these good people did attempt to deliver the intended product. The ongoing rains slowed them, and a tornado made it completely impossible. I would say that the terms make it clear. The contract is open for renegotiation."

The Vandermark family and workers broke into cheers. G.W. hugged Lizzie with such enthusiasm that Jael couldn't help but laugh and clap her hands. She met Deborah's smiling face. Apparently prayer did work. So many times of late, God had helped her in times of trouble. Jael's faith had grown in each situation.

Stepping forward, Jael took the contract from her father's hands. "I suggest that this contract be completely dissolved." She tore the papers in two. "That way you can sell whatever you like elsewhere."

"You can't do that," Stuart protested. "My lawyers will see to it that you honor the terms. It changes nothing."

She smiled and handed him the pieces. "Oh, but it does . . . *Husband*. It does." Stuart clearly noted her emphasis. He looked at her for a moment, then drew a deep breath and nodded.

He turned to look at his father-in-law and then Arjan. "Very well. Let us start anew."

Jael smiled. "I think that would benefit everyone."

CHAPTER 30

SEPTEMBER 1887

Summer's end brought many changes. Deborah and Christopher moved back to the doctor's house in town and received provisions to reestablish the infirmary. This was thanks to Jael's father, who had forced his son-in-law to sell his shares of the mill town. Together with Zed Perkins, who was back at the helm, Mr. Longstreet promised to make Perkinsville even better than before. To honor this pledge, the people voted him mayor.

"He's never been happier," Jael told Deborah.

"You seem quite happy yourself."

"I am, Deborah. I truly am happy."

Deborah knew the reason for this. Jael had been quite pleased when Stuart announced that his father needed him back East. Deborah had been there when Jael had told him firmly that she would stay in Perkinsville. Stuart hadn't been surprised, but he did seem concerned. Jael promised him that she would remain his faithful wife. She would write to him, so his father would see that they remained wed. Deborah argued that he didn't deserve her generosity, but Jael told her she desired to forgive Stuart the past and move forward. Her words humbled Deborah—Lizzie too.

"Who knows," Jael had told Deborah. "If God is as powerful as you say He is, then He can bring love even to our hard hearts."

Many of the families returned to Perkinsville. Margaret Foster came back with one of her sons and his wife. Their young children quickly befriended the Kelleher siblings. Little by little, many of the other regulars came home, as well. Zed reinstated each crew member with promises of a bigger and better mill. He split the workers between rebuilding the black town and getting the mill up and running. The progress lifted everyone's spirits.

Perhaps the greatest joy, however, had been the well-attended wedding of Robrecht Vandermark to Miss Mara Shattuck. Only an hour earlier, Deborah had stood at the depot with her family, waving good-bye to the couple as they caught the train to Houston. Rob had agreed to pastor a church in the area, and Mara had great plans for the Sunday school. Even Pastor Shattuck was delighted with the couple's plans, although Mara was worried he would grow lonely.

"I do fear he won't eat properly," she told Deborah as they bid each other farewell. "You will look in on him, won't you?"

"Of course," Deborah assured her. "And you can bet that my mother will, as well. She isn't about to see anyone go hungry."

But with everything falling back into a normal routine, Deborah couldn't help but wonder if that might allow for her and Christopher to have a little time to themselves.

"Haven't you finished in here yet?" Christopher teased.

"I'm daydreaming," Deborah said, glancing over her shoulder. "I often do so when I'm cleaning the examination room."

"And what are you dreaming about?"

She halted her work. "You do realize that we've never had a proper wedding trip? I thought that with Miz Foster back in town, perhaps we could get away for a week or two. She would surely be willing to treat folks while we were away. Wouldn't it be great fun to go to Galveston?"

"Goodness, woman, you think I'm made of money?"

Deborah put her hands on her hips. "I happen to know that my family paid you quite well for your service before and after the storm. And they paid me for my work. If you would check the new bank at the commissary, you would find that we have quite a nice bit of savings."

He laughed. "And it's burning a hole in your pocket—is that it?"

"Not exactly, but I think it would be awfully nice to be alone with you." She put down the cleaning cloth and walked toward him with a provocative smile. Reaching up, she trailed her fingers against his cheek and down to where a hint of chest hair peeked out from his unbuttoned shirt.

"Just imagine it. We could stay at the Tremont Hotel. I've heard it's absolutely beautiful since they rebuilt it. We could have a lovely suite and order room service." She stretched on tiptoes to brush his lips with a kiss. "Just imagine—an entire week alone."

He took hold of her. "Go on."

"Of course, there's also something else that might hold your interest."

Nuzzling her ear with kisses, Christopher shook his head ever so slightly. "That isn't possible."

"Oh, but I think it could be." She pulled away and smiled.

"They are building a new hospital, and rumor has it that a new medical college will be established. The paper noted that several lectures were going to be given next week. One is on the repair of compound fractures."

He laughed. "You don't want to get away with me—you just want to attend lectures on medicine."

Deborah feigned shock. "How could you say such a thing? You know perfectly well that I am the kind of gal who wants it all. Why couldn't we have both? After all, lectures only last an hour or two at the most. We needn't leave our room for much longer than that."

"You are positively scandalous, my dear." He drew her back into his arms. "And that's what I love most about you. You are a woman without boundaries. No one tells you no and gets away with it."

She shrugged and smiled. "At least not for long."

"Docs! Come quick!" someone yelled from outside.

They went quickly to the door. "What's wrong?" Christopher asked, pushing open the screen door.

"There's been an accident at the mill. Otis done cut himself up on that new-fangled saw," one of the young Foster kids declared.

"I'll get the bag and bandages," Deborah told her husband. "You go on ahead."

He nodded and shot out the door. Deborah hurried to grab what they would need. This was indeed the life for her—the life she loved. Working alongside her husband to help others. There was no way of knowing what the future held, but her hope had been rekindled and her heart overflowed with joy. And that—for now—was entirely enough.

LETTER TO THE READER:

Dear friends,

So many struggles plague people these days. From time to time, my readers write to tell me about a particularly difficult time or heartbreak that they've endured, reaching out to share when the world seems to turn a deaf ear to their pain.

My heart has been touched so many times by your letters, and I felt it was only right to share my heart with you now. I pray that the books I write will encourage you to lift your eyes to Jesus. That your hope will be rekindled in the promise of God *to never leave you or forsake you.* If you haven't yet put your hope in Him and accepted His free gift of salvation, then I encourage you to do so now.

The world tries to convince us that it is no simple process to yield your heart to the Lord. The world tries to tack on all sorts of other requirements, but the Bible makes it clear in Romans 10:9–13 that receiving salvation in Jesus is quite easy:

That if you confess with your mouth, "Jesus is Lord," and believe in your heart that God raised Him from the dead, you will be saved. For it is with your heart that you believe and are justified, and it is with your mouth that you confess and are saved. As the Scripture says, "Anyone who trusts in him will never be put to shame." For there is no difference between Jew and Gentile—the same Lord is Lord of all and richly blesses all who call on him, for, **"Everyone who calls on the name of the Lord will be saved"** (NIV, emphasis added).

I'm praying that these verses will bless your heart and bring you to a richer life in Christ Jesus. God bless you!

Tracie Peterson

More Adventure and Romance from
Tracie Peterson!

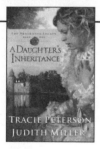